Keeper of the Flame

The Carly Sisters Series

Mary Kay Tuberty

MRP
Mantle Rock Publishing
www.MantleRockPublishing.com

©2016 Mary Kay Tuberty

Published by Mantle Rock Publishing
2879 Palma Road
Benton, KY 42025
http://mantlerockpublishing.com

Printed in the United States of America

All rights reserved. No part of this publication may be reproduced, stored in a retrieval system, or transmitted in any form or by any means—for example, electronic, photocopy and recording— without the prior written permission of the publisher. The only exception is brief quotation in printed reviews.

ISBN 978-1-945094-07-1 Print Book
      978-1-945094-08-8 EBook

Cover by Diane Turpin

Published in association with Jim Hart of Hartline Literary Agency, Pittsburgh, PA

for Jessica Tuberty
Kyle Tuberty
Nicole Tuberty
Chris Tuberty
Alex Tuberty
Jack Kiehl
Gaby Kiehl

The *Keeper of the Flame* story, Book Three of The Carty Sisters Series, grew out of family lore, the author's imagination, and the letters Anne, Julia, and Kate Carty received from their family in Blackwater, Ireland. The letters are included in the tale just as they were written some one hundred and fifty years ago.

Mary Kay Tuberty

Acknowledgements

I owe supreme gratitude to:

My husband, Larry; children; and grandchildren.

My brothers and sisters: Susan and Jerry Spann, Betty and Tom Pisoni, Tom Duff, Pat and Janet Duff, Ellen and Stan Poniewaz, Mike and Joyce Duff.

My family by marriage: My amazing sister-in-law Marge Miller and the Miller and Menke nieces, nephews and cousins.

My Carty and Duff cousins, nephews, and nieces, scattered throughout the world, with whom I share these amazing, courageous ancestors.

The folks of Blackwater, Ireland, whose culture and traditions make up such a strong part of our heritage and who have so graciously supported the Carty Family story.

The St Francis girls: Barb, Carol, Cathy, Dot H., Dot Z., Elvira, Ginny, Ilene, Jean, Joan H., Joan M., Joan S., Joan T., Joyce, Maggie, Mary Ann, Nina, Ramona, Rita, Shirley, Theresa, and Valerie.

Special thanks to:

Jim Hart; Hartline Literary.

Kathy Cretsinger and Diane Turpin, Mantle Rock Publishing.

Praise Be To God!

Chapter One

St. Louis, Missouri
January, 1869

Kate Carty trudged up the rain-drenched hill from the mission, two empty wicker baskets swinging from one arm, an umbrella on the other. She raised the umbrella high above her head, shifted it to the left, then to the right. The driving rain soaked her bonnet, and droplets ran along her face. Useless. When she held it in front of her, streams of frigid water rushed beneath the collar of her coat and soaked her clothing and skin.

Keep yourself calm, Kate. Promise me. Love. Forgive.

She peered in every direction, straining to make out anyone…anything…on this dark, murky night. The voice was Lizzie's. The words, her little sister's final message before she died. She had given Lizzie her promise, but she had failed. "I will keep myself calm, Lizzie." Her words rang out through the wind and the rain. "I will forgive. I will try."

"Kate! Kate! Hold up there. I've come to take you home." The bakery wagon pulled up alongside her, with Walter Dempsey seated in the driver's seat. "Sure, and the devil himself must have ordered this dismal night."

"Walter? It's good to hear your voice." She turned toward the street…unsure…unsteady. "I can barely make out the wagon."

"Whoa, Josie, hold up." With the gentle old mare halted in the road, Walter, Kate's landlord and benefactor, jumped to the street. "The gaslights are out, plunging the city streets into darkness. I've heard complaints everywhere I've traveled today."

"A ride home will be welcome." Kate shook water from the umbrella and headed for the front seat.

"Hold on a moment." Walter rounded the back of the wagon. "Allow me to help you."

"Jonas' whale!" Kate stamped her foot, sending a spray of water all about. "Would you wish me to stand in the road and drown, while I wait for you to perform the proper niceties?" Ignoring Walter's extended arm, she tossed the bakery baskets into the wagon. Crashing to the floor of the empty wagon bed, the baskets made a louder thump than she expected.

The horse lurched.

Kate grasped the door frame and climbed up to the seat. "Easy, Josie. I am sorry I startled you." She leaned out the front opening of the wagon, but she came only close enough to feel a swish of her tail. "Sorry, girl. Steady now." She took a firm hold of the door handle, as the horse veered toward the side of the road and the right, front wheel rolled into a slight ridge. The wagon tilted and then rolled back to the left.

"Ho!" Walter settled his powerful frame in the driver's seat. "Easy now," he called out to the horse.

Josie quieted.

"'Tis a bitter night to be out on the street. If you lingered at the mission, I could have collected you at the door. I meant to save you from the soaking I see you received." Walter took up the reins, and with a cluck to the horse, they went on their way.

"Walter, I am sorry. I did not intend to throw the baskets so hard and frighten Josie." Kate settled back in her seat, as water dripped from her raincoat and shawl, pooling on the floor of the wagon.

Walter's hearty laugh rang out through the dark night. "Josie's fine. She was already undone by the rain." He sobered quickly and pulled a towel from beneath the wooden seat for her. "You look a bit bothered yourself. Is something wrong?"

"As I climbed the hill I was lost in thought, and then I imagined Lizzie called to me. The words were hers. The sound of her voice seemed so real." Kate blotted her face and hair with the towel, and then rubbed the soft cloth along her cloak. "I do not wish to burden you with such depressing thoughts."

"When my parents died, I missed them greatly, but I never heard their voices again." Walter's deep brown eyes held compassion and caring. "Did the experience frighten you? Are you all right now?"

"I am fine, Walter. Please forgive my outburst." Kate lowered her chin to her chest. If only she could take back her cross words. Would she never learn to curb her tongue? "You could be resting inside your warm comfortable parlor rather than sitting here drenched while collecting me from the mission. You surely did not deserve my thoughtless tirade."

Ah, my, she had been seeking a few private words with him. She had an enormous favor to ask. Now the opportunity presented itself, and rather than a thank you for escorting her home, she had lashed out at him. Was her cause already done? When she glanced toward him, rather than anger, she beheld the kindest face she ever encountered. Courage rose up within her. "You see—"

"So, why has the owner of Kate's Dressmaking Shop been out delivering baskets of baked goods to St. Vincent's Mission on such a cold, rainy night as this?" Walter's strong voice boomed over the pounding rain. "I told Mary I would drive you girls on these bitter cold nights. No point in anyone becoming ill."

"I volunteered to carry the day-old goods to the mission." Kate held the towel before her, attempting to shield herself, but the rain poured in from every direction. It soaked the cloth and her. "Grace suffers from a cold. And in spite of the marvelous meals we all enjoy at Dempsey's, the poor girl is thin as a stick. This evening's fierce wind and rain could knock her clear about." She leaned closer, searching Walter's face. "Why, may I ask, is the proprietor of Dempsey's Bakery out on this cold night?"

"Eddie has Grace's same cold, so I volunteered to handle the last delivery of the night for him." When the horse and wagon attained the steepest part of the hill, Walter relaxed his hands on the reins. "I suspect my bakery helper and my shop girl may be spending some time together. What do you think?"

"I pray with all my heart there is truth to it." Kate chuckled, the tension slipping from her shoulders and limbs. "Our poor Grace has been despondent since she came to America and that fool Will Stapleton jilted her. If Eddie offers her some measure of happiness and contentment, I love him for it myself."

Kate drew in a deep breath. Their conversation had veered in a different direction. She could not allow this rare time alone with Walter to pass. Even if he was a bit upset with her, she must make her appeal. "I have a great application to make to you. Ellen and I have the possibility of a grand, new order for draperies." Kate paused, gathering courage. "Janey Flynn already works for us half days, and I am considering hiring another girl. Actually, it is Gus Mueller's daughter, Charlotte."

"Gus and Tilda Mueller will be pleased." Walter leaned through the side opening, peering out in all directions. "How did you come to hire Charlotte? Do you know her well?"

"I met her a few times at St. Vincent's." Kate swiped at her face with her glove, but the rainwater continued to drip from her hat and roll along her cheeks. "She told me you worked with her father during the war, supplying baked goods for the Union Army."

"He and I forged a friendship many years ago." Walter pulled the wagon to the shoulder of the road to avoid an oncoming cart. "We met well before the war."

"Janey sang Charlotte's praises for her sewing skills, and we have used her help when we were overwhelmed with orders," Kate said. "I have judged her to be a talented seamstress."

"Will the fact that her family is German bother your customers?" Walter raised an eyebrow.

"When they discover what beautiful dresses and curtains Charlotte will create for them, they will respect her." Kate straightened her shoulders. "If not, it is their loss, and there's an end to it."

"Good for you, Kate. I have met Charlotte on a few occasions and found her to be a nice, sweet girl." With the horse now returned to her usual, even gait, Walter focused his attention on her. "And, the new business?"

"Palmer House." A trickle of pleasure coursed through Kate. She covered her smile. "Of course, it will not be settled until they sign an agreement."

"A good bit of sewing work?" Walter removed his cap and shook it out the window, sending streams of water out onto the road.

"It could develop into a large order. Draperies, bedspreads and table coverings," she said.

"That is grand, Kate. I admire what you've done with your shop." He pushed his cap down on his head. "Why, in just these few years, you have grown from a small, one-person place to a flourishing business. Freeing our Ellen from her position in that dress factory is a grand achievement. Working with you changed her life. Then you hired Janey Flynn, and now, Charlotte Mueller. It is a wonderful thing."

"Thank you." Had the compliment from Walter brought this warmth that crept along her face? Fortunately, the darkness of this miserable night would hide her blushes. She shook herself vigorously. They had digressed from the subject, again. She could not allow herself to be swayed from her mission.

"I must speak with you before we reach home." She pushed her earlier thoughts of her little sister and her concerns about her rain-soaked clothing from her mind and added strength to her voice. "You see, with a fourth seamstress, my small shop will grow a mite crowded. The girls work well together, and I would like that camaraderie to continue. I wish to rent additional space. Do you suppose we could arrange it?" With his nod, she grew confident he could hear her over the pounding rain, but still, she worried. Could she hold a businesslike conversation with Walter, while water dripped from her hair and streamed along her face?

"I should have thought of it myself." Interest beamed from Walter's eyes. "There is a world of empty space at the back of our bakery building. Expanding your shop would pose no problem."

"I will, of course, pay more rent." They had drawn near the bakery. When the horse rounded the corner, they would be across the road from the shop. Little time remained. There would be no chance for a conversation of any importance, once they had been drawn into the general stir and commotion of a Dempsey's supper.

"Ride along with me, while I take the horse and carriage over to Donovan's. We'll have more time." Walter turned Josie toward the livery. "We will not need any increase in rent

Keeper of the Flame

money. The room adjoining your shop stands vacant, gathering dust." He gestured in the air, his hand still holding the reins. "You will be putting the place to use and keeping it cleaner than it is now."

The horse stamped in the road, waiting.

Walter handed Kate the reins. He jumped down and swung the door open.

She maneuvered the horse and wagon through the wide entryway.

He stood before her, offering his arm, a firm, serious expression across his face. "You pay rent for your room in the attic and for your dressmaking shop. I will not accept more."

"No, Walter. I cannot allow that. I will pay additional rent." She ground her foot into the wagon's top step. "I must handle this business on my own." Once the words were out, her indignation faded. A rush of regret enveloped her. This good man had just agreed to help her with the expansion of her shop. Had she offended him again?

"Your determination and impatience never fail to surprise me, Kate. I admire a girl who is not afraid to speak out." When Walter looked down at her, rather than the look of displeasure she expected, his face held a grin.

"Forgive me. As usual, I permitted my tongue to rule over my sound judgment." A wave of shame swept through her. Her wont of speaking out before thinking brought about many of the troubles in her life. Would she never rid herself of this distasteful habit?

"Ah, Kate, I feel confident I will survive your fierce attack." Walter extended his arm to her again. "I appreciate your good business sense. Let's explore what your needs will be. Then, we will discuss terms."

She accepted Walter's arm and leapt down. "I'll see to Josie while you take the wagon."

"Evening, folks." The livery owner, Jed, approached them. He and Walter released the horse from her traces, and the two men backed the wagon toward its storage space across the passage.

She led the mare away, humming softly, and eased her into a stall. Working by the flickering lantern light, she removed the harness. She leaned into Josie's soft mane and dried her with a thick, sponge-like mat. "You're a good girl, Josie. I'm sorry I startled you."

The stable's familiar animal scents enveloped Kate. She smiled…remembering. Hadn't thoughts of her dear Lizzie been with her all through the day? Now, she pictured her family's old horse back home in Blackwater. The little ones loved her, shaggy mane, wobbly legs and all. Lizzie named her Gerald, even though she was a mare.

Kate drew her lips together. Father sold Gerald…he could no longer feed the horse…they could not allow her to starve.

She reached for a currycomb set on a ledge above her head. "All right, girl, time to—"

"Allow me to finish up." The stable owner appeared in the stall, sliding the comb from Kate's hand. "I'll manage things from here." The tall, slim young man bowed to her. "I've brought fresh hay, and I'll brush our Josie down, good and proper."

"Thank you, Jed." Walter appeared outside the stall, Kate's bakery baskets slung over his arm.

"Goodnight." Kate waved a farewell to Jed as they walked through the wide doorway. "Ah, the bitter cold and rain have not abated."

"Wait…I have forgotten your umbrella." Walter retrieved it from the wagon, and taking her arm, he guided her into the road.

The square, three-story building loomed before them. Walter had connected two abandoned factories and renovated

Keeper of the Flame

them to create what had now become the bakery building. The imposing structure held two oven rooms, a bakery shop, private family quarters, rooms for boarders, and Kate's dressmaking shop. While the majority of the city sat in darkness, the large "Dempsey's Bakery" sign hung just below a gas light that operated perfectly.

As they passed beneath the lamp, Kate scrutinized Walter. Why had she never noticed the fine, sharp features that defined his face? Why had she never appreciated the depth and caring resting in his warm, brown eyes?

She shook the thought away. She would not allow herself to be swayed by a genial, well-looking man. Her time alone with him was drawing to an end. She must stand firm…settle her business transaction. "You are being exceedingly kind and generous, but it is too much."

"On the contrary, Kate. Your shop is of great benefit to our bakery. Women of the neighborhood apply to you for dresses, and before heading home, they walk around to the front of the building and shop in the bakery." Walter shook out her umbrella, and once they stepped through the door, he placed it in the stand.

"True, true, but that works both ways. Customers from the bakery often make their way around the side of the building to my shop." So many arguments could be brought forward, if only she could find the right words. But, it was too late. They were already passing through the darkened bakery shop.

"You are most generous in declining to increase my rent. I do appreciate the offer, but I cannot accept." She halted her steps. She must make one final attempt. "I would like the shop to be all one area. Some work would be involved in tearing out the wall between the two rooms. There will be city permits required and additional taxes. I must bear the cost of these expenses. I cannot conduct a proper business if I do not pay my own way." She looked over her shoulder. "'Tis terribly quiet in here."

Walter nodded. He placed a hand on her arm and turned her until she faced him. "Come to my office first thing in the morning, and we'll draw up a sketch. We will settle our differences on the business then. Agreed?"

"Yes. And, thank you." Walter had stymied her for now, but she would persevere. She had developed a plan for her new space and figured the costs. She would hold firm. She would pay her own expenses.

They walked toward the archway at the rear of the room. Oh for a quiet supper tonight…and perhaps an opportunity to change to dry clothing and smooth her hair?

Chapter Two

"Happy birthday! Best wishes! Happy birthday!" A clamor of clapping and cheering erupted as Kate approached the doorway to the dining room with Walter right behind her. She gasped. No quiet supper tonight. A crowd of family and friends were gathered around the table.

She leaned against the wall. Her birthday. She had forgotten her twenty-fourth birthday. Since her beloved little sister died, she had buried herself in her dressmaking business. The weeks and months blended together.

Kate sought out Anne and Julia, her two married sisters, who sat with their husbands at the far end of the long table. "Well, is this not a lofty scene? You have found a grand way to make that fresh start we resolved on."

"God be with you, dear." Julia's voice rang out across the room. She moved toward Kate, her long, slim arms outstretched, her soft, brown curls bobbing all about.

Kate forced a smile across her face and stepped from the darkness of the hallway into the glowing dining room. Cream-colored walls accented by the near-matching draperies that she and Ellen created added warmth to the large room. Light glimmered from the gas lamps mounted on the outside wall. Tiny flames flickered from the masses of low candles arranged in an intricate pattern along the center of the table.

"I did not expect to see you all." She hugged Julia and then moved toward Anne. She stopped short when she reached the end of the table. "Where are the children?"

"All four are sleeping peacefully in Mary's parlor." Anne, slight of figure despite being the mother of two, her thick brown hair arranged in a perfect bun, moved back to her place beside her husband. "We're taking turns checking on them." Her deep blue eyes rested on Kate. "We thought you would never come. What took you so long?"

"It was Walter's doing. He captured me and took me to the livery to put the horse up." She grinned at Walter, who moved toward the head of the table. "You were in on the secret, eh?"

Walter winked at her. "Happy Birthday, Kate."

"Happy birthday, dear." Mary Dempsey, Walter's sister and the heart of the entire Dempsey's operation, placed her arm across Kate's shoulders.

Kate leaned against Mary, allowing herself to be swept into the warmth of her twinkling, blue eyes and smiling face. Not all softness and good humor, though, Mary possessed an astute business mind Kate sought to acquire one day.

"Come now, hurry and wash up. Our dinner is ready." Mary bustled off, rearranging steaming bowls of food on the table and adding additional ones.

Kate hurried to the alcove off the dining room to wash her hands. How grand it would be to rush up to her attic room and change to a dry dress. She shook her head. No time. Supper awaited. Examining her likeness in the small mirror above the wash stand, she recognized the resemblance to Anne. The one exception was that her hair and eyes were a shade darker than her sister's. But, could this thick, brown hair pressed against her head, the dull, tired eyes, and the slack skin belong to her? Her sisters had been right. The face gazing back at her appeared tired and sad. Lizzie would never approve. It was well past time to push aside her grief and begin to live again.

Hurrying back toward the table, she swerved to avoid a collision with Grace. "Oh, sorry, dear, I nearly toppled you. Will I take that heavy platter?"

"Of course not, Kate. It's your birthday. You must hurry right over and sit at the place of honor beside Walter." Grace hunched her shoulders, a tiny expression of guilt growing across her face. "Did we surprise you?"

"Hah. Kate placed a fist on her hip. "Do you even have a cold?"

"Here's Cara now with the last of it." Grace's frail form, once bent down with sorrow and despair, moved with ease and confidence. She avoided Kate's gaze. "I've made room for the potatoes here, Cara."

Cara arranged her bowl where Grace indicated. The tiny, reserved young woman had lived and worked at Dempsey's for many years, devoting her life to keeping the place spotless. She stepped toward Kate. "Happy birthday, my dear. I trust you've had a fine day."

"Just imagine, Cara. Our Kate did not even remember her birthday." Ellen, Kate's helper in the dressmaking shop slipped into a chair. Her blue eyes sparkled, and when she shook her head, bright red curls flew about.

"I cannot imagine anyone forgetting their birthday, Kate. Sure, you did make it easy to keep this dinner party a surprise." Ellen bestowed a radiant smile over her. "Happy birthday, dear girl. I pray this day marks a new beginning for you."

"You managed a magnificent surprise. I had not given a thought to my birthday." Kate rested her eyes on Grace and attempted a stern look. "You've avoided my question, but I will not allow you to slip free. Are you truly ailing? Or was your cold an act meant to remove me from the house?"

"I do have the sniffles." Grace laughed.

"Ah, you possess a fine silver tongue." Kate inclined her head toward Grace. Moments ago she had giggled. Now she actually laughed. The sound was wonderful to hear after all these many years of sadness. Could she follow Grace's example and straighten her life around? Perhaps, the trick played on her would be well worth—

"Happy birthday, Kate." George, who had worked with Walter in the oven room since being assigned to help during the Civil War, took a place beside Anne.

"Best wishes to you, Kate!" Eddie, Walter's helper for many years and Grace's rumored romantic interest, patted Kate's shoulder and circled the table, extending a greeting to everyone. "We have not had this festive a celebration at Dempsey's in a long while." He saluted Kate. "We have you to thank for it, my girl."

Kate followed Eddie's progress as he continued around the table. Did he stop a moment longer at Grace's chair than anywhere else, before taking his place beside George? It certainly seemed so. Kate touched her napkin to her mouth to hide her smile.

Walter cleared his throat. "We have all resolved to pick up with our lives. Your birthday is the perfect time to begin, Kate. Shall we offer our thanksgiving?" Silence descended around the room.

Kate bowed her head. Her heart swelled and thumped with gratitude for her dear family and friends. And then... Lizzie's sweet face rushed before her. Ah, my, wasn't her little sister delivering the same message she heard from Anne and Julia? "Move forward...live."

When a chorus of "amens" reverberated around the table, Kate jumped. Distracted by the vision of Lizzie, she had missed much of Walter's prayer.

A hum of conversation filled the room. Kate sat back in her chair. Worries over damp hair and wet clothing fell away. How comforting to be enveloped in the familiar aromas and sounds of a Dempsey's supper. She shook herself, hoping to dispel the sadness that remained with her.

"Before I even begin to eat, I'll rush over and peek in on the children." Julia eased the parlor door open and leaned her head inside. "All is well." She slipped back into her chair, her blue eyes shining. "Our twins are curled up together on a blanket. Your wee Nell is sleeping soundly in the crib, Anne. Young Tom is against the wall, keeping as far from the girls as possible, I suppose."

"That's my boy." James Duff's voice boomed out across the room.

"I believe he snores." Julia grinned at her brother-in-law. "There is a decided rumble in the parlor." The room erupted in laughter.

"Will this commotion wake them?" Kate raised her eyebrows and directed her questioning look to her sisters.

"Well, if they do hear us, they will just join the party." Anne's often serious face held warmth and calm. "Do not worry, Kate. Enjoy your celebration."

"We all wish you a wonderful birthday, Kate." James raised his water glass, and the others around the table followed his example. "May you enjoy a happy and prosperous year."

Calls of: "God keep you! Long life to you!" and "A world of happiness!" rained down on Kate from everyone around the table.

Kate eased back in her chair again. After months of sadness, joy filled her being. And was this a genuine smile that threatened to explode across her face? What a wonderful gift! An insistent gnawing in her stomach distracted her. Ah, more than grins had returned. This grand celebration brought the awakening of her appetite after so many months. She tasted a few morsels of the smooth, creamy potatoes and then a few green beans seasoned with a hint of bacon. Delicious.

"Thank you all for this wonderful party. I am feeling better than I have in a long while." Kate gazed at each of her dear ones. "Besides the rekindling of my appetite, I made another step forward today. Since we are all together tonight, I will share my plan with you. On our ride home, I discussed it with Walter." She wrinkled her nose at him. "Besides tricking me by taking me along to the stable, he has agreed to help me expand my shop."

"Congratulations, Kate." Martin Tobin, Julia's husband raised his glass. "A more deserving person could not be found. Your hard work is bearing results."

"Best wishes, Kate, Ellen." James banged a spoon against his glass.

"Congratulations. Good luck. Good fortune." Good wishes came from her dear ones seated at the long table.

"Thank you. I appreciate your kind words, but I must extend my gratitude to Ellen. With her help, our business has expanded tremendously." She bowed to her helper. "While I was mired in sorrow over losing Lizzie, Ellen saw to it that our orders were met. Because of her fine work, we anticipate an abundance of new business."

Sitting across from her at the table, Ellen blushed. "Thank you, Kate. That is fine praise, but—"

"You deserve every word of it." Observing Ellen's discomfort, Kate worried. The girl was unaccustomed to praise. Orphaned and sent to America at a young age, she spent her first few years in St. Louis working in a garment factory. Her difficult start had not tamed her high spirits, though. Ellen, always ready with a laugh or joke, could often be found at the center of the girls' schemes. Still, she would not embarrass her dear friend.

A new subject slipped into her thoughts. "Surely, you were in on the surprise this evening. Am I right?" Ellen's sheepish grin satisfied Kate. All was well.

She glanced around the table. "As our business grows, our little shop seems to be shrinking. With Janey Flynn coming to help us half-days, we've managed to push our sewing machines and tables together well enough. Ellen and I agree we have sufficient trade to hire her on a permanent basis."

"Oh that is wonderful news." Julia twirled her fork about as if waving a flag. "Does Janey know about this? Does her mother know? Oh my, Mrs. Flynn will be so happy."

"Janey does not know. Ellen and I wished to work it out with Walter first. The other part of the story is we have decided to bring in Gus and Tilda Mueller's daughter, Charlotte." She rejoiced to see the smiles coming from all around the table. "Charlotte will take over Janey's hemming duties and eventually become a full-fledged seamstress."

"Oh, how grand." Julia placed her fork on the table with an enthusiastic clunk.

"And so, on our long trip home tonight," Kate grinned at Walter, "we talked over the possibility of expanding our shop. Ellen and I will meet with him tomorrow to work out the details."

As her head swiveled, she caught an expression of sadness clouding Ellen's face. "What is it? You look stricken."

"'Tis a shame to toss bad news onto your birthday celebration." Ellen bowed her head. Silverware stopped in midair, and the raising of water glasses and passing of platters ceased.

"We may as well know the bad news." Kate's heart commenced to thump, but she reached across the table and squeezed Ellen's hand.

"Mr. Smith from Palmer House came to the shop after you left. The hotel management turned down our proposal for the draperies. They decided on a larger company." Ellen dipped her head again.

"Ah, don't even think of it." Walter slammed his hand on the table. "I hold a world of confidence in you girls. Your reputation is spreading throughout the city. You'll soon be that larger company, the one all the smaller places will attempt to outdo."

"Thank you, Walter." At his praise, a soothing balm slipped through Kate's mind and heart. A tiny shiver flitted through her.

"Do not worry, Ellen. Though the loss of the hotel business we were expecting is a disappointment, we hold prospects enough to go ahead with the expansion. With supporters like our Walter here, things cannot help but work out." Kate reached across the table again, but when Ellen pulled her hand back, she drew in her breath. Had her earlier squeeze been stronger than she intended?

"If my opinion counts, I echo Walter's confidence." Eddie stood and bowed, bringing a laugh from everyone. "Your business flourished without Palmer House, and it will continue to grow and prosper. I am sure you'll have many new clients come calling on you."

Anne tipped her glass to Kate and Ellen, and everyone followed her example.

Another rumbling in her stomach reminded Kate of the marvelous meal before them. "I am still hungry, Ellen. That is a sure sign everything will work out well." She lifted her fork, determination swelling within her, to sample each wonderful dish.

"I am proud of you, Kate," Anne said. "You accepted this setback in a steady, businesslike—"

At a sharp knock, a brief, loud rap at the bakery door, Walter headed toward the darkened shop. Silence hovered in the room, until he reappeared.

"A messenger delivered this for you, Kate." Walter pulled a clay pot from behind his back that held a tall, unusual looking plant.

"It is a beautiful...well, interesting...flower." She pushed her chair back and rose from the table. Taking the pot in both hands, she held it away then drew her arms back for a careful examination. She turned to Mary, an eyebrow raised. "I am not a gardener. Do you have any idea what flower this is?"

"Some species of orchid, I am sure." Mary pulled her eyeglasses from her pocket as she approached Kate.

"Go way out of that." Walter shook his head. "In the middle of January?"

Standing beside Kate now, Mary pointed her finger toward the flower pot. "These plants grow in New Orleans or somewhere to the south of us. They are transported up the river by steamboat to St. Louis."

"For a pretty penny, I suppose." James poured himself a glass of water, then gestured with the pitcher to those nearest him.

Kate held the plant out in front of her again. Unusual. A sturdy green stem was centered in the substantial clay pot. A cluster of slightly darker green leaves grew from either side of the stem. Nestled at the core of each cluster was a bulb, about the size of her little finger. A white silk bow had been affixed to the rim of the flower pot. Who would send her such a thing?

"Ah, orchids." Julia rested her chin in her hand, a dreamy expression slipping across her face. "They are lovely in full flower. Do you think they will bloom here in St. Louis?"

"Perhaps." Mary moved back to her chair. "You must keep the plant warm and moist, Kate."

"There's a card." Walter gestured to the small, folded sheet attached to the ribbon. "What thoughtful person sent you such a gift on your birthday?"

Kate read the note, her mouth tightening to suppress a grimace. "It is from Francis Reilly. He wishes me a happy birthday." Why would Francis do this? He had courted her for a time and proposed marriage, but after brief consideration, she refused him. Why would he not allow the matter to rest?

Looking toward the end of the table, she read the concern in her sisters' eyes. "Do not spend one moment worrying, girls. The business with Francis is all in the past. It was a thoughtful gesture. That's the end of it."

Kate stepped away from the table. With all eyes fixed on her, she must hold her voice even. "I will find a place for the flowerpot in the kitchen, if you have no objection, Mary. With the warmth from the oven and a touch of your magic fingers, it will surely bloom there." Her hands trembled. Without warning, the damp flowerpot slipped from her hands. She stood, bewildered, watching the plant glide toward the floor.

Her brother-in-law Martin slipped to his knees and caught the flowerpot in his one good hand. "No harm done." He grinned as he handed it back to Kate.

"Oh, thank you, Martin. Your presence of mind and quickness amaze me." She shook her head. Martin, Julia's husband and a true hero, lost his left forearm saving the life of a young boy who had fallen under the wheel of a horse-drawn bus. In the two years since the accident, Martin rehabilitated himself and obtained a position as a purchaser for a successful, downtown shoe business. His dexterity had certainly served her well just now.

"You are surely the most agile man in the room." Walter applauded.

Keeper of the Flame

"Amen to that." James stood and clapped with him, and everyone around the table joined them.

As she started off for the kitchen again, Kate's emotions overcame her. Oh, for the end of this eternal day. She bit down on the inside of her cheek to stifle her tears, but they would not be pushed back. "Here I am making a scene. I do apologize. It has been a wonderful birthday celebration. Mary, Cara, Grace, your meal was delicious. I've no reason to take on so."

"Now, now, everyone grows a tad weepy on their birthday." Mary took the pot from Kate and pulled her into a hug. "Leave the flower here for now, Kate, and let us continue with our party. You'll be right and smiling in no time."

James pounded his fist on the table, demanding Kate's attention. "I will be happy to help with any work that's needed for the expansion of your shop."

"Thank you, James. I appreciate your offer." She dipped her head. "And…the welcome change of subject."

"I am sure my trusty aide will come along?" James looked over to Martin.

"Well, if you need the services of a one-armed man, I offer you my help." Martin's words were said with a smile.

"That is grand of you, Martin." How kind he was to join in James's attempt to shift attention away from her, when he usually sought to avoid the subject of his injury.

"You will provide a tremendous service to us." Walter's eyes shown. "None of us possess your skill at cabinets and shelves. And, Kate will be thrilled at the results of your work. The other fellows and I will appreciate your help every bit as much."

"Is there anything I can do, Kate? You know, I wish to be of service." Grace walked up behind her and tugged at her sleeve.

"I speak for your seamstresses. We are all standing by to help," Ellen said.

"Do not forget your sisters." Anne turned to Julia, and together they bobbed their heads in agreement.

"Everyone who works at the bakery will be ready to assist you." Mary inclined her head toward Kate.

"Thank you." She gazed around at everyone. How kind and caring they all were. Her words came with difficulty. "You have all been wonderful—"

A great crack and then a tiny wail sent Julia and Anne running toward the parlor. "Oh my, they will all be awake in no time." Julia pushed open the parlor door.

Chills rushed along Kate's arms when another loud cry erupted, followed by a softer murmur. And then, silence. She looked to Mary and Grace for reassurance, but they, too, shook their heads.

Anne and Julia reappeared, holding a child in each arm. James and Martin moved quickly to their wives, forming two small groups, murmuring to the children in soothing tones.

Kate watched, transfixed. These beautiful children Anne and Julia now hugged, patted, and cooed over required their constant attention. Her sisters, while they had grieved over the loss of Lizzie, were allowed precious little time to dwell on their sorrow. She, on the other hand, spent the good part of her day working needle and thread through assorted pieces of material. Was it any wonder she experienced more difficulty rising above the anguish?

Mary and Cara had been collecting the emptied dinner plates and transferring them to the kitchen. She had not even noticed. They returned now, Cara juggling dessert plates, silverware, and napkins and Mary bearing a tall round cake, covered in frosting. White icing, her favorite. Mary remembered. The slicing, serving, and tasting of the dessert distracted Kate. "The cake is delicious, Mary. Thank you so much."

Keeper of the Flame

With the clearing of the dessert plates, Kate rose from the table and followed along to the kitchen behind Julia. Her sister's two squirmy babies roused her into action. She pulled up a chair for Julia and settled her in with the babies. "'Tis a beautiful thing to watch them snuggle against you so peacefully." She ran a finger along the silky, soft cheek of each wee girl.

"I must stay and help with the dishes tonight," Mary said. "I do not wish to miss out on a moment of time with these beautiful children."

Kate pulled up a chair for her. "Are your arms strong enough to hold two sturdy babies, girleen?" They all giggled with Mary while Kate helped her arrange Anne's sleepy babies in her arms.

"Come, Anne, we'll show these lasses how to do the task the right way."

"Ah, Anne and Julia," Ellen carried a kettle of boiling water to the sink, "it is grand to have you back in the kitchen. When you've finished drying the dishes, Anne, you might dance a magnificent jig for us. And, if you have any interesting stories to share, Julia, it will make our work move more quickly."

Grace raised her head from her task of shaving slivers of soap into the water. "Though we are all truly happy for you, with your fine husbands and babies and homes of your own, we do miss you."

"My stories have changed some." Julia balanced one baby on her knee while she cuddled the other into her shoulder. "My adventures now range from twins, to infant clothes, and back to baby girls again. I could tell you all about Elizabeth's attempts at sitting alone and Maura's first baby words."

"We would all love to hear those stories, Julia." Kate paused in her dish-drying and tickled her sister under the chin.

After she stacked the clean dishes in the cupboard, Ellen faced Anne with hands on hips. "With so many helpers, the cleanup is proceeding quickly. What we would like, young mother, is an exhibition of the latest dancing steps. We'll all need to practice before we attend the church social next month."

"Sing something for me, and I will have a go at it." Anne moved to the open space between the table and the outside door. "Come Grace, Ellen, lead us. Sing 'Shake Hands with Uncle Tim.'"

Kate sang along with the others. "Shake hands with all the neighbors…" Was this her serious, determined Anne, dancing with abandon? A contradiction, indeed. Anne's face glowed and her feet moved at a furious pace.

"Slow down, Anne." Kate stood beside her sister. "The step is complicated. How did you learn this?"

"My neighbor, Irene, mastered all the latest dances from her cousins, when she and her husband traveled to New York." With the song ended, Anne lifted Tom from Mary's arms.

"You are barely winded. That is amazing." Holding baby Nell, Kate followed behind Anne as her sister led them through the hallway to the parlor.

"I have blankets and bunting at the ready." James held out arms draped in wool. "Place Tom in my arms, Anne, and we can wrap him securely. Will you manage Nell, Kate?"

"Allow me to take one of the twins." Ellen lifted a baby from Julia's arms. "I watched James and Anne. I will imitate their technique."

"I'll fetch the carriage." Walter appraised the two small family groups. "I believe we'll squeeze everyone in." He headed out the door.

"Good night, Kate." Julia pulled back a cover to allow Kate one last kiss of soft baby skin.

She moved to Mary. "Thank you for the wonderful celebration." She lowered the blanket again to give them an opportunity for one last peek at the sleeping baby. "Goodnight, everyone."

Kate stepped back and watched. Her heart, soul, and body trembled with a new feeling of exhilaration. She welcomed this long-forgotten joy that suddenly appeared in her. Were Lizzie's words earlier that evening foretelling of this new peace that now filled her being? Could she, indeed, manage to rally her spirits and improve her life? Was it possible the changes were already beginning?

"Here's an old letter from Father, dear." With a question in her eyes, Anne held an envelope out to Kate.

"I will read it as soon as I reach the attic room, I promise you." Kate bowed her head.

A smile crossed Anne's face as she passed through the door.

Holding a flickering candle before her, Kate climbed to her third floor attic room. She arranged the candle in a holder on the table beside her bed. While changing into her night clothes, she took a look around her dear little room. Three beds had been lined up along the inside wall of the tiny space, a reminder of the time when she, Julia, and Lizzie shared the room. A massive wardrobe filled one entire side wall. The trunk Kate brought to America rested beneath the two small front windows. Against the fourth wall, interrupted by the doorway, were the desk and chair where each of the Carty sisters sat, at one time or another, to write letters home.

Kate sat back on her bed and unfolded the many creases in the wide sheet of paper. Could this be the word she and her sisters longed to receive? Would the message the letter contained inform them their young brother and sister were coming to America? Of course not. Anne had said an "old" letter. If it had been a recent message, bearing news of anyone coming, Anne and Julia would have been jumping for joy this evening. Resigned, she held the paper beneath the candle's flame.

December 12, 1868
Blackwater, County Wexford, Ireland

Dear Anne,
I am glad to have the pleasure of writing to you once more. I thought you were after forgetting us altogether. It was so long since we heard from you and we now return you the most sincere thanks for the present you sent in Julia's letter. I hope this letter will find you all in good health as this leaves us all here at present, thank God.

Dear Anne, I hope you won't be so long without writing for the time to come. It is a great comfort to us to hear from you. Tell Julia to send the picture of herself and Martin and the children in the next letter.

Remember us to Kate and tell her to write and let me know particulars about her occupation. I hope with God's help all is well with her.

Dear Anne, I want to let you know the way we are circumstanced here. Michael is in the one place this three years, his time will be out soon. His wages are small, only #12 per year. He is a good boy. Anything he has to spare he gives us. He would like to go to America but we won't give him consent and the reason is your Father has been helpless. He is scarce able to do anything. We are striving to help him in every way for it is hard to pay a man now the men are scarce. I am posting a letter to Julia today. I hope you will get them in due time. Aunt Mary wishes to be remembered to you.

Write soon and I will send you a longer letter. Please let me know if you have any account of Grace Donahoo and also James Brien. Johnny Doran of Ballinard is dead, may the Lord have mercy on him. A great many of the neighbours are sick and dying.

No more from your mother,
Mrs. Carty

Folding the letter, Kate shook her head slowly. It had been written by her mother actually. Difficult to understand, just like Nell Carty. Oh dear, there went every positive resolution she had made that evening.

The image of her father came to her. It had been years since she had seen his face in her dreams. Her heart filled with yearning. Why had so many months passed since they received a letter in Father's hand? Was he ill or injured, and thus unable to write? She made a decision. She would walk to Anne's tomorrow and appeal to her for another one or two of Father's old letters.

Chapter Three

Kate stared at the detailed drawing spread across Walter's board. "You have begun already?" A lump rose in her throat. "Aw, didn't I wish to help with the plan?" She ground her fingers into the small scrap of paper she held in her pocket. She had worked on her sketch most of the night. Was Walter's plan finished entirely? Would her ideas matter at all? Was she to have no say in the design of her own shop?

"'Tis only a rough layout." Head bent to the table, Walter continued to draw. "I've also created a smaller version. I thought you might take it back to the shop to show the other girls." He held up a simple, stationary-size sheet. "Go ahead. Look it over. James and Martin helped me last night, while you worked with the girls in the kitchen."

Had Walter not heard her words? Was he ignoring her disappointment? Kate grasped Walter's smaller rendering and stepped backwards until she banged into the doorway. A wave of tremors raced through her. Without even a thought, she left the room and headed along the dim hallway that led to the back door. She reached for the door latch, but she could not locate it in the darkness. Her shoulders sagged. A huff of air slipped from her mouth. Nothing for it, but she must retrace her steps and return to the office.

Halfway along, she paused in the archway that led to the oven rooms. Her breaths coming quickly now, she leaned against a table just inside the door. Bright rays from the gas lamps, the ovens, and the tall windows across the room afforded enough light for a clear look at Walter's sketch. The details of the drawing and the care he had taken with it brought a new wave of chills. She covered her face with her hand. Wonderful! More than I could ever have dreamed.

She walked back toward the office. What strange malady had taken over her senses? Why had she run out on Walter? Likely she had offended him again. She straightened her back as she reached the doorway. He had every right to be angry. Would he accept her apology, once again?

Standing at the table, working still, he waved Kate over. "Come on up to the table. Let's have a thorough look at this project." He grinned. "I know you are vexed with me. I hear your heels grinding into the floor. Bear with me, now. This is a basic floor plan. You will have free reign of everything within this dark outline."

"Walter, please forgive me." She moved closer to the table. "I had no call to rush out in such an abrupt manner. My attempts at drawing were feeble, a poor excuse beside your fine work. What you've done is magnificent." She eased closer to the table. "There is nothing simple or basic about this layout. The depth and detail are amazing."

"Is Ellen coming?" Walter pushed back his chair and faced her.

She shook her head. "Ellen is working with a customer. A couple with a new home awarded us another substantial drapery order. I'll show this smaller copy of the plans to her and Janey later." She bent over the table for a closer look.

"I thought your present work space could be used for laying out patterns and cutting." Walter pointed out each of the items on the sheet. "The tables could be placed beneath the light fixtures. Martin suggested shelves on the far wall. Then, in the new area—"

"It seems massive. This new space looks to be almost twice the size of our existing room." Tiny bumps rose along Kate's arms. "Oh, excuse me for interrupting."

"Sure, it will be an imposing room, but the far wall is already in place. I see no need to move a wall, just to make it smaller. Do you?" Walter took her hand and guided it along the board to the top of the table. "Here at the outside wall, we could cut two additional windows. That was James's suggestion."

"Is that possible, could it be done?" Kate's breathing accelerated. "Would it be expensive to cut through the brick?" She wrinkled her forehead. Would this grand plan cost more than her limited funds could bear?

"We learned to do the windows when we renovated the oven rooms." Walter dropped her hand and faced her. "With four, you could position a sewing machine at each window. James will ask Mr. Flynn for his assistance. He is an expert, you know. With his help, I believe it will work out. We'll talk about costs later."

"Unfortunately, we have only two machines. Well, I will manage, somehow." She trailed her fingers across the board to the squares to the right of the windows. "And these small boxes?"

"Cabinets." Walter leaned closer, his voice rising. "This is Martin's doing. Shelves here." His pencil tapped the opposite end of the layout. "And another batch of cabinets over here. Our expert offered a few excellent ideas. He is enthusiastic about the plan, but he seems to need reassurance that we want him to help."

Kate read the caring in Walters' deep, brown eyes. "I welcome Martin's help. I did not even dream we could have cabinets and shelves. Rest easy. I will make a point of telling him so."

"No heel grinding?" Walter laughed.

She had become so caught up in her inspection of the drawing, her outburst of temper slipped from her mind. A feeling of ease coursed through her, and she shared a moment of laughter with Walter. "My shoes are silent." She turned back to the plans. "And this marking on the inner wall, across from the existing door?"

"That is a small space partitioned off for a changing room." Walter rapped the board with his pencil.

"A marvelous idea. I did not think of it." Kate ran her fingers along the sleeves of her woolen dress. "I wonder, though, if it would not be better back in the corner of the old space. I think the women might be more comfortable trying on garments if we placed the room in a somewhat darker area at the rear of the shop. Could that be done?"

"An excellent suggestion. I will make the change with no trouble at all." Walter scribbled a note on a small sheet tacked to the wall. "I thought there would be space for two upholstered chairs at the outside wall of the old area, across from where we will move the dressing room. Two others could be placed in the new room, opposite the windows."

"Oh, how grand." She faced Walter. "The entire plan is magnificent. I never even considered windows or a dressing room. And cabinets and shelves. It will all be perfect. The thoroughness of your layout amazes me." She slipped her own amateurish scribbling into the pocket of her apron. "After my outburst, I would not blame you if you abandoned the project altogether. I behaved abominably." Kate lowered her head. "I do apologize."

"Ah, Kate, it is no mind." Walter dropped his pencil on the table and took her hand. "We all understand the turmoil you've experienced this past year."

"All the same, I appreciate your work. It is more than I ever imagined." Kate turned back to the sketch. Beginning at the left edge and following the lines across the board, she examined each detail.

"Ach, my girl, your own suggestions have been excellent." Walter sharpened his pencil with his pocket knife. "You and I will be a grand team. And you know I like nothing better than drawing up plans, unless it is the construction work itself. Now, let us move on with our business."

Kate stood beside him, reviewing the sketch once more. "I can almost picture the finished shop now, Walter. It will be wonderful!" She had been squeezing her lips to hold back an insistent grin, but she relaxed now and allowed it to spread across her face. "I cannot stop gazing at your drawing. Cabinets and windows, just imagine. How will I ever repay you?"

Walter had been sitting with his shoulders hunched over the wide work table. He straightened now and waved his hand in front of his face. "Your brilliant smile is payment enough."

Kate quivered, but there was no time to examine this new and unsettling sensation. She squared her shoulders. "We must discus costs. I have an estimate worked up." She withdrew the paper from her pocket again and placed it on the table with her calculations showing, her amateurish drawing faced down. "I intend to pay for all necessary costs."

"James, Martin, and I propose using building materials left over from our own remodeling projects." Walter read her list, following along each line with his pencil. "That should help with the cost of some of these supplies."

"I appreciate that, I really do, but I must pay for materials you purchase. I insist." Kate's right foot stamped a little harder than she intended. Did Walter hear? "On this point, I stand firm."

"I bow to your wishes, Kate. I made a list of what we will need to start the project and here's my estimate of the costs." Walter handed her a sheet with rows of numbers lined neatly across the page. "The expenditures will change from day to day, as we discover what's needed and what we each have on hand.

"With the offers of help we've received from all sides, there will be no labor costs." Walter placed a firm hand on her shoulder. "I am sure you understand. These good men are our family and friends. No one will accept payment for their work. Certainly not Mr. Flynn. It is his daughter you are providing with employment, after all. On this issue, it is my turn to hold firm." He held her eyes with his own.

She recognized the determination in his gaze and the strong set of his jaw. It was useless to argue. "Very well. I will concede this point. I will, however, take note of each purchase and reimburse you."

"And now, the matter of rent." Kate picked up her own list from the table and pointed to the section marked charges. "The area that makes up the new part of the shop more than doubles the space I now let. You must agree to an increase."

"I will agree to pass on to you the cost of operating the gas lamps for the new area and any additional taxes or permit fees levied by the city." Walter rose from his chair, arms folded high across his chest.

Kate returned his steady gaze. "I believe we have a deal."

Walter placed his pencil on the table with a thud. "My hand to you."

She accepted the hand he offered. Settled at last.

"You're a fine businesswoman, Kate." Walter moved away from his work table. "I am relieved our negotiations are concluded, and we can set to work. I would like to begin this evening. We do not wish our fine friends to forget their offers of help."

"To think it was only yesterday that I approached you on this matter of increased work space." Things surely moved swiftly at Dempsey's. Oh, what bliss.

Kate's eyes wandered all around the room. While Walter provided everyone at Dempsey's with fine accommodations, his office appeared stark. Simple wooden floors and brown windowless walls formed the backdrop. A bookshelf, two long tables, and a desk and chair were the only furnishings. She glanced at the second table where another drawing had been spread out.

Walter followed her gaze. "That is another scheme entirely." He touched her elbow. "Come, look at my latest project. Some years back, when prices were low, I purchased a parcel of land a few city blocks from here. Now, I am attempting to convert the area into a sports field. I marked the dimensions here for hurling. I am also researching the game of soccer, which is increasing in popularity here in the city. If it is possible, I intend to use the field for both sports."

"Will my shop expansion interfere with your plans?" Kate crossed the room to the second table.

"No. The field is in bad shape." Walter increased the flame on the gas lamp, affording Kate a better view. "I must wait until the weather improves and the ground is leveled and seeded."

"And what of your other projects?" With her negotiations completed, Kate conversed with ease. "The air vent that brings a fresh breeze into the bakery shop? The mechanical fan?"

"I have a vent, similar to the one in the bakery, ready to install in the Flynns' home. The fan is not proceeding so well." Walter grinned and shoved his hands in his pockets. "I decided to push that contraption to the far corner of my work room, out of sight. Place some distance between me and the wicked thing, you see." His hearty laugh filled the room.

"Well, I wish you luck with your sports field. I'm sure the project will be a success. As for me, I am thrilled, Walter. I cannot thank you enough. I must run now and discuss it all with Ellen." She headed for the door, then turned and faced him with a wide, unguarded smile. "I cannot wait to show your drawing to the girls. They will be as giddy as I have become. I thank you again, with all my heart."

Walter raised his arm in a wave. "I'll leave the drawing spread out on the table until the work is completed. Bring Ellen and Janey around when they have a moment. I welcome their ideas and suggestions."

Chapter Four

Early the next morning, Kate and Ellen entered the shop and were met with an enormous surprise. The wall between the two rooms had been torn out completely, and the chairs and tables had been moved against the far wall. Kate walked along the entire area. "They certainly worked quickly, did they not?" She stopped in the center of the room, pretending not to notice the layers of dust and plaster everywhere.

"The room is even larger than I imagined it would be." Ellen passed from the old shop area into what would soon be the new space. "Is this not an exciting moment, Kate?"

"I know it will be magnificent once the renovations are complete." Kate raised her hand. "I hereby resolve I will not utter one word of complaint."

"Well, it is a frightful mess." Returning to the center of the room, Ellen ran her fingers along the dusty tabletops.

"Perhaps we could allow ourselves one moment of fretting before we go to work." Kate lifted a canvas cover spread over one of the sewing machines. "Come and look, Ellen. I do not believe the situation is as dreadful as it appeared at first glance. James's suggestion that we cover our sewing machines and material will save us hours of labor and our work from being buried in the dust."

Keeper of the Flame

"Your sister has a splendid husband." Ellen twirled around the room. "Still, there is much to be done. How shall we—"

"We've come to help." Walter's helper, Eddie, entered the room. A short, smiling young man, with already-thinning brown hair and kind, dark eyes, he came armed with two buckets of soapy water and a mop.

"I am here to cart away refuse." George, the second of Walter's bakery helpers, followed behind Eddie. Tall and lean with thick blond hair and intense blue eyes, he held several cartons, large enough to haul away a mountain of trash.

"I apologize for the disorder." Walter moved into the room, arms filled with brooms and a shovel. "By the time we finished tearing out the wall last evening, the hour had grown late. I insisted the men go on home. This debris will be the worst of it, I assure you." He gazed around the room, rubbing his jaw with the palm of his hand. "Ah, the truth is, I cannot promise there will be no dust. From now on, though, I will endeavor to finish in time for a complete cleanup."

"You need not worry. Ellen and I will manage the dust." Kate took up a bucket and an armload of cloths. "Let's begin with the original part of the shop and make it ready for customers. We'll push the refuse toward the empty area." She unlocked the outside door. "Ah, here's our Janey, come to help."

"I see I am just in time." Janey, a slight, dark-haired girl with a strong voice and enthusiastic personality, burst into the room. After a brief examination of the new work space, she took up a broom and began to sweep. "Our new shop will be enormous. I cannot wait to see the place without this mountain of dust." Her chatter exploded through the room, the sound bouncing across the walls of the large, empty area.

Kate and the girls swept and dusted and mopped in a grand united effort, while the men carted away boxes of rubble.

"With this grand help, we've finished the task in good time." She waved to Eddie and George, who pushed the last carton of rubbish through the doorway. "Thank you for your help."

Kate grinned as she handed Walter the buckets and mop. "It seems all I ever do is thank you. Unless, of course, it is to apologize."

"You are welcome, Kate." Walter surveyed the room. "I believe this room will work well for you."

"It will be magnificent." Kate spread her arms and whirled around in a circle. "In all my dreams, I never imagined we would have this much space."

"I do believe our Anne could give dance lessons right in the center of the floor." Ellen paced the length of the room, her bright red curls flying all about. "What do you think?"

"The women of the neighborhood could learn the latest dance steps and then be fitted for new dresses for the next church social." Janey Flynn caught Kate's arm and sent her for another spin.

"I have taken in so many new orders this past week, I cannot help but worry a bit." Kate removed the cover from one of the sewing machines. Folding the cloth, she shrugged her shoulders. "I just pray we will be capable of completing our work in the midst of this chaos."

"This disorder makes me a tad lonesome for the garment factory." Ellen spread a length of cloth along the table beside Kate. "Of course, this bit of confusion could never compare with the enormous, noisy machines, the crowding together of the workers, the stale air of the place, and of course, the cruelty of the foremen." Ellen's expression sobered.

"What is it, Ellen?" The girl's stricken look drained the laughter from Kate.

"I thank God every day for making it possible for me to leave that miserable factory. I am also thankful to you, Kate, for providing me with a job in your fine shop." Ellen wrinkled her brows. "It's just that I worry about the girls I left behind. Some were so young. And they were treated with such unkindness. Perhaps this new union movement we've been hearing about will improve the working conditions."

Ellen's smile blossomed again. "I do believe this dusty room is my favorite place in the entire world." Her joyful laughter resumed, lacking in strength but echoing around the room, bringing giggles from Kate and Janey.

"We will dedicate our efforts each day to gaining additional business, until we have the need for yet another seamstress." Kate bent her head over her sewing machine. "Perhaps we will be capable of hiring one of those girls, or even more, away from the factory."

"Thank you, Kate. That is a wonderful goal." Ellen tapped her scissors on the table. "I do have a suggestion to offer. Perhaps, we could work out an agreement with our Mary. This evening after supper, one of us could spend time working here in the shop cleaning up after the men. The other could double her efforts with helping the girls tidy the kitchen."

"That is a splendid idea." Pulling pins from a length of cloth and placing them in her mouth rendered Kate silent. When she had fixed the pins safely in the cushion, she turned to Ellen. "I am sure Mary will agree to your plan. If we do not keep a step ahead of the dust, it will eventually creep out into the oven rooms, the shop, and even Mary's lovely parlor." Kate reached out to touch Ellen's arm. "You always manage to discover new ideas and plans. What would we do without you?"

"I will return after supper to help." Janey had settled in an easy chair. Her hand flew as she hemmed a wide pink skirt. "I, too, have been saved from a position in a dreaded garment factory. I will gladly come every night if you will have me."

"Thank you, Janey." Kate rose from her chair to arrange the finished dress across the ironing board. "We will accept your help with pleasure. One or two evenings a week will be fine, if your mother will spare you."

❄ ❄ ❄

"Once again, you've come to our rescue, Mary." After discussing their cleaning project and obtaining her blessing, Kate walked from the dining room directly to her shop. Ellen had agreed to stay back and help with the kitchen work.

When she entered the room, Walter held up a long strip of sandpaper. "We are repairing the rough edges laid bare by our demolition of the wall last night. We'll try to hold down the dust, wherever we can."

"Do not worry." Kate placed her cleaning equipment on the table and tied an apron around her waist. "The girls have all volunteered to help with the cleaning, once the kitchen is returned to order." She dipped a cloth in the bucket and squeezed out the excess water. "With the wall removed now, we are able to dream a little. Each of us holds an idea of a color scheme for walls and curtains. We will work without ceasing to make our fancies come true. It is the least we can do."

"We appreciate your hard work, Kate." James Duff approached, holding an empty container. "However, I must warn you, Mr. Flynn has agreed to come next weekend and help with the windows."

"Ah, you are right, James." Walter ceased sanding and walked over to join them. "That project will create a tremendous mess. We must consider moving you and your girls out of here, Kate, while we tear out the areas of the outside wall needed for the windows." When Kate opened her mouth to protest, he held up a hand. "I will talk this over with Mary."

Recognizing Walter's resolute look, Kate said no more. She wiped walls and table tops, following behind the men as they worked.

Janey Flynn arrived and swept and mopped each corner of the shop. After working for over an hour, she stopped to knead her neck and shoulders. "I'm amazed our cleanup progressed so quickly. The men have completed the sanding, and we have rid the place of every speck of dust."

"I'll be right back." Kate held out a hand to Janey. "I'll just be gone long enough to dump out this bucket of dirty water. Please do not leave until I return." When she rushed back to the shop, Janey had buttoned her coat, and the men were slipping into their own jackets. Walter was turning down the gas lights.

"Good night. Thank you." She waved to James and Eddie as they went through the door.

"See if you like this material." She handed a package to Janey. "Mrs. Smith left it for our use, and I thought this green could be the perfect color for a dress for you."

"It is lovely. I cannot wait to begin sewing." She hugged Kate then ran for the door. "My father is likely on his way to fetch me. I'll hurry and meet him halfway. Good night. Thank you for the material."

"You certainly need some rest, Kate." Walter took the mop Kate held and tucked it under his arm. "I do have a small favor to ask. There is a parcel in my office Mary will need first thing in the morning. Will you take it to her?"

"Of course. Will Mary be awake, still?" Kate checked the outside door, making it secure for the night.

"You will likely find her doing some hand work." Walter rushed out. While she checked the windows, he reappeared and handed her a thick envelope.

"I will be happy to take this to her." Kate held the envelope with both hands. "Good night, Walter. Thank you again for your work."

"My pleasure, Kate." Walter moved along the hallway toward his office, his hand held high in a salute. "Good night."

❊ ❊ ❊

Kate climbed to the second floor and knocked on Mary's door. "It is Kate, Mary." She spoke quietly. The Dempsey girls were surely asleep in their dormitory-style room down the hall. There was no need to disturb them.

"Come in, Kate." Mary's response was barely audible.

Pushing open the door, Kate remembered Walter's prediction. Mary sat in her comfortable upholstered chair, a crochet hook held securely in her right hand, otherwise covered from her shoulders to her toes by a voluminous, green afghan.

Kate gazed all around. "I had forgotten how lovely your room is." Everything in the place was white: walls, curtains, furniture, and bedspread. Miniature white rugs placed around the room softened the light, polished wood of the shiny floors. Against this pristine background, the brilliant green of the afghan provided a striking splash of color.

"I brought this envelope from Walter." She moved closer. "Oh, Mary, how beautiful. This color is marvelous."

"Thank you, Kate, for the parcel and for the kind words." Mary continued to work the green yarn. "It is meant for Eddie. He performs so many kind deeds for Walter and me, I wish to show him my appreciation." She held up one corner of the afghan. "Do you think he will like the color?"

"He will love it." Kate knelt beside Mary for a closer look. "Your stitches are perfect. I had no idea you possessed such talent. I would love to learn." She brushed her fingers along the soft wool. "Will you teach me?"

Mary pulled a pillowcase from behind her chair and handed it to Kate. "Choose a color you like. You will find a hook at the bottom of the bag. If you wish, I'll show you right now."

With Mary guiding her hand, Kate labored over her first row of slip stitches. "This pale rose color is lovely. Are you sure you do not mind my using it?"

"Of course I don't mind. In truth, I enjoy the company." Mary sat back a moment, holding Kate's work in her hands. "Ah, your stitches are nice and even. Let us start you on the next row."

Kate grew silent, concentrating on the double crochet stitch Mary demonstrated for row two. As she began the third row, though, she held a hand across her mouth, unable to suppress a yawn. "Sorry. I suppose this long day has made me weary."

"You poor dear." Mary brushed hair back from Kate's face. "You look tired. Is the work on the shop going well?"

"I believe so. I worked alongside the men tonight, cleaning up after them. I carried warm water from the kitchen stove to the shop and scrubbed everything I could reach. If they held an objection to my being there, I did not hear it. They asked my opinion from time to time, and I felt free to make suggestions." She placed needle and yarn in her lap and sat back. "Janey Flynn came in and helped. I found the work a joy, and I'm sure she agreed with me. We were on hand to observe each improvement as it was made. And the place is clean. The other girls volunteered their help, but we were finishing up for the night, and I sent them on to bed. There will be no surprises now, when the seamstresses arrive in the morning."

"Well, you are working hard, that's sure," Mary pulled a sack from a side pocket of her chair. "Why not take the yarn along with you and experiment with it as time permits?" She took the yarn and needle from Kate's hands and placed her work in the bag. "Come by anytime, dear, and we will have another lesson."

"Thank you for showing me the stitches, Mary. I love crocheting." Kate could not suppress another yawn. "I suppose I am more tired than I realized. Good night."

"Good night, Kate." Mary waved her needle in Kate's direction. "Visit me again soon. I've enjoyed our time together."

Kate rushed upstairs to her room. One thing more before her day ended. She fingered the rough edges of the envelope that had rested in her pocket throughout the day. A letter from her father, nearly ten years old. Anne had received it shortly after she arrived in St. Louis.

After preparing for bed, she settled in, holding the paper beneath the flame of the candle.

22nd September, 1859
Blackwater

My dear child,
We hasten to acknowledge receipt of your welcome letter. We are rejoiced at your recovery from ill health and beg you to return our thanks to those friends who sheltered and attended to your wants in the hour of need. Present our thanks to Mr. Fortune, to Walter Dempsey and sister, to Miss Donahoo and brother, and all we can do is pray for their welfare. We are sorry to hear of the uncertainty of your departure for Oregon. The voyage will be expensive from St. Louis and I wish we could be of help to you. It is kind of your Uncle James to send you money toward your passage and we hope, my dear, when you do reach him you will do all in your

power to repay him.

Before leaving St. Louis, write to us and let us know what route you will travel. Is it all a sea voyage or across the Isthmus of Panama or an overland journey?

My dear child, I am happy to inform you your mother's health is good. Kate is at your Uncle Martin's. He and family and Aunt Mary are well and send their love to you. Julia is at home. We are all thank God in the enjoyment of good health. John Donahoo and family are in good health. James Dempsey and family are well. We had a drought here this summer in consequence of which the potato and barley crops are short.

Your mother, sisters, and brothers and I join in sending our love,
John Carty

Chapter Five

February, 1869

"Lovely to come home and find you here, Mary." Kate rushed to the hearth and held her hands near the fire. "It is surely the coldest day of the year. Even with these thick gloves, my fingers are stiff." She reached for the poker and stirred the flames. "Shall I fetch the measuring tape and fit you for a dress?"

"Thank you, Kate, but you've supplied me with dresses aplenty. I've come to see how you are weathering the construction work." She faced Kate with a determined gaze. "The men will begin cutting into the outside wall for the windows tomorrow. You must allow them to move the sewing machines into the parlor. It will be impossible to work amid this dust and grime."

"I admit I've held back." Kate moved dust cloths from the nearest chair and offered it to Mary. "Though I attempted to keep up with the cleaning, the shop is in complete disarray, and grime has materialized everywhere. And we received an order for floor length draperies. Ellen will go and take measurements tomorrow."

"Oh, Kate, that is grand." Mary jumped up and headed for the door. "Is the order large enough to ease Ellen's worries over losing the Palmer House business?"

"No, it is not a hotel. Still, it is a grand home. A good bit of work. It would be near to impossible to spread out the lengths of cloth and complete the measuring and cutting in here. If we are to complete the project in good time, we will be forced to move out of our shop." Walking along beside Mary, Kate reached out and tucked a curl beneath her friend's cap. "I did not wish to push you from your own parlor, but I must relent and accept your kind offer. I assure you, we will all take care to keep your beautiful room in perfect condition."

"Don't give it a thought." Mary waved her hand in front of her face as she stepped out into the hallway. "With so many coming to help each evening, the work will be finished in no time, I'm sure."

"That's what Walter tells me. I pray he is right. Sure, the girls will be pleased to work in a quiet space again…wait, Mary…" Kate rushed to the shop again and came back with a heavy burlap sack. "I had almost forgotten your coins."

Mary shook the bag in the air, the coins inside clinking together. "Thank you for picking up change from the bank for me."

"'Tis the least I could do."

※ ※ ※

"I have scrubbed everything I could reach. I am finished for the evening." Kate settled into a chair in Mary's room. "I need your assistance again." She pulled a small afghan from her bulky sack. "I believe this is a good size for a girl as tiny as Nell, but I would like to add a trim. Would fringe work?" She spread the small coverlet across the end of Mary's bed.

"Ah, it is lovely, Kate. Your stitches are perfect. When did you ever find the time to complete this? With your growing business and the cleanup in the shop, you must be exhausted when you climb to your room at the end of your long day." Mary took the ball of pink yarn from Kate's hand. Her fingers flew. Measuring and cutting short strands of yarn, she demonstrated how to slip the pieces through the edge of the afghan and tie them to form a fringe. "Here is one possibility. What do you think?"

"That is perfect. Allow me to give it a try." Kate sat beside Mary and copied her example. She undid her first effort and tried again. "Actually, the motion of the crochet needle and the feel of the soft yarn soothe me." Satisfied with her second effort, she bent to her work. "I often experience trouble settling down to sleep at night, but after a short time with the crocheting, I climb into bed and drift right off. Before the work on the shop is completed, I may have created an afghan for each of my nieces and the girls in the shop, as well."

"You surely take grand care of your workers." Mary dropped her needles and yarn into her basket. "Do you mind, dear, if I ask you a personal question?" When Kate shook her head, Mary scooted forward until their knees touched. "Do you suppose your time working at that miserable Hogan's place back home benefitted you in a small way? Did the harsh conditions you endured and the cruel treatment you received there lead you to become the conscientious shop owner and kind employer you are today?"

"Well, I thank you for the compliment about my workers." Kate stilled her fingers. Why had Mary's suggestion never occurred to her? "I did not think any good had come from my father sending me to work in that place. You know, I blamed the dreadful conditions at Hogan's for Lizzie's illness. I am attempting to forgive my father. At times I believe I am succeeding. Your idea that I learned something there may help me. I will think on it, I promise you."

"Ah, you're a good girl, Kate. I only wish to help you move out of your sadness. If any small thing I said will be of assistance, I'm happy for it." Mary pulled a handkerchief from her pocket and blew her nose. "You know, I loved our little Lizzie. I miss her. And, I love you and your sisters. Each one of you is dear to me. If there is anything at all I can do, please tell me."

❦ ❦ ❦

An easy, joyful breeze stirred deep within Kate as she sat with Mary again the following evening. This fresh, peaceful state had certainly not been brought on by the fierce snowstorm raging outside the window. Was her tranquility caused by the crocheting? Or perhaps her quiet talks with her dear friend?

"The men are making quick work of the expansion, and they seem to be doing a fine job." Mary held a teacup out to Kate, but when she shook her head, they went back to their work. "Your shop will reap the benefits of the experience Walter, James, and Martin gained when they worked together on the remodeling of the bakery building and the renovation of Anne's home."

"So many others have offered their help." Kate rummaged in her bag for scissors. "Eddie, George, James's brother Ned, and Martin's brother Patrick all volunteered their help. Several men from St. Vincent's have come to lend a hand. And now, Mr. Flynn directs the work on the windows each night." Finding the scissors, she opened the sharp blades wide for Mary's approval.

"Is that the pair you brought from home?" Mary tested the blades with her thumb. "Nothing like County Wexford scissors."

"You must come and see the work Martin completed on the cupboards and shelves." Distracted by a picture that entered her mind of the goods stored on the shelves at Hogan's, Kate quieted. Shaking herself, she tucked the scissors away and took up the yarn. "Though Martin is limited with what he can do, he guides the others in the project. He accepts his role of sometime teacher, sometime helper with grace and good cheer."

"Julia's husband is a wonder, that's sure." Mary said.

"Walter, of course, is there every evening. He tells me the building is his priority, and I bow in agreement." Kate nudged Mary's elbow and winked. "I know the truth. He wishes to help me. I am eternally grateful for his kindness."

"I know Walter, James, and Martin are accustomed to your working beside them, but are the other men surprised to find you there?" Mary rose and spread her afghan across the end of her bed.

"I assume so." Kate chuckled. "I rarely work there alone. Janey Flynn helps some evenings, and the other girls come in once the kitchen work is done. They were all there one night when the talk turned to Walter's sports field." Kate walked to the bed and ran her hand along the soft wool of Mary's afghan. "It is lovely, Mary. Will I help you press it?"

"No, I'll bring it to the parlor tomorrow and use your iron." Mary folded the cover and sat back in her chair. "Did the men approve of the sports field?"

"Oh, yes. Eddie is convinced they will all be getting grand exercise running up and down the field. Martin knows all about hurling, and Walter spoke of missing the hurling matches from his days back home. Most admitted they have never seen soccer, or football as it is called back home." Kate packed her work in her bag. Time to go. She needed rest. "James brought hearty laughter all around, when he suggested a wager on how many months would pass before one of them kicked the soccer ball through the goal."

❁ ❁ ❁

Keeper of the Flame

Kate knelt on the floor of her shop, scrubbing away with a brush and soapy water. Ah, my, would the accumulation of dirt never end? She sat back to rest her shoulders against the wall. "I was surprised to learn you are a prodigious reader, Walter." He was sanding the wood around the new windows, preparing the surface for painting. "What type of books do you prefer? Tell me some of your favorites."

"I enjoy the adventure stories. James lent me a few of his." Walter stepped down from the ladder and dragged it across the floor to the next window. "James Fenimore Cooper's 'The Last of the Mohicans' is my favorite, and I have just purchased Dickens's 'Oliver Twist.'"

"You're good to share your thoughts with me." Kate moved to the window Walter had just vacated. Dipping a cloth in the soapy water, she scrubbed the new woodwork. "I was also pleased to discover you listen to what I have to say and encourage me to express my ideas freely. How refreshing that is."

"Well, of course, I wish to hear your views." Walter removed his hat, and brushing his fingers through his thick, curly hair, he studied her intently. "You have much to offer, Kate. Why would I not want to hear your ideas?"

"Our friend, Mr. Reilly, believed women should be silent and keep their opinions to themselves." Ah, no. If only she could push back her words. Why had she brought that man's name into the conversation?

"He's an ejit. And this evening is not the first time I have thought him so." Walter's hearty laugh rang throughout the shop.

She laughed with him. "I believe you are right." She had been kneeling, scrubbing the lower edges of the window sill, and the unexpected mirth sent her toppling against the window.

Walter walked over and offered his arm. "Allow me to help you." When she held his arm lightly and sprang up, he reached out and touched her cheek.

Such a gentle gesture. She shook her head, wondering.

Without a word, he moved back to his work. A few quiet moments passed, and then Walter spoke again. "You know, Mary and I arrived in St. Louis some eighteen years ago, after our parents died of cholera back home in Ireland. I will never be able to thank her for her hard work and support. Our early days in St. Louis were wrought with trials, and she has been a real partner to me through all these years."

"You'll receive no argument from me on that score." Was Walter speaking of Mary because he considered her a safe subject? Her curiosity pressing her on, Kate edged closer and gazed at him until he looked her way, a tinge of pink across his cheeks. Not wishing to cause him embarrassment, she backed away. But she couldn't help but wonder. What prompted him to reach out and touch her? And why had the gesture discomfited him?

"Mary and I often spend an hour or so together, before I retire for the evening. I have come to believe she is the kindest, most generous person I have ever known." Kate stole another glance Walter's way. Had he recovered his composure?

"Mary is that." Walter bent to his work, sanding the window frame with vigor. "We have been family for one another these many years. Still, I long for a home of my own." He chuckled. "I am sure you know all about Mary's matchmaking efforts. I have begged my sister to allow me to manage these things myself. In truth, I have not given up hope that one day I will be blessed with a family."

Walter moved to the window where she worked and addressed her with a twinkle in his eyes. "And you, young lady, are you to be a businesswoman all your life?" he asked. "Do you hold my same dream of a home and family?"

Warmth rose up within her. Her own cheeks had likely turned pink now. She had no response ready for him. She opened her mouth but could not form one intelligent word. She pressed her lips together.

"And what of our good Mr. Reilly? It seems he has not forgotten about you. Is there any hope for him at all?" When he turned toward her, all teasing had vanished, and his deep, brown eyes held the kindest expression she had ever seen.

"Breaking off with Francis last year did not cause me sadness or heartache." She exhaled. If only she could thrust away this talk of Francis, as easily as she had blown out her breaths. "As I have already mentioned, Francis had no intention of listening to anything I had to say." She shook her head. Why had it become so important to her that Walter know the truth about Francis Reilly? But she wanted him to know. "He is searching for a wife who will stand a pace back from him and agree with his every word and deed. We were wrong for each other, entirely. His absence in my life brings only relief, I am sad to say." Kate halted her cleaning and faced Walter.

"Our falling out last year over Francis doing business with the man who stole money from my sisters was only the beginning of our differences." Kate dropped scrub brush and rags into her bucket and placed it on the floor. "Oh, I was angry with him over the matter, to be sure. He gave no consideration to the fact that the money Fortune stole from Anne and Julia was meant for my passage to America. He seemed not to care that I was forced to remain in Ireland, working at Hogan's, while my sisters saved for my passage all over again."

She searched Walter's eyes. Was it the kindness and caring she found there that drew her to him? "It is good of you to listen to this story, Walter. The poor, foolish Mr. Reilly, while a perfectly kind man in some ways, believes a woman should speak out only when asked her opinion." She had confided most of the story to him. Perhaps someday she would summon the courage to tell him the rest.

"Somehow, I cannot picture you standing back, waiting for permission to speak, Kate. I agree you did the right thing in ending the courtship." Walter grinned a little, and when she raised an eyebrow in his direction, his laughter rang out again.

❋ ❋ ❋

Kate worked with Walter, scrubbing the walls and floor of the new dressing room the men had completed. After an hour of steady work, she placed her brush on the floor. "Would you like some tea or water?" She lifted a pitcher, tilting it in his direction.

"Tea, please." He sat down in the nearest chair and accepted the drink from her. Taking a sip, he leaned back. "I know you have heard that I have taken the pledge."

Kate filled her cup and walked over to sit beside him. "How old were you?"

"I was just a lad of fifteen. Too young to have any idea what it meant to never take a drink during my entire lifetime." Walter rolled his head slowly from side to side. A tiny frown crossed his face.

"Are you angry with your father for insisting you take the pledge? Have you regretted giving your word?" Kate leaned closer. Here was a subject she struggled with each day.

"No. I loved my father. I miss him." A shadow crossed Walter's eyes. "I know he wished a good life for me. I could never be angry with him. I sometimes wish I could have made the decision on my own, though."

"I am trying still to forgive my father." Kate paused. The words were difficult to say, nearly impossible. "I loved him dearly. I suppose I still do. But, I cannot understand how he could send me to that terrible Hogan's Dry Goods Emporium to work. He pretended everything was fine, but he knew the truth. It was not.

"Each week, when I came home to spend Sunday with the family, I told Father every detail." She rose and paced the floor. "The workers, all children, shared space in a shack behind the store. We slept on straw pallets on the dirt floor. Mice and insects came through the holes in the wall and pestered us throughout the night. We worked from sunup to sundown, with only scraps of bread and gruel for sustenance. Mr. Hogan beat anyone who complained or laughed or stopped to rest."

"I am so sorry, Kate. Your father must have been desperate." Walter placed a hand on her arm.

"When I left for America, I begged Father not to send the younger girls there. I showed him the scars I bore from Mr. Hogan's cruel stick." Kate wrapped her arms around her body. "When he sent Lizzie there, I knew she would not be strong enough to withstand it. By the time she arrived in St. Louis, it was already too late. A terrible cough had settled deep within her, and she never did recover. I hold Father and the Hogans to blame for her death."

"And your mother?" Walter spoke softly.

"Oh, of course, it was all her doing. She pushed him to send us out to work. But Father loved us. He never failed to tell us so. He should have been strong enough to stand up to my mother. He should have known better." Kate bowed her head.

"Will you ever find it in your heart to forgive them?" Walter's eyes held steady, never leaving her face.

"I am trying. I discussed it with Mary. She thinks releasing the anger at Father would free me to move forward. I recently began reading a few of the letters Anne received from him when she arrived in St. Louis. Father's words are so filled with love. I miss him so, Walter, but—"

"Perhaps, if you continue to read the letters, talk to your sisters, talk to me." Walter took her hand and held it between his. "If it helps you at all, I am ready to listen, anytime."

"It does help." Were her breaths already coming easier? Perhaps, she could forgive. "Thank you. I will remember you offered to listen. I long for peace. I do not wish to go through my life burdened with anger."

Chapter Six

March, 1869

"What will we do for our Mary?" Kate sat with her patient, while Dr. Gallagher checked for fever, listened to her breathing, and prodded for pain.

Snapping his bag shut and fastening the buckle at the top, he stepped over to Kate. "She will be fine."

"I suspect you have the grippe." The doctor touched Mary's shoulder. "I'll see you again tomorrow."

He wrote a few sentences on a small paper and passed it to Kate. "Will you insist she rest in bed for two full days?"

As the doctor's footsteps retreated toward the first floor, Kate helped Mary to a chair. "I'll place fresh sheets on the bed and fetch a clean gown for you."

"Thank you, dear." Mary's voice was no more than a whisper, and her eyelids blinked shut, as if they contained heavy weights.

"You rest now." Kate helped Mary back into bed, and as she pulled a sheet around her, she drifted off to sleep.

She found Walter at work in the oven room. "The doctor believes Mary's ailment is the grippe. He prescribed bed rest for two days and assured me she would be fine. He will come again tomorrow." She handed Walter the doctor's instructions. "Before I left the room, she had already fallen asleep."

"Ah, Kate, you are so kind to care for Mary." Walter placed a tray of biscuits on the counter.

"'Tis nothing at all. I love Mary. You know that." Kate stood still, measuring her breaths. Surely it was the run down the steps that winded her. A few words of praise from Walter would not leave her gasping, would it?

"Could I ask an additional favor?" Walter held his baker's hat, passing it from hand to hand. "Will you help in the bakery for a bit? Our little Grace is doing her best out there, but a crowd has gathered. I hesitate to pull you away from your own work any longer, but you are experienced out in the shop. You would be a great help to Grace." He placed his hat on his head. "I will send Delia to assist you, after we remove these loaves from the oven."

Kate gave Walter a questioning look. "Grace performs well in the shop, does she not?"

"She makes a valiant effort to emulate the outstanding work of the Carty sisters in the shop, but the task is daunting." Walter grinned. "She is shy and retiring by nature, and you and I know the anguish she suffered when that fool suitor of hers back home failed to join her in America. She lost all confidence in herself." Walter lifted several large cartons from the counter and followed Kate to the door. "I've tried to bolster her belief in her own abilities, but she needs constant reassurance. Perhaps, if she had family here, they could help. What has happened to her people, do you know?"

"Her brother, who came to America with Anne and Grace, is now Father Edward Donahoo and serves a parish outside Kansas City. I have not seen him in a long while." Kate touched her forehead in salute. "Well, I will go out and help. I remember how busy it can be in the shop early in the morning. And you know, any small opportunity to repay you and Mary for your kindness brings me pleasure."

❦ ❦ ❦

"I will be working in the bakery for a time, Ellen." Kate leaned her head through the doorway of the parlor and addressed her helper.

"How is our Mary faring?" Ellen shook out her sewing work and rose from her chair.

"Mary is resting comfortably, but a crowd has formed in the bakery, and Grace needs help."

"You run along." Ellen approached Kate and squeezed her arm. "We will be fine here."

Kate found the shop filled with customers. She stood beside Grace and wrapped baked goods, placed them in the women's shopping baskets, collected coins, and made change. An hour flew by before all had been served and the shop restored to order.

"Thank you." A wan smile spread across Grace's face. "Wasn't I about desperate out here with no Mary to assist me and so many wanting my help?"

"Business has grown since I last worked in the bakery." Kate collected empty trays and stacked them on the table against the wall. "I have never attempted to serve so many at once. I've gained a new measure of appreciation for your work, Grace. You do a grand job of it."

Kate gazed around the room, admiring the look of the bakery. Determined their shop must be spotless at all times, Walter and Mary had painted the walls, floors, shelves, and counters a gleaming white and kept the place clean with constant scrubbing. A few months ago, she had convinced Mary to allow her to experiment with fresh, new window coverings. The result was remarkable. The white cotton curtains, with thin diagonal stripes of bright red and blue lent a cheerful, homey touch to the room, while maintaining the crisp, clean look the Dempseys desired.

"Your curtains brought joy to our Mary." Grace followed her gaze and reached high to touch the material. "Not a day goes by that she does not remark how much she admires the colors and how talented she believes you to be."

"Thank you, Grace. Nothing could make me happier than pleasing Mary." A customer came through the door, and Kate rushed to assist her. Then she moved on to the next woman who entered the shop…and the next.

A little before noon, Delia, the newest Dempsey helper, walked through the archway from the back of the building. "I am here to replace you, Kate."

"Well then, it is time to take my leave." With the shop quiet and Delia in place behind the counter, Kate removed her apron. "I am impatient to return to my sewing machine."

The bell over the door jingled, and as Kate turned toward the sound, the sun touched the windows with its full brilliant force. A short, stocky young man with rather wild brown hair pushed the door open. The bright light obscured his face momentarily, but a tiny stirring of memory touched deep within her and she shivered.

"Is it our Kate, then?" The young man moved to the center of the room.

Those words, the language of home, brought a stinging to her eyes and caused a dryness to form inside her mouth. She ran her fingertips along the row of buttons at the front of her dress.

"Have I found you, after all these years?" The bearer of a quality of voice peculiar to Blackwater, Ireland pushed the door closed.

"Michael. Can it be?" She spoke with great effort. She pushed one foot forward…then, the other.

"It is." He stepped closer.

"Oh, my word." With her heart pounding and tiny spurts of wind rushing through her ears, she ran toward her brother and wrapped her arms around him. "Praise be to God! You have come, at last."

He leaned down and rested his head on her shoulder.

His gesture, so intimate and so brief no one but her would have noticed, brought a cry of joy to her lips. The sandy brown hair, a faint, far away memory, touched her shoulder and tickled her chin. She could not still her fingers. She stroked the soft strands the way she had so many times when he was a child.

"Well, I have made my way to you at last." Michael took a step away. "I arrived in Boston two months ago and worked for a time to earn train fare. I stopped again in Chicago and found employment there. What fine cities they are, with the grand tall buildings and the great crowds of people in constant motion." Michael placed his patched, canvas bag on the floor. "Bless me, though, if St. Louis does not appear the finest of them all." He pulled his fingers through his thick hair. "Forgive me for going on so. I cannot cease my ravings over everything in America. I will calm myself, I give you my word."

His smile dissolved the passage of years and the pain and sorrow of their separation. Though Kate recognized the happy-go-lucky little boy she once called in from play and scrubbed to meet their mother's approval, little remained of that carefree lad. Here stood a toughened, weathered young man, the lines of his face revealing a youth spent taking on much of the support of their family. Ah, and he no more than a lad. Michael's dark brown eyes sparkled, though, and his warm and wonderful smile had survived.

"I expected to gain no more than directions here, and now with God's fine intervention, I have found you." Michael gazed around the shop. "My good fortune holds with me."

"How are Father, Mother, and Maggie?" Kate held her brother's arm with a firm grip.

"They are all well, thanks be to God." Michael patted her fingers that still grasped his arm.

"Oh, Michael, I am near speechless with the surprise and joy of seeing you. It is astonishing. Magnificent." What should be done first? Kate moved toward the rear of the shop, then stepped back to her brother. "We must inform Anne and Julia you are here. It will be a while before you meet the Dempseys, though. Walter is off on his delivery rounds, and Mary is upstairs recuperating from a mild illness."

"I have a letter with me from the Dempseys' aunt and uncle." Michael lifted his bag from the floor.

"I remember Mr. and Mrs. Dempsey well." The faces of the elderly couple, who lived a short distance from their home passed before Kate. Such kind folks…of course, they were kind…they were related to Walter and Mary. "How are they?"

"Grand." Michael opened his bag. "Mrs. Dempsey is convinced letters to America are dumped in the deepest reaches of the Atlantic. She would not be satisfied until I promised to hand her letter to her niece and nephew personally."

"You will see Walter before the day ends, I am sure, and you can deliver it to him then." Another strong shiver surged through Kate. Had the splendid shock and surprise she experienced when Michael walked through the door rendered her a blathering fool? "I am forgetting my manners. Right here behind the counter stands our Grace Donahoo, herself a fine Blackwater girl. Sure, I know you were young when she and Anne left Ireland together. You likely do not remember her, but she will be so pleased to see you. We all love to talk with anyone newly arrived from home."

She led Michael toward the counter at the center of the room. "Allow me to introduce you to Grace. And here is Delia, our newest bakery helper, and Rosie, sister to my seamstress Janey. You will have an opportunity to come to know them all, but for now, we will be brief. I must take you to Anne and Julia."

"Well, a roomful of Irish lasses. Sure, I believe I've captured a rainbow." Michael favored each of the girls with a splendid smile. He approached Grace and extended his hand. "And here's a lovely Blackwater girl. It is grand to see you again, Grace, after all these many years. And sure, I came bearing particular news for you." He rummaged through the valise again and pulled out a wrinkled envelope. "From your brother William. I spoke with him the night before I left home. He asked that I deliver the note to you as soon as I arrived in St. Louis."

Grace opened the envelope and pulled out a single sheet. "Thank you, Michael. After my father died, I worried I would never hear a word from my family in Ireland again." Tears rolled along her cheeks as she read the letter.

Kate placed an arm around the girl's shoulder and attempted to comfort her. "Well now, you've received news, at last." Impatient to reach her sisters, she took in a sharp breath. When Grace finished her letter and her tears turned to smiles, Kate moved away and took Michael's arm.

Walking through Dempsey's hallway with her brother sent a new chill coursing through her. He had come at last. The touch of him and the sound of his voice brought home right back to her. She had missed him so. She pinched her arm. She must halt this rambling.

"Your own shop, that is grand. You've had some success here already, have you not?" Michael followed Kate past the dining room to the parlor. "I never doubted it, though. You always were the determined one."

"The Dempseys helped me. They help me still. I will be forever beholden to them." Kate placed her hand on the door. "Walter is expanding my dressmaking shop, and Mary has allowed us the use of her parlor while the place is in disarray." She took a step back and lowered her voice. "Prepare yourself, these girls are none of them the retiring sort." A giggle escaped. Wasn't she still silly with the shock? "Once again, you will be scrutinized, admired, and prodded for information.

"We will not linger, though. As soon as I check on things here, we will hurry to Anne's. I cannot withhold the news of your arrival from her any longer." Kate stepped inside the parlor and pulled Michael along with her. "Our dear sister has been waiting for someone from Blackwater to come and stay in the lovely home James Duff rebuilt for her. She will insist you reside with her, you know."

❀ ❀ ❀

"Young man, will you deliver a message for me?" They walked out the door of Dempsey's, headed for Anne's. Kate waved to a boy sitting on the step, whittling away at a stick. She handed him a note for Julia and gave him explicit directions to her house.

"Here, young fellow." Michael tossed a coin his way, and the lad ran off to deliver the dispatch. Then Michael took her arm and they walked on.

Kate pointed out places of interest for him along the way. A grin spread across her face as Michael exclaimed over each building. She pointed to the right and they turned the corner. "Those are fine places, but I cannot wait to observe your reaction upon your first sight of the Duffs' home."

"Which house?" Michael gazed along the street.

"It is the place at the end of the road. I must also prepare you for the folks you will find in residence there. James's brother Ned lives with them. Of course, you know James and Ned, two excellent Blackwater lads. Julia's husband, Martin, stayed at the Duffs' for some time after the tragedy that took his arm. You know about the accident, do you not?" At Michael's nod, she went on. "His brother, Patrick Tobin, moved in with them to help care for Martin, and Patrick remains now as a boarder."

She clung to Michael's arm. Even the brisk walk could not brush away the shock and surprise that lingered with her. Smile...he has arrived. The strong pinch she administered to herself earlier had not jarred her into accepting this miracle.

As they came upon the house and climbed the first step, he slowed, turning his head from side to side, taking in the span of the porch across the front of the house. "Whew." Michael's strong whistle would have startled the neighbors, had anyone been on the street at midday

"Michael?" When Anne opened the door and found him standing on the porch, her face paled.

"Easy there, Anne." Worried she might topple over, Kate reached out to steady her, but Michael reacted quickly. His strong hold of their sister allowed Kate to step back and observe the reunion.

"I cannot believe it!" After a fierce embrace, Anne pulled Michael inside. She maneuvered her head around him and fixed Kate with a stare. "Is this a vision?" Leading the way, through the hallway toward the kitchen, she moved on a few paces then turned back again. "You must meet my Tom."

"What a magnificent home." Michael followed Anne, moving slowly, examining the parlor and dining room. Finally they entered the bright, roomy kitchen. "Did James Duff do all this?"

"Every bit of it." Kate stretched her arms all about to include every corner of the room. "You cannot even imagine the dilapidated condition of this place when James purchased it."

"Walter, Martin, and many other friends provided him with help." Anne's smile shone with pride.

Kate noticed her sister still trembled. "Perhaps you should sit, dear." She took Anne's arm. "Our surprise nearly put you off your feet. I understand it. I am only now beginning to recover myself."

"I am so happy to see you, Michael. I will not allow the shock to overtake me for even a minute." Anne hugged him again. "How are Father and Mother and Maggie?"

"He says they are well Anne." Kate pushed her sister into a chair. "When Julia arrives Michael will supply us with all the details.

"You know, Michael, no one deserves this moment of joy more than our Anne." Kate continued to hold onto her sister. "It has been Anne, after all, who saved money all these many years since her arrival in St. Louis. We suffered disappointments, again and again, when Father spent the passage money we sent to pay the taxes on the land in Ireland. Julia and I often grew discouraged, but Anne never gave up. She continued to save and urged us on as well."

"Aw, Kate, you and Julia did all you could to help." Anne bounced up again. "Come, I'll make tea and you must describe the crossing and tell us about everyone at home."

"I will make the tea. Our walk from Dempsey's has placed me a few steps ahead of you in clearing my head and recovering from the surprise." Kate took up the teapot. "Perhaps you are calm enough to introduce Michael to wee Tom here?"

Michael walked over to where Tom sat with eyes wide, observing the adults. He knelt on the floor beside the chubby, sandy-haired little boy. "I am your Uncle Mike, lad."

Kate felt her heart might jump outside of her when her brother extended his hand to the child. She watched Tom hold out his toy train to Michael, and with a serious, solemn face, demonstrate how the whistle worked.

Keeper of the Flame

Quick footsteps crossed the back porch, and Kate rushed to the door.

In a great explosion of energy and excitement, Julia swept into the room. She carried a baby girl in each arm. "Michael! I cannot believe it. We prayed you would come. We waited and prayed." She hugged him, squashing the two babies between them.

Hearty squeals burst forth from tiny Elizabeth and her sister Maura, making them all laugh.

Another wail came from the direction of the nursery.

"Ah, it's Nell." Anne hurried across the hall.

Kate took a baby from Julia's arms. Maura? She could never be certain. "Michael, meet Elizabeth and Maura. I'll leave it to Julia to inform you which twin is which."

"'Tis the lovely Maura you hold, Kate." Julia wrinkled her nose at her and turned to Michael.

"Now tell me please, Michael. Everyone at home, are they well?"

Kate could not hold back her giggle, as Anne approached holding a bundle wrapped in blankets, the tiny face peeking through the folds bathed in tears. Baby Nell's cries brought on wails of sympathy from Julia's twins. "Well, one thing is certain, they have joined together in a magnificent greeting for you, Michael."

With his right hand, Michael caressed the cheek of the tearful, dark-haired baby in Anne's arms and stroked the curls of each blonde twin. He bent down and used his left hand to help Tom pull his train along the tracks. "Ah, sisters, they are all grand."

Questions for Michael had been forming in Kate's mind. If only there was time. "I wish to stay and hear every word you say, but I must leave you and return to my shop."

"It will not be for long, Kate. I've decided that, with Mary ailing, we will hold Michael's 'welcome supper' here this evening. Will you please invite everyone at Dempsey's for me?" Anne had settled Nell on the floor in the center of the room, and Kate placed Maura beside her baby cousin.

"I am so sorry our Mary will not be able to attend." Julia added Elizabeth to the group of babies on the floor. "Please tell her I will visit tomorrow."

Kate pulled Michael up from the floor for one last hug. "I wish I could stay. Promise me you will discuss naught but the weather, until I return."

❀ ❀ ❀

Back in her temporary shop, Kate settled herself in her chair, taking deep breaths to calm her still skipping heart. She hemmed a dress and then pressed it.

"May I help you?" Janey Flynn took the gown from Kate and hung it on a hook her brother-in-law Martin had installed beneath a row of high cabinets.

"Yes, please, Janey. Mrs. O'Brien will bring her own box when she comes to collect the dress. Just help her fold it carefully. She will wish to return in the morning and pay for it. She has her own decided way of doing things, and that is fine. As one of my first customers, she has earned some leeway." After a fleeting glance at the soft blue gown, she headed for the door. "I must see to Mary."

She rushed up the stairs to the second floor. She could not go another minute without sharing with Mary all that happened in these few short hours. "How are you, dear?" Kate rested her hand on Mary's forehead. "Ah, your skin feels cool. That is grand." She sat in the small chair beside the bed.

"I am much better, Kate." Mary pushed back her covers and raised herself to a sitting position. "I believe I will be capable of coming down to the shop in the morning."

Keeper of the Flame

"Two days of rest, girleen." Kate held up the written instructions Walter had placed on the bedside table. "These are your orders. I promised Dr. Gallagher I would see to it, you know."

"Yes. I know. But I am already missing out." Mary held out a hand to Kate. "What a grand surprise it is, though, to hear your Michael has arrived. I look forward to meeting him, at long last."

"Oh, Mary, I am so happy. In truth, I am still a little shocked." Kate held her arm out to demonstrate how she trembled still. "Poor Anne, she was shaken with the surprise. Michael will stay with her, of course. And we will be going there for supper. I only wish you could attend the celebration. I will miss you." Kate felt herself bouncing, and she eased back in the chair to prevent it from vibrating.

"Julia will be here to see you tomorrow, and Anne intends to bring Michael to meet you as soon as you are well. Ah, my, 'tis a wonderful thing. He is every bit as fine a lad as I expected him to be."

Kate stood and smoothed the covers. "Shall I brush your hair? Bring fresh water?"

"I want for nothing." Mary gave Kate a push. "Go now, and come back tonight with a full report of the entire grand party. Off with you. I will rest until you return."

Kate extended Anne's supper invitation to each of the Dempsey folks, rushed to her room to refresh herself, and started on her way to the Duffs'.

Chapter Seven

"I am here to help." Kate found an apron behind the cupboard door and tied it around her waist. "What will I do for you?"

"I'm glad you have come, Kate. Will you sort the silverware and arrange it beside the plates already on the table?" Anne stood at the kitchen table, carving a roast and heaping the slices on an oblong platter.

As Kate gathered forks and spoons and placed them in a small straw basket, she heard footsteps on the back stairs. Gazing out the window, she watched Julia and Martin cross the porch, each holding a baby girl. "Good evening, Martin. Did you not receive a grand surprise when you returned from work this evening?"

"Good evening, Kate, how are you faring?" Martin held the door, and Julia entered before him.

"We are all in a stir, are we not, Julia?" Taking up her cutlery basket, Kate led them to the dining room. Anne followed behind them, bearing the heavy platter.

Settled in a chair at the far end of the room, Michael helped young Tom stack blocks on the table. "You'll make a splendid builder one day, lad—"

"Michael, I've brought you my husband." Julia pulled Martin along the length of the table.

"It is wonderful to have you here with us, Michael." Martin offered him a handshake with his good right hand, while the smiling baby Maura nestled in the crook of his arm. "Sure, we have heard your name mentioned a time or two by your sisters. And it is grand to hear your family in Blackwater is well."

"Ah, Martin, 'tis magnificent to make your acquaintance, at last." Michael rose from the chair and met them halfway along the table.

Kate moved to the other side of the table, placing knives, forks and spoons beside each plate while observing the scene unfolding around her.

Martin's brother, Patrick, part of the family at the Duffs', slipped into the room. "I feel as though I know you already, Michael. And, aye, if you don't sound just like home."

"I agree with that." James Duff came in, just home from work, along with his own brother, Ned. A great round of handshakes and "welcomes" followed.

Listening to the men's talk, Kate inclined her head toward Anne, who had come up behind her. "Will our Michael not hold a decided advantage, arriving in America with relatives and friends already here? And, living with you and James, he will enjoy the company of Ned and Patrick. Ned is a few years older, but the two did know one another back home." She and her sister watched as the young Blackwater men included Martin and his brother Patrick into the group.

A stir erupted in the hall, and then Walter appeared in the doorway, followed by Eddie, Grace, Ellen, and Cara. He glanced all around before directing his words to Kate. "I have been charged by Mary to assure you that Cara volunteered to stay back with our patient. You know our Mary, though. She would have none of it. She insisted she was fine and Cara must come with us."

Walter crossed the room and shook Michael's hand. "Aye, I am pleased to meet you. You are so dear to your sisters." He looked over again at Kate then back to Michael. "It was Lizzie, most recently from your home, who spoke so warmly of you."

"Pleased to meet you, Walter. I assure you I've heard your praises many times. Ah, and your mention of Lizzie, reminds me…" Michael pulled a small, weathered envelope from his pocket, and after unwrapping the faded brown covering, presented Kate with a sketch of their young sister. "This picture comes to you from the hand of Nell Carty."

"Ah, Lizzie was just a child. It is an excellent likeness." Kate passed the worn paper to her sisters, who gathered beside her. "While the rendering brings a tug of sadness, we cannot allow anything to spoil the joy of Michael's arrival." She inclined her gaze to Anne and then Julia. Surely they experienced this same exhilaration that had taken over her being. "We have longed for Michael to come for all these many years. We will celebrate tonight."

"You are right, Kate," Anne said. "I am incapable of sadness tonight. And yes, it is a wonderful likeness." She handed the picture around for all to admire.

"It is marvelous!" Julia took a sleepy baby from Martin, and with a twin in each arm, she headed for the nursery across the hall. "I will be right back."

Kate wrapped the picture again and placed it in her pocket. Then she and the other girls followed Anne to the kitchen. When she returned to the dining room, bearing a platter piled high with steaming vegetables, silence had fallen over the room.

"Take a seat now, everyone." At Anne's urging, feet shuffled and chairs scraped along the floor. "Sit beside Kate, Michael." Then the room quieted again.

James, their host for the evening, led them in prayer. "We thank thee, Father, for the fine meal...we offer our special thanks for Michael's safe arrival—"

"Amen" and "praise be to God" circled around the table. A hum of conversation interspersed with clinks of silverware and thumps of bowls and platters being passed from place to place.

Kate cleared her throat. She could not wait. She must hear it all: family, Ireland, everything. "Begin with your crossing. Of course, we have all made the same journey, endured the same discomforts, and suffered the same distress. But the harshness of it fades."

"It was a grand adventure, Kate, the roar of the sea, the pounding of the waves against the ship. The crowds of people in New York and the constant bustle and noise are a memory that will stay with me forever." Michael ran his fingers through young Tom's thick hair. "And the trains, my boy, they are amazing. And yes, lad, the train goes very fast. Zoom!" He thrust his arm in the air, exaggerating the sound effects.

"Was this the same journey I made? My recollection is of filthy straw pallets, the rocking and grinding of the ship, the noise, and the poor, sick people." Kate trembled. "Ah, the memory has not faded entirely."

"Tell us about the latest developments of ships and trains." James worked in the railroad yards, and his expression held interest equal to that of his son.

"I believe the smoothness of the sail improved somewhat, and the travel time has been shortened a few days. They've done nothing to soften the bunks, though." At Michael's wry grin, the table erupted in laughter.

"Tom follows Michael's every word." Kate leaned across her brother to whisper to Anne. "Surely he is not old enough to understand a bit of it, but he listens with rapt attention."

She turned to Michael. "And you've been wonderful to him. You have answered his questions patiently, many times the same query again and again. Ah, and the sound effects." The three laughed together. To think she had just shared a chuckle with Michael and Anne. How many years had it been?

Kate and Cara poured coffee for everyone and served the dessert brought along by the folks from Dempsey's. "Tell us about home, Michael—"

"You all sit back. I'll collect the dessert plates," Cara said.

"Cara and I will wash up the dishes," Ellen said. "You folks take some time for a family talk."

"I'll help." Grace headed for the kitchen, her arms laden with dishes. Eddie followed behind her.

Kate settled back in her chair. What a thoughtful thing they had done. She studied Michael. Sadness lurked behind his brave smiles. When he cleared his throat, she braced herself. He had more to tell. She knew it.

"The struggle to obtain food consumes everyone in Ireland. All over the land, folks suffer great distress. Father plants his crops and toils each day to cultivate them, only for rot or flood or drought to destroy his work. These last few years, he endured a malingering illness. His sad condition brought a terrible time for us all." Michael paused and sipped his coffee.

"At the farm, where I was indentured the past three years, the old man worked me like a slave from dawn until past dark." Michael folded his arms across his chest, and a grim expression crossed his face. "He paid me little for it, but in fairness, I'm sure he lacked the money. Each Sunday, I helped at home all I could. While I worked throughout the day, I tried to thrust aside the thought that come morning I must go off and leave them all." Michael lowered his head.

"Surely his report cannot grow any worse." Kate whispered to Anne, wiping at her tears with a napkin.

"Father did not wish me to sign on with old Mr. Roach. He begged me to stay and work our own place. Though I am not a farmer at heart, I would have done so rather than sign away three years of my life." He halted again and nodded to Kate, Anne, and then Julia. "Mother insisted I go. The question of my indenture caused resentment and dissatisfaction in our home, until Father became too weak to oppose the idea. Not wishing to bring about further pain, I relented."

"Holy angels and saints!" Kate jumped up and walked to the side table to retrieve the coffeepot. She could not be still. Stopping behind Michael's chair, she poured hot coffee for him and then continued around the table refilling cups. "The woman persists in sending her children off to do slave work."

"Do not think ill of our mother, my Kate." Michael reached out as she passed by and tugged at her sleeve.

"This terrible injustice brings back memories of my experiences before I came to America." She must gain command of her emotions. She should not be speaking ill of her family. Why could she not break free from the bitterness that threatened to consume her?

"Did you know Anne writes and sends money each month, Michael?" Julia's clear voice broke into the silence that had descended over the room. "Our mother complains she never receives letters, but Anne has written each month without fail since she arrived in St. Louis. Lizzie suspected Mother hides the letters, and I'm convinced of it." She sent them all a rueful smile.

"I am not faithful in writing like my sisters, but Anne and Julia have persisted all these years, though they almost never receive an acknowledgment of their letters." Kate bowed her head.

"I must agree with you." Michael took the coffee pot from Kate, and placing it on the side table, he claimed both of her hands and held them with a fierce grip. "When Father's illness slowed him, I was forced to finish some bookkeeping work he could not handle. While I searched cabinets and shelves for the proper papers, I discovered a packet of mail our mother had hidden away."

"Oh my word!" Julia reached across the table and clasped Anne's hand. "Do you believe it?"

Kate's tears poured forth. "And, the passage money?" Her sisters had denied themselves for so many years. "I have been helping to save since I arrived four years ago, but Anne has been here for ten years and Julia eight. Again and again, they struggled and scraped to gather enough for our entire family to come. They sent the money, only to have no one arrive in return."

"I cannot explain what malady has invaded our mother's mind, or why she would withhold the letters and money from us. Before I left, I handed over the entire batch of mail to Father, so he will have in hand the words he has been missing from his beloved daughters." Michael continued to rub Kate's hands between his own weathered ones. "I took the funds I recovered from the letters and settled their outstanding accounts. At least for the present, their taxes have been paid and they are out of debt."

"'Tis a shocking thing." Anne sobbed against James's shoulder.

"You girls have earned the right to be angry. Still, we must show compassion." Michael released Kate and moved back to the table. "With Father incapacitated, Mother has lived through the torments of hell. Rather than sitting in her chair and tending to her sewing, she, with Maggie's help, performed the majority of the heavy chores on the place. Even with her fingers bent with arthritis, our mother handled the plow and weeded the garden."

"Ah now, we knew nothing of that." Julia rocked from side to side." We are so far removed from our dear ones." When Martin placed his arm across her shoulders, she ceased her swaying.

"The money I found was not enough to meet the payments for the hired land. They have let it go. 'Tis just as well." Michael fidgeted, his coffee cup shaking. "The work is too much for them, and after the rent and taxes are paid, there is no decent living in it."

Kate watched him carefully. Was there still more?

"Father now appears to have overcome his illness." Michael's countenance brightened. "His resilience amazes me. We thought he was done for and would never resume the rigorous farm work, but he rallied and returned to his former strength. He has taken on the heavy load once again. When I gained release from my contract, there was nothing for it, but I must go. He would not be dissuaded."

"Oh, Father." Kate's tears flowed freely now. "We did not know how ill he was." She pulled a handkerchief from her pocket and buried her face in it.

"Again, Mother opposed it." Michael reached out to Kate and held her against him. "She wished me to remain at home, but with the return of Father's vigor came a determination I have not seen for a long while. He demanded I leave, and he would not hear any argument. Father feels I can help you save passage money for Maggie, and with God's help, enough for fare for all three of them."

Kate blew her nose. "Lizzie told us the same story of Father's strategy." She sat back, listening to Michael's talk. A new, nagging touch of irritation grew within her, an ache of disappointment that would not be held back. "Your arrival has filled me with such joy, Michael." She straightened her shoulders and held her voice firm. "But, we have been building a fund to bring you all out together once your indenture was satisfied."

"Have I spoiled your plan by coming now?" A question loomed in Michael's eyes.

"No, of course not. Praise God you are here, at last." Kate's smile returned. Sure, the joy of her brother's arrival had not left her. Everyone around the table nodded in agreement. "It is just that...ah, my...I cannot help but wish Maggie could have come with you."

"I begged to be allowed to bring her, and she longed to accompany me." Michael sipped his coffee again, his warm, open expression revealing the thought behind his words. "Again, our mother would not hear of it. When I left for Cork, Father promised he would send Maggie next year. I know he means to keep his word, and I intend to hold him to it. I will not rest until they are all out of that desperate place."

Michael rose from his chair and walked along the table until he faced James. He shrugged his shoulders and cleared his throat. "I hold more sad news that must be shared, and I cannot delay any longer. I am sorry to bring you this dreadful word." He looked across the table to Ned. His voice fell to a near whisper. "James…Ned. Just before I left, your dear father died."

"It cannot be!" James jumped up from the table. His face had turned red. He marched about the room, swinging his arms. "Was he ill?" Back and forth, he paced. "We did not know of it."

"Did he suffer?" Ned remained seated, but his voice quivered with shock and dismay.

"Oh my dears, I am so sorry." Anne rushed to pour the two men a small cup of whiskey.

"I am so sorry you lost your father." Sadness filled Kate's being. James and Ned loved and admired their father. "I remember on many evenings, when I came here to supper, you told stories about your father...of the wealth of knowledge you gained from him...of his kindness...and of the fun and adventure he brought to your lives."

Murmurs of sympathy came from everyone around the table.

"Though he must have borne some pain, your da was a fine, brave man. He never uttered a complaint." Michael reached out to clasp James's shoulder. "His time of suffering was brief. You can rest in the knowledge that he endured but one week of sickness."

"What can you tell us of our brother Dan?" Ned walked around the table to stand with his brother and Michael.

"Your Dan is fit, though sorrowful over your father's death, of course." Michael touched Ned's sleeve. "He had begun to see to all the arrangements before I left. He will be here, once he has disposed of the house and the smithy. And didn't he take me to Cork and see me off there?"

When the Dempsey Group returned home that evening, Kate stopped at Mary's room and discovered her patient fast asleep. As she continued on up the steps, her limbs felt heavy with disappointment. She longed to share her stories of the Welcome Supper with her dear friend. Well, the good Lord willing, Mary will be improved in health and eager to hear all about it in the morning.

Chapter Eight

Kate sat in the shop with clean cloths spread on the floor, protecting the silk material she hemmed. She looked up from her work to see Walter standing in the doorway.

"Why are you here alone, while the other girls are working in the parlor?" He removed his hat, but with the yards of cloth spread all about serving as a barrier, he did not approach.

"I yearned for a few minutes to myself." She held up the paper and pencil she had placed on the table beside her. "I must develop a price for a new customer involving curtains for a three-story home. Sitting here, sewing quietly, clears my mind and organizes my thoughts."

"I hesitate to disturb you then, but I do need your assistance." Walter lifted one section of the cloth and took a step forward. "It is a great favor I'm asking. Martin, James, and I will attend a meeting this evening with city officials, regarding the construction of a new water treatment plant for the city. I would like Mary to go with us."

"She should go." Kate pushed the yards of silk aside and attempted to stand. "The improvement to the quality of our water is an important cause to her. What can I do to help?"

"Because of the meeting, we will not work in your shop this evening, and there will be no need to clean up after us." Walter held the cloth high, allowing Kate to step free. "I would appreciate it if you would deliver the day-old goods to the mission. Grace will then be free to prepare supper for everyone, and she and Cara and the other girls will clean up." Walter continued to hold the draperies, while she folded the lengths of material. "If you could see your way to it, I would thank you kindly."

"I would be happy to go." Kate arranged the draperies across two high-backed chairs. "In fact, a walk on a fine evening such as this will be a welcome change from cleaning up after my favorite construction workers."

"Thank you, Kate." Walter headed for the door.

"Thank you for your help with the draperies." She chuckled, when he turned back and bowed.

❋ ❋ ❋

"Good evening, Grace." Kate entered the bakery a short while later to help Grace fill the wicker baskets. Day-old bread and rolls were sold in the shop at half price. What remained at the end of each day, Dempsey's donated to the mission at St. Vincent's, where an evening meal was served to newly-arrived immigrants. "The wonderful aroma of freshly baked bread out here reminds me I have had scant food today."

"Do you not enjoy scents aplenty from the baking room right across the hall from your seamstress shop?" Grace held a tray stacked high with cinnamon biscuits.

"Working in Mary's parlor, we are tucked away from the enticing aroma of the oven room," Kate said. "When I walked through the entryway here, that fresh-bread smell struck deep in my heart."

"Help yourself to a biscuit. There is no need to go hungry. Such a thing is not allowed at Dempsey's." Grace waved the tray beneath Kate's nose. "Or, if is bread you wish, I will cut a slice for you?"

Kate shook her head. "I believe I will hold off for now and hurry to the mission. I heard a rumor we will be enjoying ham for our supper. Am I right?"

Grace nodded vigorously. "Your favorite, is it not?"

"It surely is, and I will try to survive until then. But thank you." Kate retrieved an empty wicker basket from the hallway and placed it on the counter.

"Fill the baskets to the brim." Mary called to her from the doorway. "Take a third basket, if you will, Kate. If there are not enough day-olds, fill it with fresh bread and biscuits. I heard three ferries arrived at the riverfront today, loaded with immigrants. Those poor souls will need a decent meal." Mary backed out into the hallway. "Well, I'm off now. I must rush upstairs to dress for the meeting."

Kate left the shop a few minutes later. She stepped out into Park Avenue, her arms laden with the three wicker baskets filled with bread and baked goods. March winds rushed toward her, blowing her cloak about. Brr…chillier than she had expected…at least the sleet and snow have departed. When she approached the first intersection, she encountered her good friend, Bridget Rice. "I am happy to have someone to walk with." She raised her arm in greeting, but hampered by her bulky load, her wave proved feeble. "I am surprised to see you. I thought you would be at the mission, already at work."

"My mother is not feeling well. She suffers from a severe cold." Bridget was wrapped in a voluminous cloak with a wool shawl around her head, revealing only one errant blond curl. She reached out and relieved Kate of her heaviest basket. "I prepared our dinner, and since Mother was napping, I decided to rush to the mission and help Mrs. Flynn."

They approached the entry, and Bridget held the door while Kate passed before her with her two baskets. "I will be happy to stay and assist Mrs. Flynn."

"Sure, and it is high time my two fine helpers arrived." Mrs. Flynn called to them from the kitchen alcove. Standing before a huge oven, she bowed to each girl as they approached. Though dressed in a simple blue frock, she managed to add a creative touch to her ensemble. The full white apron that protected her dress had been covered, from her chin to the top of her shoes, with row after row of brightly colored, cloth hearts. As she turned to greet the girls, the hearts flowed outward and fluttered all around her. "Of course, I am but teasing." Mrs. Flynn's grin spread across her face. "How is your mother faring, Bridget?"

"She has been sleeping for much of the day, but I believe she is somewhat better." Bridget removed her cloak.

"And you, Miss Kate, what is our city's finest seamstress doing delivering bread?" Mrs. Flynn helped her lift the baskets and place them on a low counter.

Kate rushed to wash her hands and went to work. She sliced the bread and arranged it in small tins. "Mary is attending the meeting about water improvement, and Grace is preparing supper for everyone." While she talked with Mrs. Flynn, Kate surveyed the room. Nearly every table was filled with folks appearing exhausted and hungry. She bent to her task as another large group came through the door.

"Good evening, Kate, Bridget." Father Ryan, the young priest who operated the mission in conjunction with the Irish Benevolent Society, approached the counter where they worked. "Thank the Dempseys for me, Kate. Mary always knows when we need extra bread. Thank you all. The poor folks here will welcome this magnificent meal."

While Mrs. Flynn stirred her pots of stew, Kate filled bowls with the wonderfully-smelling creation, and Bridget handed them around to each one seated at the tables.

After they had worked together for over an hour, Kate untied Bridget's apron. "Go on home and look after your mother. I will help Mrs. Flynn clean up."

"Thank you, Kate. I believe I will run on home. With Father working late tonight, I do not want to leave Mother alone for long." Bridget hung her apron on a hook and headed for the door. "Good night, Kate. Good night, Mrs. Flynn, Father Ryan."

Kate filled a platter with iced biscuits and cinnamon rolls and walked from table to table, offering the sweet treats to the grateful folks.

"It was a splendid meal, Kate." Father Ryan accepted a biscuit from her. He sat at a table surrounded by a family with several young children.

"We do thank you, miss." The young father dipped his head to Kate. "It has been many weeks since we've tasted such fine fare. And now, here's Father Ryan arranging a place for us to stay for a few nights."

"You are welcome." Kate tickled the chin of the tiny boy who leaned against her. "But, it is Mrs. Flynn, back in the kitchen, who prepared the food. She has been here most of the day working on the meal."

"We will stop at the kitchen on our way out and thank her." He and his wife bowed in unison. "We will never forget your kindness."

Kate stood for a moment, watching the young children. They were engaged in a game that involved lengths of twine wrapped around their fingers. She recalled playing the game with her sisters and school friends back home in Ireland. The words "cat's cradle" came to her, and she tried to remember more. Ah, it was useless. She turned back to the young father. "Where are you from?"

"Rosslare, a grand place." He crushed his hat between the fingers of his right hand. "We sailed out of Cork."

Kate nodded her head. Visions of Blackwater rushed in, so unexpected, so sharp. She shook the memories away. No time for sad thoughts or longing for home. Waving to the children, she hurried to assist Mrs. Flynn with the cleanup. She stood at the counter, drying cups, when Walter arrived.

"I should at least provide you with a ride home, Kate." He went right to work himself, scrubbing the large cooking pots. The three of them worked in the kitchen, and Father Ryan cleaned the tables out in the dining area, until the place had been put back in order.

❀ ❀ ❀

Riding along in the wagon with Walter, after delivering Mrs. Flynn to her doorstep, Kate stretched her shoulders. Sure the long day had worn her down. "I am not sure if my count is accurate, but I believe we served supper to one hundred twenty people. Mrs. Flynn is amazing. She did not even appear weary, while I'm wondering if I will possess strength enough to taste my favorite supper.

"Father Ryan is a wonder as well." Walter held the reins loosely, and Josie ambled along on this beautiful, clear night. "I'm not sure how he finds places for those poor folks to stay, but he always manages to care for everyone."

"Does the Benevolent Society assist with money for rooms at boarding houses?" Kate eased back in the seat, relaxed at last.

"I believe they provide some funds." Walter studied her, his eyebrows raised. "I've been meaning to question you about your Uncle James. Do you mind?"

"No, of course not." The wind had settled, and the evening's crisp air and gentle breezes soothed her. Little would disturb her tonight. "Why do you ask?"

"When Anne and her family came for dinner the other evening, she mentioned your Uncle James. I remembered that when she arrived in St. Louis, she intended to travel on to Oregon to meet him." Walter stared out through the window frame. "I understood they still planned to continue on out west after Julia came." He brought his gaze back to Kate.

"Anne received a letter from Uncle James shortly after her arrival here. We've heard nothing from him since, though she has written every year. 'Tis a mystery." Kate straightened and regarded Walter. Why had he questioned her?

"With Anne and Julia both married and settled here with their families, I don't suppose they are thinking of moving on." Walter sat back, fingering his cap, unbuttoning his jacket. "What about you, Kate?"

"When I arrived in St. Louis, I intended to stay only long enough to gather fare money to go on to Oregon. But things have changed for me as well." Kate studied Walter's expression. "My shop is successful beyond all my dreams, and soon the place will be larger and more beautiful than ever. Even more important, I am surrounded by wonderful friends at Dempsey's. I no longer feel the need to strike out on my own."

"I do have one more question for you." They had reached the corner, and Walter allowed Josie to maneuver the wagon while he faced her. "Will you ride on to the livery with me?"

She raised an eyebrow. "It is not a surprise birthday celebration, is it?"

"No more parties, I promise." Walter clucked to the horse and pulled back the reins as they reached the livery. "I thought this might be a good opportunity to ask about your shop. Are you pleased with what has been done? Are there any changes you would like to suggest?"

"Oh, Walter, the place is magnificent. The windows are marvelous. I am amazed at the amount of light that comes through, even on cloudy days. You and the men will soon grow weary of hearing my endless thanks." She took the reins from Walter, and he jumped down from the wagon seat. "We cannot wait to move into our new quarters. That would be my only question. How much longer will it be?"

Walter pulled open the wide livery door. "At least three or four more weeks. Of course, with Michael helping us each evening now, the work has been proceeding nicely."

"Good evening, folks." Jeb came to greet them, and he and Walter released the horse. Then, with Jeb seeing to Josie, they headed out the door.

"I have been talking too much. I did not allow you an opportunity to report on the meeting." Kate held Walter's arm as they crossed the road to Dempsey's. "Did you feel progress was made?"

"No. Not much was settled. Only the mayor and one alderman attended. The others sent along one excuse or another." Walter quickened his strides as a carriage passed by. "The completion of the new waterworks has become entangled in money shortages and partisan battles. Some worry that involvement in this project will have an adverse effect on their political futures. It proved a frustrating evening. However, an order will go out tomorrow requiring residents to boil their drinking water. That one issue was settled." Walter held the door for her as they entered the building. "Tomorrow evening, while we work in your shop, I will give you a full report."

"I also have a few more questions about the shop," he said. "The color you wish to paint the walls is one of the important matters. We must make a decision on color very soon."

❀ ❀ ❀

April 28, 1869 dawned amid bright sunshine and glowing skies. Kate left her bedroom early that morning, walked to the first floor, and entered her newly-enlarged, renovated shop. She strolled all through the room, inspecting every inch of the place. At last, some time alone in the new shop. What a remarkable transformation the men had accomplished. How beautiful it looked.

After days of discussion, she settled the question of the color, choosing cream. "The fabric our customers bring in will look wonderful against the neutral background." She had spoken firmly, hoping to convince the girls, and then she worried over her decision. Concerned they were disappointed with the pale color, she agreed to some brightness in the curtains. The fabric was stretched out now across a long table, ready to be hung. She spun all around. Magnificent…the shop of her dreams.

A sharp knock drew her back from her thoughts. Unlocking the door, she discovered Mrs. Flynn. "Good morning. What brings you to my doorstep so early?"

"A shop warming gift." Mrs. Flynn marched across the room and emptied her roomy bag on the cutting table, arranging a row of vases in a line. "The blooms will not last, but I will replace them as soon as my iris and daisies open."

"They are lovely." The eight matching vases, their vivid blue reminiscent of the lapping waves of the ocean, held sprays of magnificent white blossoms. Kate brushed her hand against the end vase, and then…she could not resist…she touched each one. "You are so kind." She threw her arms around Mrs. Flynn and hugged her.

The dear woman pulled away from Kate. A blush growing across her cheeks, she fidgeted with the flowers, pinching off a dead leaf, positioning the blooms. "I am indebted to you, Kate. My Janey is so happy working here. I can never thank you enough." Mrs. Flynn hesitated. Her expression grew uncertain. "There is something more I must talk to you about before the others arrive. I wish to send over our sewing machine for Janey's use. My Tim will deliver it to you on Saturday."

As Kate opened her mouth to protest, Mrs. Flynn unbuttoned her cape. It was only then that she noticed the cloak. Pressing her lips down hard, she suppressed a laugh. Mrs. Flynn was fond of wearing unusual creations, but today's outlandish ensemble soared beyond all expectations. At the front, the peculiar garment was so long it trailed on the floor. How had she managed the three-block walk to the shop? Oh my word, that must have been difficult. When Mrs. Flynn turned slowly around, Kate discovered the back hem stopped just below her waistline.

"Surely, Janey did not make your wrap?" Kate clapped her hand over her mouth. Too late. The words had already escaped.

"I thought you might refuse to accept the sewing machine, so I wore this marvelous garment I created for myself." When Mrs. Flynn turned back to face Kate, she stumbled over the abundance of material at the front of the coat. "Does this absurd cloak convince you I will have little need for a machine?" She patted Kate's hand. "Janey will put it to good use here."

Kate's laugh rang out. "You could not have made a stronger argument. We cannot have you stumbling all over the streets of the city. Of course, I will accept your gift. I thank you with all my heart."

"Good morning, Kate. Happy new shop day...or congratulations...or something." Julia entered the room from the inside hallway. "Good morning to you, Mrs. Flynn. 'Tis grand to see you."

"Hello Kate. Mrs. Flynn, how are you?" Anne placed a large bag on the floor against the wall. "We've come to help with the curtains and whatever else you need."

"Anne, Julia, Mrs. Flynn has offered us her sewing machine for Janey's use." Kate shook her head from side to side.

"That is so kind." Anne picked up a curtain panel.

"'Tis a wonderful thing to do, Mrs. Flynn." Julia's curls bounced in agreement as she followed Anne to the window.

"Well, I must go." Mrs. Flynn buttoned her coat. "I have marketing to do." She draped her empty bag over her arm.

"Good-bye, Mrs. Flynn. Thank you for the flowers and the offer of the sewing machine." Kate closed the door behind her, still shaking her head.

"Oh, my!" A catch in her throat made it impossible to say more. Her first inspection earlier this morning had revealed a fresh new shop, all cream-colored and bright and shinning. Now, with only one panel of the beautiful curtains hung at the window, the place had been transformed to a warm, colorful room.

"It is lovely." No more words came forth. She placed a handkerchief over her mouth.

"Have we made you cry?" Julia walked up behind her and pinched her ear.

"Did I hear someone mention tears?" Walter entered the shop, just back from his morning deliveries. "It is time we moved you in, is it not? I'll summon my helpers, and we will bring the sewing machines and tables in from the parlor."

"Ah, this is an exciting moment." Julia rushed to the table and took up another curtain panel. "We've come in at just the right time."

"Just direct us, Kate." Eddie came through the doorway bearing one end of a long table, with George behind him holding up the other end. "We will place these tables wherever you wish."

"In the far corner, please." She led them to the spot she intended for the table. A sudden grip of tension and unease enveloped her? Why? She searched deep in her soul for the answer. The place had been in an upheaval for weeks, tables and sewing machines shoved aside and then finally moved to Mary's parlor. Soon, she and her seamstresses would work in a clean, cheerful space. It was done. Why had this feeling of melancholy swept over her?

"Kate, my dear, you are looking sad. Are you not feeling well? Is it the curtains? Is the color wrong?" Anne stepped back from the window and touched her forehead, like a nurse checking for fever. Shaking her head, she took Kate's hand.

"Oh my, no. It is not the curtains." Kate submitted to her sister's ministrations, her distress lessening some. "The girls created them on their own. I love the colors. My favorites, blue and green. The dramatic change they bring to the room stunned me. The color alters the sameness of the cream paint. The shop is more beautiful than I ever dreamed it could be." Kate forced a smile for Anne.

"Are you bothered by something other than the shop?" Julia walked toward them, the curtain rod for the smaller window in the door held firmly in her hand. "Can I help you?"

"I wish I knew." Kate took a step back from Julia and her curtain rod. "I began the morning filled with joy, because the shop is finished at last and looks magnificent. I am so grateful for the help everyone has given me. And then, Mrs. Flynn came in bringing flowers and offering her sewing machine. Suddenly, for no discernible reason, my spirits plummeted. Why, at this perfect moment, am I experiencing sadness? I cannot understand it at all."

"Are you still upset over your breakup with Mr. Reilly?" Anne squeezed Kate's hand firmly as she looked deep into her eyes.

"No. It's not Francis Reilly. Of that, I am absolutely sure." With Anne continuing to hold her gaze, Kate found it impossible to escape her scrutiny. "I have gone over all of that in my own mind. I am relieved the entire business is over."

"Then, what?" Julia asked. "Is it Lizzie? We have resolved to move forward. I thought you were progressing so well." Julia shook the curtain rod she still held.

Kate watched her sister move the rod from her left hand to her right, twirling it in a small circle. Surely, she did not intend to—

"Are you thinking of the folks back home?" Still swinging the rod, Julia backed away and moved over to the chair where the last curtain panel had been stretched out.

"Ah, Julia, you are good for my spirits." Kate laughed. "My worry over being assailed with your curtain rod chased the ill feelings clear out of me." Her sisters were laughing with her now, but she observed the quizzical expressions still present in their eyes. If only, she could explain her lapse to them. She wished them to know—

"Tell us what you mean, Kate." Julia turned back, her laughter disappearing abruptly.

"I suppose I am thinking about home, a little. It came to me this morning that Mother should be here. She could be one of the seamstresses working in this very room." Kate paced the floor in front of the newly-hung curtains. "Her stubbornness about leaving Blackwater holds them all back. They should have come long ago." She wished for a curtain rod of her own to shake, but stamped her foot instead. "It is infuriating. I understand her attachment to our homeland. We all miss Ireland. But, they could make a good life here. Still, they endure the poverty, the sickness, the droughts, and the rot. I cannot bear it."

"We have all experienced times of impatience and frustration over their not coming to America." Anne stepped back and examined the curtain panel she and Julia had just hung. "I keep searching for something to bring us hope.

Michael is here now. Surely, if we send the money to James's brother, our folks will come with him." She pulled Kate over to the window. "It's what we have been saving for all these years. It is what I've been praying for."

"You are right, of course, Anne." Kate reached out to stroke the beautiful material. So colorful, and yet so soft. "You are much too kind. Perhaps, instead of patting my hand, you should jostle me a little or shake the curtain rod at me, as Julia did. I deserve it. If only, I possessed a small measure of your patience."

"I volunteer to do the task." Julia stepped closer, the last empty rod held high. "As soon as I have this last curtain hung, I will administer a thorough shaking."

"Who is shaking?" Mary entered the room, bearing a tea tray. Ellen, Janey, Cara, and Grace followed her, each girl carrying some part of the treat.

"Oh my, it is so lovely. The curtains are beautiful." Tears glistened in Ellen's eyes. She placed the cream and sugar pitchers on the corner of the table. "If you all could have seen the dreadful factory I worked in." She walked over to Kate. "I cannot thank you enough for bringing me out of that place." Ellen wrapped her arms around Kate's shoulders and began to cry in earnest.

"Now Ellen, we have decided to set aside all worries and cares today. This is to be a happy shop." Kate held Ellen away and wrinkled her nose at her. "Be on your guard. Our Julia has one curtain rod not in use, and she threatens to thump away at any sadness." Seeing Ellen's smile break through eased the tension churning within Kate, and a delightful stream of joy rushed through her.

"Here are Eddie and George now with the first of the sewing machines." Kate gave Ellen a little push. "Will you direct them in placing the machines?"

"Come, let us prepare our tea." Mary arranged a cloth on one of the empty tables. "A nice cuppa will do a world of good for all of us."

Grace and Cara busied themselves with plates, forks, and napkins, while Julia and Anne sliced the cakes and passed the treats around. Anne retrieved her shopping bag and placed a large bowl on the table.

"What is this?" Kate leaned closer to the bowl and sniffed. "It smells like bananas."

"It's banana pudding." I've just learned to make it. My neighbor, Patricia, taught me the method. She has chickens and thus an abundant supply of eggs, and James obtained a large bunch of bananas at the market." Anne spooned a portion on each plate. "See if you like it."

"It is wonderful. Wouldn't our family back home love this?" Kate took another spoonful then turned to the soda bread.

"This is grand, as well, Grace. You know I cannot resist the cinnamon." Kate sat for a moment, relishing the fine treats, deciding which delicacy to taste next.

"There are iced biscuits too, Mary's specialty." Ellen, smiling brightly now, sat beside Kate and reached out for a treat. "We would not wish to injure anyone's feelings."

Kate rose from her chair to sniff the cakes on the sparkling silver tray at the center of the table. "Ah, apple, another of my favorites." She shook her head. "Perhaps later."

"I agree with Kate about the curtains." Anne sat beside them. "You chose a wonderful pattern, Ellen. They add lovely warmth to the room."

Cara and Grace walked to the far wall, and Grace pulled open a door and stretched to admire the highest cabinets. "You will have ample space for all your sewing supplies and equipment. Your husband is a marvel of a cabinet maker, Julia."

"Thank you, Grace." A tiny blush accompanied Julia's smile.

While the girls examined everything in the room, Kate sat back and sipped her tea. She imagined the end of their celebration and the moment when the seamstresses were in their places and work was moving ahead.

Chapter Nine

May, 1869

"These two dresses are the last of the lot." Kate sat in her shop with Ellen one sunny morning finishing hems. "Our gowns will be the most beautiful at the Mission Benefit next week." Kate nudged Ellen's foot with her own shoe and waved away her stern look. "I know, I know. I will repress my pride in our work and fix my thoughts instead on the help the proceeds will bring for the mission."

"Your Michael is certainly generous with the time he spends working at the mission." Ellen set her needle and thread aside, and shook out the magnificent green gown that billowed all around them.

"I seldom enter the door of St. Vincent's these days without hearing praises for my brother." Kate slipped a long strand of thread through her needle and knotted it. "Anne and Julia also mentioned the reports they've received of Michael's kindness toward the poor immigrants who arrive at the mission in search of help."

"It is Julia's contention that his presence is especially appreciated by the girls who volunteer there." Ellen adjusted the ironing board and pulled the flat iron from the heating plate at the side of the hearth. "He is garnering admiration among the young girls of the neighborhood, that's sure."

Kate bobbed her head as she stitched. "I am sure he will continue to help out when he is able, but his work at the bakery and at the mission will soon be curtailed. Michael obtained a permanent position at the loading dock on the riverfront. He will begin work on Monday."

"That is marvelous news." Ellen tested the iron with her finger, and leaning heavily, pushed it back and forth across the fabric. "He will do fine. Everyone marvels at what a hard worker he is."

"Well, he has also encountered his first disagreement with one of his sisters." Kate shook her head. Anne and Michael having a difference of opinion...difficult to picture. "With steady wages, he no longer wishes to be considered a visitor at the Duff household. Despite Anne's firm stand against it, his intention to contribute financially prevailed. He has officially become their third boarder, along with Ned Duff and Patrick Tobin."

"Imagine our determined Anne Duff losing an argument." Ellen placed the iron back on the hearth and crossed the room. "I must speak with Michael and learn his secret. I have known your sister for ten years, and I have never swayed her opinion on anything."

"I suspect James intervened on Michael's behalf." A picture of the devoted couple drifted before Kate's eyes. "James is Anne's lone weak spot, you know."

❋ ❋ ❋

With Ellen off helping at the mission and the other seamstresses gone home for the day, Kate worked alone in her shop. She reached for a ledger from the high counter, a part of the marvelous array of cabinets and shelves Martin installed in the shop. From the middle shelf, she retrieved a box that held suppliers' invoices and customers' bills. How wonderful to have the papers and documents for the shop together in one area. She sat quietly, organizing her work into neat stacks.

"I am pleased to find you alone, Kate." Michael entered the shop and pulled up a chair beside her. "If you will spare me the time, I wish to talk of Lizzie. Will it upset you to speak of her? Everyone avoids the mention of her name."

"It is all because of me, Michael. For months after Lizzie's death, I could not rise above my sadness, and they try to shield me. Though I am making a supreme effort to move forward, I grieve for her, even now." Kate pushed her ledger away and leaned back in her chair. "I am not as fragile as everyone believes. I would love to talk of our Lizzie. I miss her so. It helps to say her name." Kate picked up the invoices and sorted through them.

"Will I help you then, while we talk?" Michael reached out to take the invoices from her. "I will do whatever you need to speed your work along. We children of John Carty know the bookkeeping tasks well, do we not?" He grinned at Kate as they rearranged the desk to make room for him. With only brief directions, Michael made the entries then passed the paperwork to her.

"You have a New York supplier?" Michael waved an invoice in the air. "Are you not the fine one?"

"I made contact with Mr. Ward through Father Ryan. His uncle works for the man." Kate wrote checks and addressed envelopes. She rummaged through the drawer for a seal. Was this a dream? Had Michael arrived from Ireland? And, were they, indeed, working together in her shop and discussing her suppliers? Or had she taken to wild imaginings? She steadied her elbows on the desktop. "Mr. Ward's goods have been a valuable addition to my business. I have a few well-to-do customers, and my ability to obtain material and patterns in the latest New York fashions impresses them."

"You are a treasure, and that's the truth." Michael brushed glue on the back of each envelope and sealed them. "I am proud of you, Kate."

"Thank you. Your good opinion means the world to me." She rested her pen on the desk. "Now, let us return to Lizzie."

"Tell me about her arrival here at Dempsey's." Michael fixed her with clear, strong eyes, the deepest blue she had seen in a person since she left Ireland.

"She seemed an angel, walking in out of nowhere to guide us all. She sought only to help everyone and make them feel comfortable. Though she was with us only a short while, she came to know the folks at Dempsey's and their customers, as well. She charmed Walter and his workers. Everyone grew to love her."

"That is grand." Michael pulled a handkerchief from his pocket and blew.

"With Anne married and in her own home, Julia, Lizzie, and I spent many happy hours together in the attic room." Kate sobered. She must not mislead him. "At times, we experienced some tense moments and uncomfortable silences. It was all my doing. I had not even begun to put aside the bitterness I carried with me from home. I feel the guilt of it even now. It's as if a giant bell tolls beneath my ribs." Would her brother understand?

"Aw, Kate. It was a hard time for you." Michael trailed a finger along her chin.

"My healing began with Lizzie's arrival. It was our little sister who helped lift me from my distress. Night after night, she sat on my bed, brushing out my hair and listening to my complaints. At first, the sharpness of my talk frightened her. She did not give in, though. Her tireless, soothing words reached into my heart. With her help, I allowed the resentment to slip away. Sadly, I had not learned the lesson entirely before she died."

Michael sat quietly, listening to her story, but a tear formed in his eye. He turned his head away abruptly. "It is a magnificent shop you have here, Kate. The tables, chairs, and shelves look to be of fine quality. Did Walter do all the work on the place? If I had arrived sooner, I could have been more help."

"James and Martin came most evenings, and Eddie, George, Patrick, and Ned lent a hand when they could. You have met Mr. Flynn, I believe, Janey's father?" She waited for Michael's nod. "He directed the others in the installation of the windows. I am so grateful to all of them. Walter has been wonderful to me. I despair of ever thanking him properly."

"Is he sweet on you?" Michael's eyebrows twisted into an intricate pattern. "He seems to seek you out when he enters a room. He addresses much of what he says to you and asks your opinion on most matters."

"Walter? I do not think so." Hearing Michael's words, Kate's heart commenced to bump and skip. "He is a good-hearted man, and like everyone here at Dempsey's, he treats me with kindness because of the grief I suffered over the loss of Lizzie."

She turned away from Michael and wrote her next check with strong, deliberate strokes. Did Walter care for her? Did he seek her out? Was he sweet on her? She would store the idea away. Alone in the attic room, she would ponder her brother's words.

Michael continued to make entries in the ledger, stopping to ask an occasional question. At length, he sat back. "You cannot imagine the grief everyone back home suffered, when we learned of Lizzie's death."

Keeper of the Flame

Kate rubbed her hand along his arm. "I do understand. I worried I would never be able to smile or be happy again. In these last weeks, my spirits have, at last, begun to revive." She grinned at her brother. "Of course, your coming helped me above all else."

They worked steadily for another hour. When they completed their task, Kate folded papers and stacked books on the shelves until the shop had been returned to order. "Thank you, Michael, for your help and for the talk. We have accomplished a great deal. My mind is eased, knowing my accounts are up to date, but our conversation has been the greatest achievement of the evening. Talking with you soothed my bruised heart. I missed you when I left home. At times, I believed I heard you calling me across the ocean. And now, speaking of Lizzie with you turns my memories of her to happy ones. I feel more peaceful than I have in a long while."

❊ ❊ ❊

"Why would you all go to Francis's pub?" Kate banged her heels against the floor as she followed Walter from her shop to the dining room. "The matter of Francis Reilly is over and done with." Oh, aye, the man continued to haunt her. Would there be no end to her embarrassment over the foolish mistake she made with him?

"It was Michael's idea. He learned somehow of your ruined friendship with Francis. The visit was a peacemaking effort, I suppose." Walter spread his arms wide. "Does that make you angry?"

"Not angry." She hurried to keep up with his long strides. "Well, a little impatient. It is no matter. I will just inform Michael that I have no further interest in Francis Reilly."

"You will not have long to wait. He's here. Michael and the Duffs have come for supper."

"Hello, Walter, Kate." James walked toward them, and they entered the dining room together. "Thank you for inviting us this evening."

"Hello, everyone." She searched out her brother and smiled at him. Sure, with the room abuzz with conversation, there would be no time to speak to him of Francis. But, they must talk. She intended to bring a swift halt to this matchmaking foolishness.

James turned to his hostess as soon as the prayer was finished." I suppose you heard, Mary, we visited Francis Reilly at his pub last night."

Kate's head and shoulders drooped. She had been seated beside her brother-in-law, one of her favorite people in the world. Sure, if she had known what James intended to discuss, she would have placed herself at the far end of the table. Could she somehow divert them from this talk of Francis? "Are the children asleep?"

"Francis is polite." James twisted his water glass again and again, leaving an imprint on the tablecloth.

It was useless…James had not even heard her question.

"We are not back to the easy friendship we once held. To my knowledge, he still does business with that fool Fortune in Chicago. Much as I want to end this rift for the sake of the entire family, I cannot condone such a thing. The disagreement was between Francis, Martin, and me, though, and I have urged Walter and now Michael, to distance themselves from the matter." James cast his gaze directly at her.

"Our quarrel with Francis could hurt any chance of reconciliation between the two of you, Kate. Your broken courtship was my responsibility, and I am sorry for it." A look of deep sorrow rested in James's eyes. "You have suffered your fair portion of troubles in your young life, without my folly adding to it."

So she had been mistaken in thinking Michael to be the matchmaker. It was James. Though he meant only what was good for her, could they not have discussed this delicate matter in private? Her cheeks grew warm, but she would not allow the anger to take control. If she spoke firmly…chose her message carefully…perhaps, she could persuade everyone seated around the table.

"Please, hear what I have to say. I should never have agreed to Mr. Reilly's courting me." She gazed all around, praying her look conveyed truth and determination. "I hold no romantic feelings for him. I regret that I may have caused him hurt. For myself, I feel relief the business is finished." Kate bowed her head, worried now she may have said too much.

Anne reached across James to pat Kate's hands. "Amen. The matter is put to rest forever." Still holding fast to Kate, Anne began to clap their hands together in a steady, measured rhythm.

"Anne?" What was she attempting? Would this foolish game distract everyone? With no better idea, Kate submitted to her sister.

"Come, Grace. We will outdo them." Julia clasped Grace's hands. Their former Blackwater neighbor, familiar with their childhood games, joined in the four-handed clapping exercise.

"Enough." Kate gave Anne a slight push away, and the game ended in an uproar of laughter.

"You must teach us this clappety-clappety game." Ellen moved around the table, filling coffee cups for everyone. "We never played that at home."

"Oh, yes, please." Eddie leaned across the table toward Grace. "I have waited all my life to learn to strike palms."

❈ ❈ ❈

With supper finished and the cleanup completed, Kate climbed the steps to the second floor and knocked on Mary's door. "Are you awake?"

"Come in, Kate. I anticipated a visit from you this evening." Seated in her usual chair, Mary busied her hands with yarn and crochet needle. "I know our James disturbed you. I am so sorry you were upset, but he meant well."

"The matter between Francis and me has been settled and done with for over a year. Why does his name arise in our midst, time after time?" Kate sat in the chair beside Mary. "Am I sending out a false impression? Do I appear to pine away over the lost opportunity? What should I do?"

"Ignore the talk. The idea will fade eventually. Poor James. He feels guilty because of the argument he and Martin had with Francis. You know, dear, he meant only to do right by you." Mary tossed her work aside and leaned across the space between their chairs to hug Kate. "He will never raise the matter again, that's sure."

Kate stroked Mary's soft cheek. "I suppose I was more embarrassed than hurt. Thank you. Just talking it over with you has eased my mind." She pulled a ball of dark blue yarn from the bag she held over her arm. "So, I am ready to work."

"What a wonderful shade." Mary fingered the wool. She took up a few strands and allowed it to slip through her fingers then held it to the light. "What will you do with this?"

"Since I have completed afghans for my three nieces, I should make one for little Tom." She pulled a skein of deep green yarn from the bag. "But then, I would also like to do something for Walter. I will never be able to thank him appropriately for making my wonderful new shop possible, but I wish to try. I'm not sure where to begin."

"Begin with Tom's cover. As quickly as you work, you'll have his afghan completed in no time." Mary tucked the green yarn back in Kate's bag. "Then, you can concentrate on something for Walter."

"As usual, you have the answer, Mary. I will begin with the blue for Tom." She spent some time rolling the yarn into a ball, and then took up her needle. Settling into a rhythm with her stitches, a feeling of peace descended over her. It was well beyond time she retired to the attic room. Sleep would come quickly.

❦ ❦ ❦

"Good morning, Mary." Kate entered the bakery and found Mary working alone. "How are you faring this beautiful spring morning?" She stacked biscuits on a tray, a surprise for her girls, and then reached in her pocket for coins to pay for her treat.

"Ah, I am grand, Kate." Mary stood beside her, adding additional biscuits to her tray. "I have a far more important question to ponder, though. In the years that you took a turn delivering the day-old goods to St. Vincent's…in all those times…did Eddie ever walk to the mission with you?"

"Well, we rode home together in the carriage a few times." Kate noticed the gleam in Mary's eyes. What mischief lurked behind her questions?

"And aside from that?" Mary blinked several times, but she did not smile.

"No, he never walked with me. He does spend long hours in the oven room. Surely, he has little time for walks." Aha, the answer to Mary's riddle occurred to her…the blossoming friendship between Grace and Eddie. Now she understood.

"Sure he works long hours." Mary's face broke into a smile, at last. "He is the finest helper Dempsey's ever had. But, is it not strange Eddie now finds time to walk with Grace or take her in the wagon when she carries day-olds to the mission? Is it not a wonder?"

"Eddie and Grace, you say?" Kate's laughter could be held back no longer. "Well, we dismissed Lizzie's romantic notions concerning them, you remember, because she had just arrived here and was unfamiliar with the camaraderie of Dempsey's suppers. It seems Lizzie could have been right with her predictions."

"I think it is probable." Mary giggled. "These nighttime excursions have surely encouraged some romances. Anne and James walked home from the mission together. Then, Martin Tobin escorted Julia home when she worked at the church rectory for Father Burns. Now, Grace and Eddie." She placed a hand on each hip. "I may decide to deliver day-olds myself.

"Why, just yesterday, with Eddie working hard the entire day, I volunteered to walk with Grace to St. Vincent's. He assured me many times and then once again a brisk walk would do him no end of good, clear his head and all." Mary dabbed at her eyes. "Ah Kate, can you believe what appears to pass between those two? Will this wonderful friendship growing between them blossom into love and end with a wedding? Will we experience the beginning of a new little family at Dempsey's after all these years?"

"I believe it is quite possible. But what is this new little smile? What have you held back?" Kate stood quietly, waiting. Mary could not hold her secret in for long.

Customers entered the shop, and they covered their smiles with their handkerchiefs. Kate placed her own tray on the counter, and while Mary served the first woman, she helped the next person.

After holding the door for her customer, Mary moved back to the counter. "We will observe everyone at supper this evening and see what we will see."

"And thank you for teasing me with still another new puzzle, Mary. Do not deny it. I know there is something more."

Kate took up her biscuit tray, a grin she could not conceal bursting forth as she started through the archway at the back of the shop. "I'll ponder the mystery you are still guarding while I work today."

❀ ❀ ❀

Kate entered the dining room that evening and stopped in surprise when she discovered James, Anne, and Michael. How nice to have them here again. But why so soon? Perhaps Anne wished to provide an opportunity for her to visit with Michael? Or her sister might be as curious as she and Mary about the courtship between Grace and Eddie? If only the cause was not their worry about her state of mind...or her being alone...and unmarried. Please, let it not be that.

"Good evening, everyone." Kate sat beside her sister. "Have I missed the opportunity to see the children again?" She was aware her sister responded. The sight of Eddie leaning close and talking quietly to Grace, however, caused her to miss Anne's answer.

"Are you becoming seriously involved in the labor union movement?" Walter addressed James, as he passed bowls and platters piled high with steaming food around the table. "Have you attended meetings at the Roundhouse?"

Kate listened intently to this newest distraction. The intricacies of Grace's love interest slipped from her mind.

"Ned and I have attended a few meetings." James spoke quietly, but the room had stilled and he could be easily heard. "Things are still in the planning state. Nothing important has been decided."

Kate read the anxious look that crossed Anne's eyes as James turned to her with a smile.

"It is my opinion that working women should be included in the struggle for fair wages." Grace spoke out with a forcefulness Kate had seldom seen from the girl.

"Well, little one, will you join the fight for more pay?" Walter turned his attention to Grace, and startled faces all around the table followed his lead.

"I might." Grace held her head high. "Not every place of employment is like Dempsey's, Walter. Many young women suffer poor treatment and receive paltry pay. I have not forgotten my hard life, before I came here. The mission proved one of the better places of employment in the city, but the wages were much lower than I receive from you and Mary."

Kate shook her head slowly. Was this our Grace? No blushing or lowering her head?

"She speaks the truth, Walter." The quiet, agreeable Eddie broke into the conversation, his face, neck, and ears bright red.

"You're right, Eddie. Grace is entitled to voice her opinions." Dropping his fork on his plate with a clunk, Walter's words were spoken in a strong voice. "In fact, I agree with her. Employers tend to treat women with even more unfairness than men. Forgive me for my poor manners. I meant only to tease Grace a little." He placed a hand on his young friend's shoulder. "You have every right to defend her. Now that she is your intended, we must show her the deference she deserves—"

"Intended!" Mary burst forth with a joyful squeal.

"Is it true then?" Kate studied Grace's expression then focused on Eddie. "Are you to be married?"

Eddie and Grace grinned in unison. Grace nodded at Mary, and then her happiness erupted, bringing a smile and a blush all at once.

Shouts of congratulations exploded around the room.

Kate offered her good wishes and sat back to take in the celebration. The men slapped Eddie's back and pumped his hand. The girls hugged Grace and shed a few tears. What a wonderful moment for our girl…poor Grace, no longer. This hardworking couple had earned a blessed life and every good fortune.

Keeper of the Flame

Settled in her bed a short time later, Kate gazed up at the ceiling, reviewing the events of the evening...the wonderful celebration for Grace and Eddie...the talk at the table regarding labor issues. She rejoiced for Grace. The business of unions was more difficult to understand. She must give her full attention when the men discussed the subject again. Why did Walter, a business owner, involve himself in the workers' activities? As a proprietor of a business herself, she had questions of her own for James and Walter. And then, one more question remained unanswered. What was Mary holding back? Her dear friend had not shared everything...well, she would persist until she gleaned the answer from her.

Chapter Ten

June, 1869

Spreading a pattern along coarse brown cloth, Kate glanced up to see her brother standing in the doorway. "Wonderful to see you, Michael. Have you had supper?"

He sat down at the end of the cutting table. "I had an opportunity to work extra hours, and I purchased a meal on the way home."

"Did you enjoy the betrothal supper for Grace and Eddie last evening? It was your first Dempsey's party." Kate searched in the drawer for pins and her favorite scissors. She placed several pins between her lips and began to attach the pattern to the cloth.

"I was amazed. The abundance of food and the constant hum of conversation and laughter were astonishing. The Dempseys are fine people." Michael held the cloth steady for Kate while she cut around the pattern. "Will the wedding celebration be equally festive?"

"Walter and Mary will provide an abundant wedding supper for them." Kate folded the cloth and placed her tools in a basket. "Grace intended a small, quiet wedding, but Mary will hear none of it. Now we've learned the other grand secret Mary's been holding back. Bridget Rice is to marry Walter's helper, George Blake. Since they have planned a combined wedding, I am sure we will experience one of Mary's finest feasts."

"Even for the Englishman?" Michael bounded from his chair. Disbelief radiated from his eyes as he paced the room. "I was shocked to find such a person at the bakery, and now a fine girl from our home village plans to marry him. I cannot believe such a thing. What is Walter thinking?"

"Please, Michael, allow George a fair chance." Kate ran her hand along his sleeve and felt the tautness of his arm. His face had grown bright red. Would he be capable of controlling this fury?

"I'm not sure I can do that." He ceased pacing. "I worked with him a few times in the oven room, and you are right, he does seem a decent sort. Still, I cannot forget who he is."

"I understand your feelings." Kate flinched a little. The anger still lingered in the brightness of Michael's cheeks and the stiffness of his stance. The set of his jaw brought a remembrance of Uncle Patrick's unwavering mistrust of the English. "The folks at Dempsey's experienced the same turmoil when the Army assigned George to work at the bakery during the war. A few of our regular customers refused to enter the building with him present. Even in the oven room, an awkward tension prevailed. We have been taught to blame the British for all the troubles back home. 'Tis a difficult habit to break."

"Indeed, it is." Michael paced again, his hands shoved deep in his pockets.

"George provided excellent assistance to Walter and Eddie through the difficult war years. He proved kind and helpful to everyone. The three men have grown to be good friends. Now, Bridget has come to love George." Kate checked the windows and the outside door. "Please, Michael, you are a part of our Dempsey's group now. Make an effort."

"I will try." His eyes appeared troubled, and his words did not sound convincing.

❦ ❦ ❦

"How are your wedding plans progressing?" Kate worked in the dressmaking shop with Bridget one evening, fitting her for a wedding gown. "I am sorry for the harsh criticism you are receiving." She slipped pins in the silky white fabric. "You do not deserve it." Kate helped Bridget step out of the dress. "At least your folks are trying to understand."

"My parents have not hidden their concern over the prospect of a British son-in-law, but at my pleading, they agreed to reserve judgment until they come to know George. My mother and Mary have been working together on the wedding supper. The neighbors are not as easily convinced."

"'Tis not fair." Kate covered the dress with a sheet.

"I will never give in to this foolishness." The always outspoken bride-to-be placed her fists on her hips. "Anyone who does not accept George is not my friend. We will be off to California soon and leave those poor fools behind."

Kate worried for both brides. Her unease pricked at her insides as she tossed in her bed throughout that sleepless night. Poor, dear Grace, she had overcome a deep disappointment, and she now anticipated a new beginning with Eddie. And Bridget devoted her life to assisting immigrants who arrived at the mission in need of help. Their wedding day must not be spoiled by old resentments.

❦ ❦ ❦

Kate left the kitchen one evening in late June and found Walter waiting for her outside the door of her shop. "I did not expect to see you again tonight."

"I persuaded Michael to take a walk with me and inspect the vacant lot we're converting into a sports field." Walter pushed his hat back on his head. "With the weather grown mild, I hired some fellows to work on the grounds, leveling, seeding, and fertilizing. I would like to check on the progress. Will you come along?"

"You know I cannot resist spending time with my brother." She turned at the sound of the back door closing. "Here he is."

"Hello, Michael." Walter shook his hand. "Sure, you are already recognized in the neighborhood as our hurling champion. I would like your opinion on the suitability of the new field."

"Wouldn't I appreciate an opportunity to stretch my legs?" Michael tickled Kate's chin as they headed along the hallway.

When they reached the door, George appeared.

Kate covered her mouth to stifle a gasp.

"I asked George to come along." Walter placed a hand on Kate's shoulder. "He learned to play soccer back in his home village."

With an eyebrow raised, Walter faced Michael. "He and a few of the fellows from church have been teaching the children at St. Vincent's to play the sport."

"Do you mind my coming along?" George, a tall, slim young man with straight blond hair and smiling blue eyes, carried a ball with a thick leather covering. "I would like a chance to try out Walter's field."

"Of course, come along." Kate squeezed her brother's arm until he nodded. "We are happy to have you." They walked along in near silence, Walter and George commenting from time to time, Michael saying nothing.

When they had accomplished the short, two block walk, Kate breathed a sigh of relief. "The field looks grand since it has been leveled. The grass has already sprouted."

Walter knelt on the ground and spread out two drawings. "Here is the layout for the hurling field." He pointed to the second sketch. "The other is for soccer. The rectangle at each end indicates the proposed goals. The sidelines are marked along each edge of the sheet."

Removing his jacket, George stretched it out on the ground, in the area where a goal would eventually be placed. "I will stand here and defend the goal, Michael. Kick the soccer ball past me."

Kate stood on the sidelines, while Michael kicked the ball fiercely, again and again. Did he intend to avenge every injustice imposed against Ireland with his kicks?

George proved a perfect match for Michael, as he lunged from side to side then straight up to pluck the ball from the air and defend his goal. Was he defending the honor of his own country? And had she been so preoccupied with her own affairs she had failed to notice the improvement in George's gait? His slight limp, the result of the wound he sustained in the early days of the Civil War, had disappeared entirely.

After a few tries, Michael became more adept with his kicks, taking the ball off to the side and kicking it toward George's homemade goal from different angles. Walter positioned himself well behind the goal, scooping up the ball on the few occasions when it escaped past George.

The animosity Michael held toward George had caused a quiver to surge through Kate. But as the two young men concentrated on their game, a joyous gleam replaced Michael's angry look. Was it possible he had begun to enjoy himself? Perhaps his appreciation for George's soccer skills would lead to admiration for him as a person.

Finally, after Walter caught one of the few balls that flew past George, he approached them. "What do you think?"

"It is a marvelous field." George picked up his coat and shook it briskly.

"I believe the soccer field should be wider than the hurling field. And the hurling goals are a few inches shorter than the ones used for soccer." Michael leaned against a tree, breathing rapidly but smiling.

Walter consulted his drawings and nodded his head in agreement. "Still, I maintain we could make the field suitable for both sports."

"I must admit I enjoyed the soccer." Michael turned to George. "If you will allow me to participate, I would like to come along when you teach the children. I have not had such grand exercise since I left home."

Kate's heart skipped.

❀ ❀ ❀

At noon on the day of the weddings, Kate closed her shop and climbed the steps to the Dempsey girls' second-floor room. She found Grace standing beside her bed, stroking the lace on the gown Anne and then Julia had worn for their weddings. "Are you ready to become a bride?"

"I had forgotten how lovely this dress is." A tear rolled along Grace's cheek. "Your sisters are so kind to allow me to wear it." She reached for Kate's hand. "And you, dear girl, you'll soon be wanting the gown for yourself."

"Not at all." Kate chuckled. "No suitors. No need for wedding finery."

"You will see, there will be a fine gentleman for you, Kate. And, I thank you so much for making the alterations."

"What's this talk of handsome men? Are you dreaming of your prince, Kate?" Ellen rushed through the door and began undoing the many buttons at the back of the dress.

"It is Grace who will have a fine husband in no time at all." Kate lifted the gown from the bed. "Let us prepare our girl." She and Ellen slipped the dress over her head.

"Ah, Grace, you are lovely." Cara entered the room, and drawing a handkerchief from her pocket, she sat down on an empty bed.

"She is our own magnificent bride." Kate curtseyed to Grace, and then she pinned the veil in her hair and trailed the soft lace around her shoulders and along her back.

"Your brother, the Reverend Edward Donahoo, has arrived, Grace." Mary squeezed between the girls gathered around the bride and took her hand. "Your Eddie has gone on to the church with him."

Grace smiled at Mary. Her soft grey eyes sparkled and a brilliant smile illuminated her thin, pale face. "I am ready as well."

The girls each held a section of the dress, and bumping one another and giggling, they made their way down the stairs to the parlor.

"It is a magnificent day, Grace. The sun is shining bright as can be. And it is all for you." Kate lifted the train of the dress high. "Happy thoughts on your wedding day, my girl."

❋ ❋ ❋

A long and happy celebration marked the marriage of Grace Donahoo to Eddie Kennedy and Bridget Rice to George Blake. Kate stood at the parlor door and waved to the happy couples as they took their leave. "It was a perfect day, Mary! You and Walter provided a splendid supper for the celebration."

"You all contributed." Mary sat in her favorite easy chair. "Let us sit and rest a bit."

"I assumed we'd all like a cuppa." Cara appeared in the doorway, bearing a tray laden with teapot, cups, and biscuits.

"Thank you, dear. Come sit with us now." Mary helped Cara settle the tray on the small table beside her. "Where has Ellen gone off to?"

"I looked for her." Cara pulled up a chair. "She's nowhere to be found."

Kate sat beside Mary and stretched out her arms. "Eddie and Grace worked hard on their new quarters—"

"Of course, we could not have finished in time without the help of James, Martin, and Michael." Mary poured tea, and Kate set plates and cups on the small table before them. "Be sure to visit Grace once she has settled in. The transformation of the place will amaze you. Ah, I never dreamed we would fill the open space at the back of the building, but we have done it."

"I have seen it." Kate added milk and sugar and stirred her cup. "It will be a nice cozy apartment for them. After so many sad years, Grace is happy and content. I am thrilled for her."

"God answered our prayers for our Grace," Mary said. "Eddie is wonderful for her. They complement one another."

"But, they have gone to Kansas City to visit Eddie's brother." Cara blew her nose. "How will we get on for a week without our Grace?"

"We'll miss her, it's sure." Kate leaned toward Cara until their foreheads touched. "You and I will surely be drawn into mischief on our own. And if Ellen continues to disappear, she will offer no help."

"I wish a blessed life for our Bridget as well." Mary moved the empty tray to the table at the back wall and took her chair again. "She made a lovely, vivacious bride. It is a disappointment so many of the Rices' friends chose not to come to her wedding. I pray her being surrounded by Dempseys, Tobins, Duffs, and Flynns made up for those hardened souls who could not accept George."

"Well, we have another bone for them to chew on." Kate leaned back in her chair and rested her head on Mary's shoulder. "Now that Ellen and I promoted Charlotte Mueller to a full seamstress position, she will be observed arriving at the shop each day. If folks did not approve of a Brit working here, whatever will they think of us choosing a young, German lass as our new seamstress? Buttons will pop with indignation, I'm sure.

"Will Charlotte's being here cause a problem for you, Mary?" Kate drew her eyebrows together. Sweet, talented Charlotte was perfect for the shop. But would she possess strength enough to shield them all from criticism?

"You and Ellen have declared Charlotte a fine seamstress, have you not?" Mary squared her shoulders.

Kate nodded with enthusiasm.

"Well, I know for myself what a fine girl she is. Let them bellow and posture." Mary reached beneath her chair and pulled out a pair of scissors with long, menacing blades. "I warrant if anyone desires the best baked goods or the finest sewing to be found in the city, they will arrive at our door." She waved her scissors in the air. "We will not allow such foolishness."

❁ ❁ ❁

Kate joined her family in the Duffs' kitchen a few evenings later. "A wonderful supper, Anne. Thank you for inviting me." While her sister passed around a plate of small cakes, Kate refilled coffee cups and handed around napkins, milk and sugar. With everyone served, she returned to the table.

James pushed back his chair, scraping it along the floor. "While it is too late for my father, we must send the fare to my brother and instruct him to bring your family out with him. We must act now." He nodded to Michael, Anne, Julia, and then Kate "I know my brother is eager to leave Ireland. If your father has grown somewhat stronger, we cannot wait. We do not want to lose anyone else." James placed his eyeglasses on the table and rubbed a red spot on the side of his nose. "Do you think your parents and sister will accompany him?"

"Will our mother cooperate and come with James's brother?" Kate looked around the table, waiting for their agreement. "We have all endured so many years of scrimping and sacrifice to bring our family out. Again and again, we suffered disappointment when the money we sent for passage was spent elsewhere." She left her chair and stood behind Michael.

"Now, after nearly three years of building our immigration fund, we have gathered a sufficient amount to bring our family and James's brother Dan to America." Passing behind Anne, she tugged at her sister's neat bun before returning to her chair. "It has been James's intention all along that they come together."

"We must be truthful with ourselves and with one another." Julia turned to her brother. "Even with an ocean between us, Michael, we all feel the sting of our mother's foolish disapproval of the Duffs." She looked to James and then to Ned. "I am shamed by her irrational notions. I know my brother and sisters join me in begging your forgiveness."

"Not necessary, Julia." Both James and Ned waved her apology away.

"I am embarrassed to admit it, but I know of what you speak." Michael stood between Kate and Julia and placed a hand on each of their shoulders. "You must know that our father does not hold with such nonsense. If Father is well enough to make the trip, he will control things and we need have no fear for Dan."

"I pray they will come." Anne placed her coffee cup on the table and bowed her head.

"It is my prayer, as well." Michael circled the table and wrapped his arms around Anne. "But besides what Kate calls our mother's 'irrational notions,' I sense they fear the separation from their home." He shook his head, his eyes filled with sadness.

"Sure, a reunion with their daughters should overcome any trepidation they feel." Kate paced around the room. "The opportunity to know their fine husbands and embrace their grandchildren should make up for any great, green hills they would leave behind." She shook her head. Ah my, have I grown at all in understanding and compassion? Shadows seeped over her thoughts. "They will also leave poverty, ruined crops, English rule, and unfair tariffs. I find nothing so grand in all of that." She felt the comfort of Michael's arms wrapping about her, and she allowed him to lead her back to the table.

"You know I honor our parents." Michael held the chair for Kate. "Still, I have wished to shout at them to sell every possession they own, take every pound they possess. Just leave and be done with it. I am weary to death of plans for one to come over at a time, waiting for the crop to come in, worrying about proper clothing." He shook his head, his hair flying all about. "Oh, och. I am sorry to sound impatient."

"We understand, Michael." Anne placed her hand in Michael's. "We have all experienced moments when we wished they would walk away from the farm and leave Blackwater. We wanted to go back and gather them up and march them on a ship." She walked slowly back to her own chair. "You see, I can be exasperated too."

"I assure you all, Dan will handle the situation." James remained seated, his voice calm. "We must have faith in him."

"I agree with James." Michael pulled out his chair and eased into it. "Dan is a strong, capable fellow."

The tension tightening Kate's shoulder slipped away. Fresh from Blackwater, Michael knew Dan even better than his brother, James, who had lived in America these past nine years. Did they dare to dream? Would they succeed at last in gathering the entire family together in St. Louis? She could not help herself. She held to a ray of hope.

❃ ❃ ❃

"Anne came by the shop this morning to tell me she mailed the immigration money to James's brother in Blackwater." Kate met Walter in the oven room as she returned an empty tray the following afternoon. "But, I've just had a visitor. James Brien, who has returned to St. Louis after a visit to Ireland, brought the message that my father's condition has worsened. According to Mr. Brien, Father seldom leaves his bed." Kate's arms and legs ached, as if filled with lead. Her head bobbed. Did she even possess the strength to move back to her shop?

"Ah, Kate, I am so sorry." Walter took a strong grip of her arm. "Do you need to rest? Will I help you up to the attic room?"

Kate shook her head. "No thank you, Walter." With great effort she straightened. "I must walk to Anne's and tell her and Michael. "I am not sure I can bear this news myself, but I am more worried for Michael. This blow will crush his spirit."

"You cannot go alone." Determination blazed in Walter's eyes. "I will walk with you."

❃ ❃ ❃

"It is kind of you to have us all for supper, Anne, James." Kate, Walter, and Mary sat with the Duffs, in their kitchen. Julia and Martin were there with them. "Once again, we've come to you in our distress."

"I thought if we faced this disappointment together, we could help one another." Anne extended her hand toward Michael and stroked his shoulder.

"You know I love this new life I've begun for myself in St. Louis. I have won a position well beyond any expectations

I ever held." Michael rested his chin in one hand. "I already consider the city my home." Disappointment filled his once bright eyes. His troubled thoughts were evident in every gesture. "Ah, I cannot be thinking of myself. Our father ill, our mother and sister in desperate straits. They are the ones who will need our help."

Kate leaned close to Mary, who sat beside her. "What a relief to have you and Walter with us." Sure, they had grown to be part their family.

"If you will allow me," Walter looked to James and waited for his nod before he went on. "I will go back home and bring them all out here. I would welcome the opportunity to do it for all of you." He rose from his chair and walked over to stand behind Mary, and she patted his hand in agreement.

"I will come with you." Michael pounded his fists on the table. "I must see them all safely here."

"You will do no such thing," Kate jumped to her feet. This would not do. "For so long, we all dreamed and planned and waited for you to come. And now, after many long years, you are here at last. I'll not hear of it."

"Please, Michael, do not think of leaving us." Julia had been sitting quietly, listening to their talk. Now she stood behind him and grabbed both of his ears. They all laughed, but it was a strained, hesitant response.

Kate had chuckled with everyone, but she sobered quickly. She must not allow herself to be distracted. "You cannot go either, Walter." She appreciated his kind gesture, but he could not return to Ireland. "If Father is not well enough to travel, you could be held up there for months."

"Here's what we must do…" Voices rose around the table. "Allow me to…" The volume increased to a great din. "I will take things in hand…"

"This noise will wake the children." Kate appealed to Anne and then Julia, but neither sister showed concern.

"No one needs to be going back." James strong voice interrupted them all. "You have forgotten my brother, Dan, who is there right now, ready to come. Soon, he will hold in hand the money we sent for the trip. I believe he is up to the task. My brother-in-law here, who left him only a short while ago, has assured me that is a fact. Let's ask Dan to hold off until the fall, and pray John will be well enough then to make the journey."

"If only we could be together and this anxiety and uncertainty would end." Anne shook her head as a tear rolled along her cheek.

"How many times have we all wished it to be so?" Kate stepped back a few paces. These dear folks meant well, but Father was ill. Could anything be done to help him?

Chapter Eleven

August, 1869

Heat radiated from the walls and rose up from the floor as Kate rushed along the hallway. Would opening the windows in her shop stir a small breeze? Her heartbeat quickened and the warm temperature flew from her mind when she discovered Walter standing in his office doorway, brows drawn together, mouth tightened to a grim line. "Walter?"

He moved into the room, motioning her to follow. "Aye, it gives me great pain to give you this news."

"What is it?" The thumping inside her reached to her ears.

"Michael is gone." Walter stood beside his desk, gazing down at the floor. "He left on the train early this morning, headed for Boston. He is returning to Blackwater."

"Oh no! Michael..." Kate crossed her arms in front of her. Perhaps she could create a barrier. Could she shield herself from these painful words?

"I tried to keep him here." Walter stepped closer and gripped Kate's arms, holding her firmly.

"No! No! It cannot be." She attempted to look away.

"I pledged to him I would go back and fetch your parents and sister and bring them here myself. He would not listen. He worried your father would be too ill to make the trip." Walter positioned himself directly in front of Kate. His eyes burned into hers.

"You should have come to me. I would have stopped him." Aye, her words were irrational. Her sharp tone was unnecessary and unkind. Lashing out at Walter afforded her some small measure of satisfaction, but the words would not bring her brother back. And now she had hurt her dear friend.

He released her. His hands slipped to his sides. "I attempted to reason with him, reminding him it was your father's wish that he come to America. I begged him not to go, Kate, but he stood firm. Naught would sway him. He knew you girls loved having him here. I assure you, he knew how upset you would be that he left. But with your father ill, he believed it had fallen to him to go back and help your mother. He felt it his duty to return home and care for his family."

"'Tis a bitter thing." Why had he done this? Kate wrapped her arms around her own shoulders but found no relief from the chill.

"Do not be angry with him. He did not wish to leave. In fact, he told me his disappointment that he must return to Blackwater all but overpowered him. His life in St. Louis fulfilled every dream and hope he harbored all his life. When I realized he would not be persuaded, I ceased my pleading. I gave him money enough for expenses along the way."

Kate noted the pain her foolish tirade brought Walter. His injured look pierced her, as if a bee sting penetrated all the way to her heart. If only she could take back her sharp words. She studied the floor boards. "I know you did what you could." She patted his arm, but he held himself stiff and still. She managed only a whisper. "Thank you for giving him the money. It was good of you." Shamed, she could not raise her head. *Will I never learn to control my tongue?* She moved to the door.

"Please do not walk away from me, Kate." Walter spoke quietly, evenly. "We have become good friends in these past months, have we not?"

Hope sprang forth in Kate. When she dared another glance at him, he appeared calmer, steadier. Still, a hint of sorrow she had never seen before loomed in his kind eyes. "I apologize, Walter. I hold you no blame. I struck out at you because you delivered the word to me. The shock of Michael's leaving is no excuse. Forgive me, please. I am truly sorry."

"You have not answered my question. Are we still friends?" Walter's eyes held hers.

"Of course we are friends." She managed a small grin. "If you will have me, we will be friends always."

"Thank you, Kate. I've come to value our talks. I look forward to hearing your strong opinions on whatever subject we choose to discuss." With a sweep of his arm, Walter placed his hat on his head. "I will do anything to bring Michael back. How I will accomplish it, I do not know right now, but I will bring him back to St. Louis, I promise you."

Relief rushed through Kate when she watched the barest hint of a smile appear on Walter's face. "Thank you. You are kinder than I deserve."

"I made the same pledge to Anne. Not the part about our talks, of course. I stopped to see her on my way home. She told me to tell you she will come to you as soon as Nell wakes from her nap." Walter started for the door.

"Was Anne very upset?" Kate reached for her handkerchief. "My poor sisters." Her gaze rested on a corner bookshelf. She still could not look at him.

"The news devastated her," Walter approached her again and took her hand. "She made a brave effort to hold back her tears."

"As usual, my first thoughts were of my own disappointment." She shook her head. "My poor Anne."

"Well, after I had made Anne cry," Walter's grin was wry, "I had no heart to face Julia. I will stop and see her on my next delivery rounds."

"Thank you, Walter." She looked down to see that he still held on to her hand. Warmth crept across the back of her neck, burning its way to both sides of her face. Was it the unrelenting heat? Or had Walter's touch flustered her? That could not be. The shock over Michael's departure must be the reason.

"Well, Anne will be arriving any time now. I'll leave you girls to sort out the whole of the story." Walter moved away, his step determined. "Remember my pledge. I stand ready to help you."

"My family appreciates all you have done, Walter." She followed him to the doorway.

"And you, Kate?" He leaned in close to her.

"Whatever do you mean?" His face held an odd expression. She had not seen such a solemn look on anyone, ever. "Of course—"

"I only wondered. Well now, we will save this discussion for our next talk." Without a further word, Walter walked away and left her standing in the doorway of his office.

After he left, she paced back and forth in front of his desk. She must sort her feelings and compose herself. Her thoughts lingered on her family in Ireland. Poor Michael and Maggie, what could be done to help them? She searched deep into her heart, thinking of her father and mother. While she clung to a bit of anger toward her parents, she felt a little sorry for them. Feeling sufficiently calm, she hurried to her shop and took up her sewing.

She sat in her chair, hemming draperies, when Anne came through the door, a large shopping bag over her shoulder, Nell in one arm and Tom grasping the other hand. Kate rushed to her sister and took Nell from her arms. Perhaps her turmoil had diminished some. She found herself composed enough to comfort Anne, who burst into tears when she attempted to speak.

"I do not regret one bit of the sacrifices we made." Anne sniffled between each word. "I no longer begrudge them any part of the money. Never in all these years, though, have I considered that, once here, any one of them would ever return to Ireland."

Hearing Anne's despairing words brought the anguish back to Kate. "I agree with you." She offered her sister a handkerchief and a sympathetic nod. "I understand Michael's feeling of duty. I applaud his maturity and his taking on the responsibility." A groan escaped. She could not hold it back. "It is the going back I cannot bear."

She placed Nell on a rug in a corner of the room next to Tom. Then she held Anne and tried to soothe her. Looking past her sister to the children, she saw drawn faces and troubled eyes. Moving away from Anne, she arranged a smile on her face and went to them. "Do not worry, Tom. Your mother and I will be fine." Pulling some pencils and paper from a shelf, she handed them to her nephew. "Do you think you could teach Nell to draw a picture?"

The little boy nodded, his eyes solemn.

Kate watched for a moment, as he gave Nell instructions for drawing a train. Though he looked back at the two women from time to time, Tom soon became absorbed in guiding his sister's hand. Kate turned back to Anne.

"We will come through this latest disappointment together. You are the strong sister. You saved me when I allowed my heart and mind to be filled with bitterness. You stood by and watched as I raged at Father and Mother for sending me, and then Lizzie, to work at Hogan's. When the resentment nearly consumed me, you and Julia suffered with me." Would talk of her own troubles distract Anne from her sorrow? Anything but the mention of Michael.

"While we worked together at enlarging my shop, night after night, I talked this over with Walter. His good counsel helped me. He is a kind man."

Anne moved from her grasp and walked over to the children. She smiled at Nellie and smoothed Tom's hair. She walked back to Kate, still saying nothing.

"There is something more, Anne." Perhaps, if her sister felt needed? "I would like to have your opinion. May I ask you a question?"

"No, I am not expecting." A tiny grin worked its way to each corner of Anne's mouth.

"Well, thank you for that information." Relief swept through Kate. Could they still laugh? Would it be possible?

With her sister's attempt at levity, Kate's courage grew. "It is another matter, entirely. I would like to ask you about… well…it's my sharp tongue, actually."

"Why, Kate, I never noticed any sharpness." Anne laughed in earnest now.

"That's the thing. You and Julia always rolled your eyes and then ignored my prickly retorts." Kate waved to Tom and Nellie. The two had abandoned their pictures, and they now crawled along the floor with the sheets of paper under their knees. "Mother always said if I did not curb my tongue I would grow into an old shrew.

"But now, there is something else. When Walter told me about Michael's leaving this morning, I responded badly. I showered my shock and displeasure over him. He did not become angry. Rather, hurt clouded his eyes. His bruised look pierced me. An hour has passed, and I have still not shaken myself free of my guilt over wounding him." Kate tightened her grip on her sister's arm. Anne would know. She understood people's feelings. "Why do you suppose my foolish words caused him such hurt? Why did the sadness I caused Walter matter so deeply to me?"

"Does Walter have feelings for you?" Anne stepped away and lifted Nell from the floor, but her eyes never left Kate's.

"Michael asked me that same question." A spell of tremors passed through Kate. "I cannot imagine he would think of me other than as a friend. I have nothing to offer."

"Ah, my Kate, you are a wonderful girl. Any man would be fortunate to win you." Anne gathered her children and directed them in gathering paper and pencils. "Here is my advice. Pinch your lips together, and speak as little as possible to Walter. Observe his manners toward you carefully. And then report everything to me." Anne extended her index finger and prodded Kate in the shoulder. "I will return soon for a full accounting." She lifted Nell into her arms, took Tom's hand, and headed for the door.

"Wait." She dropped Tom's hand, and reaching into her pocket, she withdrew an envelope. "Are you up to reading another of Father's letters? I brought you one written about a year after I arrived in St. Louis. I chose it because it mentions Michael."

"Of course I will read it." Kate pushed the letter into her pocket. "For so long, I refused to speak of our folks or read their letters. I know my stubbornness caused you distress. I apologize for that. I am suddenly filled with longing to see any word at all from home, even letters that are several years old. I promise you I will read this again and again, until I have memorized the words."

"That's grand, Kate." Anne ushered the children through the door. "Good-bye, dear."

"Good-bye, Anne, Tom, Nellie. Thank you for coming to talk with me. Your being here has already helped me reach some measure of acceptance about Michael's going back."

Kate held Tom's hand as he descended the steps, but he wiggled free of her grasp. "I forget you are such a great, grown boy. Good-bye, Tom."

Before her helpers arrived, she hurried to read the letter from home. Ah, my…words written so long ago.

Blackwater

24th August, 1860

My Dearly Beloved Child,
I received your kind and affectionate letter of the 28th and your check for £4. It gave your mother, brothers and sisters and me great consolation to learn you are now in the enjoyment of good health as this leaves us all, thanks be to God for His mercy.

My dear child, your cousin Edward Carty wrote a letter home just a few days before yours came to hand in which he stated that he was with his Uncle James. He states his uncle is rich and he gave him 360 acres of land together with 16 cows and 20 sheep. He seems reconciled to being settled for life and has mentioned in his letter to be prepared to let his brother and sister go out to him as soon as he would send money to defray their expenses which would not be longer than next spring.

He also said Anne Carty was not arrived yet although his uncle sent her one hundred dollars to defray her expenses to him and he daily expected her. His letter was dated the 16th of June last. My beloved child, I have written your uncle as you directed and stated to him the cause of your delay that the fare was raised so high what he sent you would have no chance of bringing you and less than 270 dollars would not bring you to him. I also stated you were most anxious to go to him and you were in a good position and earning all you could to put along with what he sent you. My beloved child, should your uncle send you money, it would be your mother's wishes and mine you would go, but we do not insist you do so. No my dear child, we leave you to your own judgment and we recommend you to go to your clergy and be directed by him and pray fervently to God to direct you to the best.

Your brother Michael anticipates beginning school in the fall. Mag often speaks of you and I know I need not ask that if you are to send a present to little Maggie you will not forget your Aunt Mary also as you know old maids grow childish.

Give our respects to Mr. Fortune and let him know his brother & family are well. Give our respects to Walter Dempsey and his sister. We never can forget their kindness.

With regard to your uncle's money which you spoke of sending to us, it would be our wish you secure it and not send it till you know whether your uncle would send any more to you. If your uncle answers my letter, I will be the better judge and will write you.

John Carty

    P.S. Give our respects to Edward and Grace Donahoo. William Kelly requests to be remembered to you and Grace Donahoo but my fingers are getting cramped, I am so long scribbling this, not being used to writing. I hope this will go safe to you.

Kate threw her energy into her seamstress business. She worked from early morning to late at night. She rarely left her shop...sitting alone...sewing...worrying. Would she ever make peace with the fact that Michael had gone? One morning, in the second month after his departure, she and Mary met in the family kitchen.

"I was just on my way to see you." Mary stacked iced cookies on a plate. "I was preparing a treat for you and your girls. Pour yourself a cuppa and we'll walk together."

"Thank you, Mary. That's so thoughtful." Kate followed Mary out into the hallway.

"Julia came in the shop earlier," Mary said. "Your sister invited us to visit her this afternoon."

"I cannot go. I have too much work to complete." Kate wrapped her apron around her cup. The tea burned her fingers.

"You must leave this shop, young lady. It is a lovely day, and it will do you good to be out in the fresh air." Mary led the way back to the dressmaking shop. "Besides, you have not seen Julia's new place and I would enjoy your company, as we walk along the way."

She could not refuse Mary. By early afternoon, she had finished her work, and she was ready to walk to her sister's. "Martin and Julia lived in that small flat since they married over two years ago." Kate huffed a little as they hurried along.

"It was time they found a larger home. With two babies, their need for space had become urgent."

"St. Louis's rapid growth makes finding a suitable place difficult." Mary shook her head. "An explosion of construction has begun to meet the needs of the burgeoning population, but the quality of the homes is questionable. Just a short distance from here, larger buildings, some housing as many as ten or twelve families, are lined in rows along block after block of hastily constructed streets."

"And have I forgotten so soon? Father and Mother raised eight children in our tiny cottage. Even so, I am happy Julia and Martin found a roomy, older place, rather than one of those newer, poorly constructed homes." Kate examined the places they now passed, sprawling homes and grassy yards all around.

"It is in a grand area." Mary motioned to the south, and they rounded the corner. "Just two blocks down. It is very old, but it is nestled between two large family homes on a quiet street."

"Julia called the place 'a pure gift from our great, good God.'" As they approached the house, Kate could see that, as Julia had also proclaimed, the place would satisfy Martin's need to rebuild and remodel.

"Hello, Mary, Kate. I am so pleased you both could come. Anne and her children are here already, and Tom and Nellie have settled in to play with the twins."

Anne held a small pail of soapy water as she knelt on the floor and scrubbed her children's hands and then turned to Julia's girls. "It is a grand home for Julia, is it not, Kate?"

"A lovely place." Mary followed behind Anne, drying off tiny hands and handing a cookie to each of the children.

"Yes…yes, it is." Deep in her own thoughts, Kate mumbled a response.

"Oh, my dear, the sadness remains with you." Julia had been preparing their refreshments, but she set her tea tray on the table and walked over to Kate. She bent down and peered into her eyes. "What can we do to cheer you?"

"Sure, the thought of Michael in Blackwater again has caught my mind under a cloud of gloom and confusion I cannot seem to push away." Kate pinched her sister's cheek. If only she could reassure them all. "I am determined to go forward, though. I try to push my sorrow aside. Much of the time, I succeed. There is one thought I cannot hold back. Michael seemed so happy here in our midst." Kate looked at Anne, Julia, and Mary and forced herself to smile.

"Ah, we all know you try." Mary brushed a strand of Kate's hair behind her ear.

"Do you all mind if I talk of Lizzie and Michael?" When they each shook their heads, she went on. "Sometimes speaking about things that disturb me helps to ease my mind." Kate lowered her voice so she would not upset the children. "I was so happy when Lizzie came. And didn't we lose her before she even had time to settle in? It all seemed like a terrible, cruel dream."

"Lizzie is our angel." Julia poured tea for Kate. "She was dear to us."

"Then Michael arrived, with no notice or warning. He just walked back into our lives. We all rejoiced to have him here. He loved every day he was with us, I know he did." Kate placed her cup in the saucer and lowered her head to the table. "Now he is gone."

"Michael felt it his duty to go back and help our family." Anne waved her napkin at Kate. "I miss him too, but he did what he felt was right."

"I know. I know." Kate took another slow sip of tea. "I learned from Walter that before he left, Michael served notice to his employer on the riverfront. Mr. Mott had been a decent boss, and Michael held great respect for him. When Walter encountered the man downtown one day, he tried to reinforce the enormity of the situation that caused Michael to leave America and walk away from the position that held such promise."

Kate passed the cream and sugar pitchers around the table. She needed a moment. It was difficult to speak. "The employer told Walter that Michael had been his best worker ever, and a position will be waiting for him when he returns to St. Louis."

"Such a dear boy." Mary waved her spoon in the air. "Whenever he had a spare moment, he offered us his help."

"Well, I am angry with Michael." Kate pounded her fist on the table. "We have not received a letter since he went back home. Did he arrive in Blackwater safely? What has become of them all? Father, Mother, Michael, Maggie, could not one of them send us word?"

"But, Kate, it has been less than two months." Anne went to comfort little Nellie, who had begun to cry.

"I know my anger is irrational. He will write, I am sure of it." Kate allowed a small smile to touch her lips. "Now I look around and see each of your worried expressions. Please do not fret about me. I have experienced this melancholy in the past. I assure you, I know the remedy. Make myself appear happy. Force myself to talk when I would prefer to sit in silence, to smile when it is easier to live in the gloom, to laugh when I would rather remain severe. I have done so for these many years, and while this method does not always show favorable results, I will continue to pursue the practice. I will not impose my misery on all of you."

"Oh, Kate, you must remain hopeful." Julia rushed over to her girls, who had joined Nellie's cries. "Please try. Have faith in God. I will pray for you, we will all pray for a recovery of your spirits."

"Do not become anxious about me, Julia. When I become sad, I'll remember the encouragement I received from my sisters. And of course, Mary, I include you among the ranks of my dear sisters." Kate settled back. Her spirits lifted. Was it fresh air that swirled through her being? "I apologize for my gloomy thoughts. I do not wish to spoil our afternoon together. I will persevere."

"I am happy you moved into this grand place, Julia." She studied the room carefully. The house was similar to Anne's, a large place in as much of a sad state of repair as the Duffs' home had once been. Could the men of the Dempsey group accomplish a restoration of this size?

"The men finished the new roof this weekend." Julia pointed upward. "Of course, we cannot see the roof, but just imagine, we are no longer forced to place buckets and pails throughout the house when it rains. They plan to work on the kitchen next. Mr. Flynn is coming to help move the fireplace."

"I do believe this is the largest kitchen I have ever seen." Kate sat with the others in one corner of the room, their chairs in a small circle with a low, round table in their midst. A tea tray rested in the center of the tabletop. No worry over space in this house. The children had calmed themselves, and they were engrossed in building a tower of blocks beside them on the floor.

"Well, Kate, have you ever seen a kitchen with the fireplace right in the center of the room?" Julia asked.

"I must say, I never have. But, I was totally wrong when I voiced my doubts that Anne's home could be made livable. I have learned my lesson. I will never question the men's abilities again. I look forward to seeing this magnificent room with the fireplace against the wall and the resulting open space for your kitchen table. It will be grand."

"It will be magnificent." Julia whirled all around the fireplace, coming to a stop before Kate in the corner of the room. She reached out and tickled her under her chin. "We have all heard your promise, my lovely lass. In about two weeks, I will be expecting you and your smiling face to accompany Anne and Mary here for an inspection of Julia and Martin Tobin's marvelous new kitchen."

Chapter Twelve

October, 1869

While Kate readied herself for her day in the shop, she felt a great sense of tiredness settling over her. She finished dressing for work and then sat in the rocker, her hands clasping the arms of the chair. Her head drifted toward the side.

"Sorry to disturb you, Kate." Charlotte, Kate's young seamstress, rushed into the attic room and stopped right in front of her. She took several deep breaths. "Ellen dispatched me to see if you were well. She said you are always the first to arrive in the shop each morning." Charlotte inched closer, leaning down, gazing into her eyes. "What is it, Kate?"

She must have frightened poor Charlotte when she looked up at her. She was a sweet girl, with strong blue eyes, a thick, blond braid wrapped around her head, and a wonderful, wide smile. Though she possessed the talent with the needle of a much older person, Charlotte was barely sixteen. Kate made a supreme effort to reassure the girl. Her mouth opened and closed. She could not form the words.

"I will run and fetch someone to help you." As Charlotte ran toward the doorway, she collided with Mary who walked in, followed closely by Walter.

"Kate, what has happened? What will I do for you?" Mary knelt before Kate's chair and wrapped her arms around her shoulders.

"What do you need, Kate?" Walter asked.

She watched as if a scene unfolded before her. Mary's worried murmurs and Walter's look of concern disturbed her. She tried once more, but still no words would come. Would she topple to the floor, if her arms could not support her? Minutes passed. She could not be sure how many. Her head grew heavy. It had grown increasingly difficult to move.

I hear their talk and understand their words. Why am I unable to answer? Wait! Do not leave me. She willed a look of pleading into her eyes. *Could they see?*

She watched, helpless, as Charlotte slipped through the doorway and disappeared down the stairs.

Walter followed behind Charlotte. He turned back. "I am going for the doctor." He retreated, his feet pounding down the steps.

Mary moved to a chair beside her and held her hand. "What will I do for you?"

Kate shook her head. Had it moved? The room grew still. She closed her eyes to rest a moment. When she opened her eyes again, Anne had entered the room.

"What is it, dear?" Anne pulled up a chair beside Mary. She held Kate's other hand, her quiet, unruffled manner matching Mary's demeanor. Anne glanced over toward Mary, concern in her eyes.

If only she could reassure her. Again, she opened her mouth to speak, but still no words came. Exhausted, she lowered her head.

"Kate?" Julia burst into the room. "Walter came by to tell me you had fallen ill." She crossed to Kate's chair and knelt down in front of her. "What is the matter? How can we help you?"

She tried to speak. Again, it was no use. She closed her eyes and turned away. She did not want them to see her tears.

"Speak to us, please." Julia threw her arms around her and gave her a forceful squeeze. "It frightens me to see you so!"

Kate attempted to form the words once more. She heard no sound come forth. Had her lips moved? She read the worry in Julia's eyes.

"Who is working in your shop?" When Kate managed no more than a shake of her head, Julia appealed to Anne, then Mary.

"Ellen, Janey, and Charlotte are at work in the seamstress shop." Mary touched Kate's hand. "They will handle things for you." Mary edged in closer to her. "Ellen insists you are not to worry one bit."

Anne moved about the room, taking charge as she always did when they were in distress. "While we wait for the doctor, I will settle Kate in bed. Will you open the drapes, Julia? He will not even be able to see her in this darkened room." Anne pulled her to her feet. With a gentle touch, she removed her dress and slipped a nightgown over her head.

Kate tried to walk to the bed. She pushed mightily on her foot, but it did not move. Her legs were too weak. Anne held one arm and Mary the other, and they dragged her the few steps from the chair to her bed.

"Do you hurt anywhere?" Tears filled Mary's eyes.

Her arms and legs ached, and it hurt to blink, but she observed the worry in their eyes. She attempted to shake her head, and it must have moved a little. Relief filled Mary's eyes. Soft-hearted Mary, she could not bear to see anyone in pain.

They were smoothing out the covers when Dr. Gallagher walked through the doorway. While he examined her, Kate focused on the doctor, and with great effort and concentration, she shook her head in response to his questions. And then, her last ounce of strength slipped away. She allowed her eyelids to close.

❀ ❀ ❀

Kate awakened to see the sun shining through the small space left open just beneath the curtains. Had she slept for a few hours? When she turned her head, the motion was not the grand effort she felt earlier. Relief swept through her, then shock. A woman, wearing a nurse's uniform, sat in the rocker beside her bed.

"So, you have come back to us." The nurse spoke softly, her voice warm and soothing. She rose and stood beside the bed. "How are you feeling?"

"I believe I am much better. The last time I attempted to speak, no sound came forth." A grin broke through. "I have regained my voice."

She examined her sleeves and realized she wore a clean gown. "How long have I been sleeping?"

"Two days. I am Patty Murphy. The doctor sent for me. He became alarmed when he found you too weak to even speak." The nurse bathed her face with a cool cloth.

"What is ailing me? Will I recover?"

"It appears you are recovering already." Nurse Murphy brushed Kate's hair back from her forehead. "The doctor suspects you suffer from exhaustion. He feels with rest you will be fine."

Kate raised her head and looked around the room. All was in order. "I wore a white nightgown the day the doctor visited. This one is blue. I cannot believe I have been languishing in bed. How many days did you say?"

"It has been three days since you fell ill," the nurse said. "I arrived yesterday morning."

"I must check on my shop." Kate pushed the covers aside.

"I do not believe you are meant to be worrying about your shop. A young girl, a pretty redhead named Ellen, came up to see you several times." The nurse handed her a drawing of a girl with red hair and exaggerated ears. "She said if you awakened I must tell you she is seeing to everything. She sounded quite capable."

Giggling at Ellen's sketch, Kate attempted to rise. "Ah, thank God, I can move." Relief poured through her, but disappointment followed. The effort to move her legs made her weary. She rested her head on the pillow. "I must return to my work. I cannot sleep the days away."

"Let's begin with sitting up. Then I will help you move to the chair." Once Kate sat on the side of the bed, the nurse pushed a chair right up to the edge of the mattress. Mrs. Murphy bore most of her weight. In truth, she all but carried her to the chair.

"That's a fine start, Kate. Your strength has begun to return. Are you able to sit there a few minutes? I'll place fresh sheets on the bed and help you change into a clean gown. Will it be blue or white this time?"

They both laughed. Kate felt a sliver of relief pass through her. The simple act of sharing a light moment with another soul brought a measure of hope.

"I remember you now, Mrs. Murphy." Kate talked while the nurse worked. What a thrill. She had recovered her ability to speak and laugh. "You are the kind angel who cared for my brother-in-law Martin after his accident. You guided him to a wonderful recovery."

"It is Patty. Call me Patty, please. And, yes, I did care for Martin. I hold no credit for his remarkable recovery, I assure you. A stronger, more determined man, I've never met. He persevered at rebuilding his strength like no one I have ever known." The nurse gazed out the window. Sniffling, she searched her pockets. "He also possesses a deep faith. With each bit of progress he achieved, he gave thanks. He holds no bitterness over the loss of his arm. He only thanks God for returning him to a normal life."

"Martin is a fine man. He would not agree with your claim that you did not help him, though. I've heard him speak highly of the care you extended to him." Kate pulled a blanket across her knees. "And now, I am fortunate to have your help as well."

"You give me more praise than I deserve." Mrs. Murphy brushed at her eyes with her handkerchief.

Kate sensed quickly that she could trust her nurse. She answered questions about her life and shared thoughts and concerns she had never before attempted to speak of, even with Anne or Julia. Their conversation soothed her, but it was all too brief. A great tiredness crept over her again.

"Come, let's move you back into bed. You'll want to rest for a time." Mrs. Murphy's voice remained soft and calm, but her tone took on a measure of assurance and command. "Your sisters and Mary will visit soon, I have no doubt. They have been here constantly. Many people have been concerned about you, my dear. How pleased they will be to find you awake and able to speak."

"Thank you. My limbs feel so weak." Kate allowed Mrs. Murphy to move her back to bed. "I must overcome this helplessness." Though she was determined she would remain alert, her eyelids would not obey her command.

❊ ❊ ❊

When she next awoke, Anne and Julia stood at the foot of her bed.

"Kate, dear, how are you?" Anne walked around to the side of the bed and reached for her hand. "Is it true you are able to speak?"

"My voice has returned. And, I am much better. This weakness frustrates me though. With the help of my wonderful nurse, I moved to the chair. I felt I was growing stronger. Yet, after sitting only a few minutes, I grew weary and was forced to go back to bed. I barely made it beneath the covers before falling asleep. How long has it been this time?" She appealed to Anne and Julia for answers. "I must regain my strength. I will not be such an invalid."

"Ah, Kate, it is grand to hear you speaking with us again." Julia reached down and squeezed her toe. "Now that you are a little cranky, you sound like your old self."

Kate wrinkled her nose at her sister. "How long?

"It has only been one day since you sat in the chair," Julia said. "You must not worry about anything. We met your nurse in the kitchen. She assured us you are much improved." Julia thumped her shoulder. "'Recovering nicely' were her words."

"The work of Mrs. Murphy, entirely." Kate raised her arm, but it fell back to the mattress. Ah, my...still, so weak. "She is a wonder. Our one, brief talk has soothed my troubled spirit. I am feeling much better. I will regain my strength and return to work in my shop in no time."

"This sickness reminds me of the maladies our mother endured." Julia said. "She sometimes sat in her chair for days and said nothing."

"I do not remember mother ever having such an illness." Anne walked to the window and gazed out.

Kate followed Anne's stare until her head fell back on the pillow. Did her sister wish to see all the way to their cottage in Ireland?

"Her condition worsened after you left home," Julia said.

"Yes, Julia is right." Kate attempted to sit up, but her head slid to the side of the bed.

"In all these years, I did not know it." Anne spun back to them. "Still, I have not forgotten Mother. She never put energy into anything but sewing, while Kate has been fighting to recover from the beginning of her illness. She has more spirit and determination than I ever saw in our mother." Anne bowed her head. "Ah, I do not wish to be critical of her." She looked at Kate and then Julia. "But we must recognize the truth."

"Thank you, Anne." Kate sat up straight in bed. "I will remember your kind words when I become discouraged because I am not recovering as quickly as I would like."

"Oh, Kate, of course, I did not mean my words the way they sounded," Julia said. "You are far stronger and more spirited than our mother. I do admire your courage. It was only the weakness I was referring to. When you did not talk, that was similar to Mother."

"It is all right, Julia. Do not fret. I take no offense." Still prone on the bed, Kate pushed her legs to the side. "I appreciate the concern you have both lavished over me."

"Dr. Gallagher could not be sure what ails you," Anne said. "He has ruled out cholera and typhoid. He was definite about that, but he admitted he is not certain what it is. There is still a possibility you could be contagious." Anne placed an arm beneath Kate's elbow, and with Julia on her other side, they pulled her to a sitting position.

Julia sat on the bed beside her. "The doctor did say you are in a state of exhaustion. Have you really been working in your shop day and night these past weeks?"

"Did Ellen tell on me?"

"You told on you." Julia giggled, and Kate and Anne joined in. "Apparently, in your feverish state, you informed the doctor that you could not keep up with your work and you were considering sleeping in the shop."

Keeper of the Flame

"Business has been brisk." Kate dangled her legs over the side of the bed. Could she stand on her own, even for a short time? "I acted foolishly, and now they are without my help at all."

"The doctor said you had worked yourself into a weakened state." Anne fixed a bed jacket across Kate's shoulders. "He feels that, in your vulnerable condition, you were susceptible to whatever germ overpowered you."

"What do my sisters believe?" All seriousness now, Kate folded her hands and looked at Anne, and then Julia. "Was it exhaustion? Or did a touch of madness come over me? Did I suffer a breakdown of some sort?"

"There was no breakdown." Anne sat next to her on the bed.

"And no madness. Do not even think of it." Julia took Kate's hand.

"We knew you were troubled, Kate," Anne said. "Since you arrived in America, you have lived in a state of anxiety. It worsened when Lizzie died and when Michael returned to Blackwater. We never thought it was a breakdown."

"We never considered that possibility." Julia shook her head vigorously.

"I promise you both I will not be abed for long. I am growing stronger." She touched one foot to the floor and then drew back. "I will be recovered in no time at all."

"The doctor recommended bed rest for you, Kate." Anne stood and folded her arms. "You must heed his instructions and take it slowly. I will help in the shop if Ellen needs me."

"We can check with the girls on our way out, but I do not believe they will want our help, Anne." Julia laughed.

"Now, you two are not bad seamstresses at all." Kate drew her hand into a fist. Not strong enough, but a beginning. "Our mother ruined your confidence in your ability. She could not abide anyone helping her who did not match her great talent." Kate swiped at her eyes with her handkerchief. "You are right. Ellen is a marvelous seamstress and she has a talent for organization. I am sure she is handling the shop every bit as efficiently as I would."

While they were talking, the nurse entered the room. "I assure you I will give Kate my best care. We will have her well and hearty in no time."

After promising Kate they would visit the next day, Anne and Julia headed for the stairs. Had Mrs. Murphy intimidated them? Hadn't she been in awe, herself, the first day the nurse spent with her? Still her heartening words must have soothed her sisters.

"She is making progress." Two pairs of sturdy shoes clomped down the steps.

"We will return each day until we feel confident she is well," Julia said.

"They did both live here in the attic room before they were married." Kate whispered to Mrs. Murphy. "Have they forgotten how well the sound travels up the enclosed stairwell?"

❀ ❀ ❀

Kate slept a great deal in the days that followed. "I have lost all measure of time. I can never be sure how long I've been asleep."

"Only a week has passed since you fell ill," Mrs. Murphy said.

During the second week, she became impatient with sitting in the rocking chair and attempted to move about the attic room. After each try, she fell back on the bed, exhausted. She detested giving in to such weakness, but she did not fret for long. As soon as her head reached the pillow, she slipped off to sleep again.

Keeper of the Flame

In the third week of her illness, she felt strong enough to spend greater amounts of the day out of her bed. At last. She sat in her chair one morning, trying her hand at the crochet needle with little success, when Ellen, Janey, and Charlotte came through the doorway. "The doctor recommended I not have visitors in case I am contagious."

"Now don't you start worrying." Ellen sat on the edge of the bed, and Janey and Charlotte pulled up chairs beside Kate.

"And the shop?"

"Your sister Julia is watching over the shop. She promised she will run up and fetch me if customers call in. Now, you must tell us how you are," Ellen said. "Janey and Charlotte have not seen you since the day you fell ill. They need reassuring."

"Yes, Kate, are you stronger?" Charlotte looked her over carefully. "I am relieved you are well enough to speak."

"I really am fine. And yes, my speech is normal, Charlotte. I am sorry I frightened you that day. I could not form answers to your questions." She reached out and brushed the soft, blue material of Charlotte's sleeve.

"And you, Janey, how are you faring? And, how is your mother?" Kate stroked an unruly curl that had escaped the young girl's bun.

"My mother is grand. She is threatening to sit in Dr. Gallagher's office until he allows her to see you." When Kate's laughter rang out across the room, she read relief across the faces of her three visitors.

Tears formed in Kate's eyes, when Ellen said they must go. The girls were so dear to her. And so conscientious about their work. "Come soon again." Remembering the races she and Julia once had before her sister married and moved to her own home, Kate added a challenge. "Tell my sister I will be timing her run up to the attic."

But it was Grace who came in to see her next. "I've brought you a treat." She strode into the room, a tray held out before her. "Mary believes iced biscuits are your favorites. I think you prefer the cinnamon, but to please her, I brought one of each. Who is right?"

"You are, Grace. I cannot resist cinnamon. Tell Mary I will save the iced biscuit for later." Kate balanced the small plate on her knee. "I am happy to see you, Grace, but whatever happened to Julia?"

"She is watching over the bakery shop for me. I begged her to allow me a visit. I longed to see you, to reassure myself that you are recovering." Refusing to sit, Grace reached out and tickled Kate's chin. "I must run back to the shop."

"Tell my sister I am still waiting to time her run to the third floor. I'm sure she is slower now that she is a mother of two, don't you agree?" Kate grinned. Julia slow down? Never!

"I will not involve myself in a contest between you and Julia. I am smarter than that. I will tell her what you said, and that is all." Grace moved through the doorway. "But, I am thrilled you are feeling well enough to tease. Bye, Kate."

"Goodbye, Grace. Thank you for visiting me. God willing, I will be working with you downstairs soon."

Chapter Thirteen

The trees were transformed, and ordinary city streets became avenues of orange and gold in the last weeks of October.

"You are a strong girl, Kate, and steady enough now to be left on your own." Doctor Gallagher took up his satchel, and with a wave, he moved on down the steps.

"Well, that is my signal to move back to my own home," Nurse Murphy said.

"After three weeks of your wonderful care, I will miss you." Sadness crept over Kate, but she also experienced a tiny shiver of excitement. Actually, she had already formed a plan.

When she awakened the next morning with no nurse sitting beside her, the idea unfolded. She sat on the edge of the bed, swinging her legs and figuring what her first move would be. A wave of weakness enveloped her. Perhaps she had been too hasty. No, she must not be swayed. She held herself still and gathered her strength. A faint tap on the door startled her.

Cara peeked inside. "Will I be of help to you?"

"Ah yes, Cara. I do believe I will need some assistance to dress. I am only now becoming aware of how dependent on Nurse Murphy's help I have grown."

"I have no experience in nursing," Cara said, "but I will try my best."

Kate discovered the simple act of preparing herself for the day was an enormous production. Every few minutes, she was forced to sit and rest. Time hung suspended.

Cara only smiled and waited.

"You are a model of patience, my girl." Relief poured through Kate when at last she felt groomed and ready to appear in public. "Thank you so much, Cara. I could not have managed on my own."

"It was my pleasure, Kate." With a shy little smile, Cara left her and returned to her own duties.

Kate sat back to rest. Perhaps tomorrow would…no! Her journey down to the shop could not be delayed. Proceeding slowly, she moved down the stairway, ten steps to the second floor. She paused to rest after each step.

"Kate, what a wonderful surprise." Ellen dropped an armful of patterns on the floor and stared.

She took a few steps forward. "Good morning, girls."

"And you looking so fit, this is grand. You are a treat for my eyes." Ellen retrieved the patterns sprawled across the floor then took a step toward her.

"You have a fine glow, Kate." Janey reached her ahead of Ellen. "You are a marvel, with a touch of pink in your cheeks and a faint sparkle in your eyes."

"I am well. Thanks to Nurse Murphy and with the help of everyone here at Dempsey's, I am on the path to a wonderful recovery. While Mrs. Murphy worked with me to strengthen my body, she also helped me revive my spirit. And, with the fine work you are all doing here, the shop seems to be running smoothly without me."

"Ah, Kate, we all missed you." Charlotte placed the iron on the fireplace grill and approached her.

"So here I am, not yet recovered in full, but prepared to make a fresh beginning. I am resolved to regain my strength and return to work." She made her way to her favorite chair. "Ah, it feels grand to be sitting here with all of you. You girls have done a wonderful job of keeping up with the orders. Now, it is time for me to step in and take on my share of the work." She inhaled a few deep breaths. "Well, perhaps, a small portion of my share."

"Shall we begin with our current projects?" Ellen carried the bulky order book over to Kate, and they discussed existing work and upcoming orders. As they talked, she directed Janey and Charlotte to bring over garments they were working on.

"These designs and stitches are excellent. What wonderful work you've done." She permitted herself a little smile of satisfaction. They were outstanding seamstresses. She could not have chosen better.

"Now, while you rest in the chair for a bit, Kate," Ellen said, "I would like Janey to show you the draperies."

"They are Ellen's work, more than mine." Janey stretched out a panel of cloth that was an exquisite blend of gray and silver. "Ellen measured and cut, the most difficult tasks. Do you not agree?"

"Ah, this cloth is marvelous." Kate beamed. To be back with her girls...examining such lovely material...the answer to her prayers. "Yes, I agree with you about the measuring and cutting, Janey. Our Ellen is a wonder. I also see your own fine hand in the stitching. It is your usual excellent work.

"And, do you have a project in the works for your mother?"

"I do. You know I love creating something new for my mother. With the cold weather coming on now, I am making a winter coat for her. You remember that dreadful cloak she made for herself with the uneven hems?" Janey paused until Kate nodded. "I cannot allow her to wear that again. I took the new coat home last night for a fitting, but I will bring it in tomorrow to show you."

"Thank you, Janey. I look forward to seeing the new coat."

Charlotte approached, holding a bolt of magnificent white silk. "My mother commissioned me to make a dress for my sister, Barbara, for her confirmation." Charlotte placed the cloth on the cutting table and spread it wide. "I am so happy to see you back in the shop, Kate. The pattern for this dress is intricate, and I will need your advice as I proceed with the sewing."

"I plan to be here every day," Kate said. "I will help you in any way I can."

"That's wonderful, Kate." Charlotte unfolded the pattern, and they spent some time going over the instructions.

She tried her hand with sewing, but it was not a happy experience. As she attempted to hem a simple skirt, her fingers trembled. Within moments, she had pushed the needle into her thumb. Had her walk down to the shop drained her sewing ability as well as her strength? And how would she ever climb back up to the attic?

At that same moment, Walter appeared in the doorway. "I heard your voice." He walked in the room, pushing his white baker's hat to the back of his head. "It is wonderful to see you downstairs. How are you faring?"

"I'm afraid I am a bit weary." She decided she must be bold or she would be forced to remain in the shop overnight. "And, haven't you come at the best possible time? Could I bother you to help me up the steps?" When he offered his arm, she took it right away, and with a wave to the girls, she left the shop.

Climbing each step presented a struggle. At last… the second floor landing. Her legs shook. She gained a new appreciation for Walter's strength. As they neared the third floor, she was placing her full weight on him. "I would never have made it all the way to the attic room without you."

Keeper of the Flame

Walter settled her in her chair and turned to leave.

"Will you sit with me a moment? Do you have the time?" Kate eased back, pleased to have made the trip down to her shop to visit with the girls, happier still to be back up those steps to her bedroom. "I am so thrilled to be moving about again. I just wish to share the delight I am feeling right now. I want to shout with joy. I am recovering! Sure, I am a bit weary, but I have regained a little of my strength."

Walter pulled up a chair beside her. Sitting in her bedroom, his knees resting close to hers, did not seemed to daunt him. "You had a grand nurse. She seemed to help you recover your strength."

"Indeed, she is a wonder. Though I barely knew her when she arrived, I found I could confide in her. In my weakest moments, all the troubles that haunted me over the years spilled forth. She listened to my ramblings, never criticizing and never passing judgment. I will miss her soothing manner."

"It is grand that you felt comfortable enough to speak freely with her." Walter took her hand. "It is wonderful that you are speaking at all."

"She suggested I must exercise more. She recommended long walks in the fresh air." Kate gazed out the window. "I suppose spending all my time in the shop does not lead to good health."

"I would be happy to accompany you on your walks. I could profit from some exercise myself." Walter rose from his chair and stepped away. "I must admit to an ulterior motive. I have missed our talks."

"Have I seen you since the first day I fell ill?" Kate searched through what few memories she retained from her three disoriented weeks.

Walter shook his head. "I did not wish to disturb you when you were so ill. And you know I would not intrude. Now that you are recovered enough to make your way downstairs, I have hopes. I wish the friendship growing between us while we worked together on the expansion of your shop to continue."

"I have missed you too." The admission caused Kate to sway with surprise. "Walking with you will be my next incentive. I will work to become strong enough for an outing."

When Walter departed, Kate undressed and slipped into bed. Nestling her head into her pillow, she spent some time organizing her thoughts. Why had it taken such an effort to walk down the same stairs she had run up and down without a care for almost four years? And how long would it take to grow strong enough to make the run once again? And then another more perplexing question presented itself. Why, with her head resting on her pillow and with each bone and muscle in her body aching, was she unable to prevent a smile from spreading across her face?

❊ ❊ ❊

"How are you this bright, sunny day, Kate?" Ellen pulled up a chair beside her. "You manage to arrive earlier and remain longer each day. Sure, you are growing stronger."

"Today I dressed myself. Are you not proud of me?" Kate allowed an unladylike snicker to escape. She pushed her feet forward. "Except for the shoes. I could not bend down to tie my shoes. Will you help me?"

"Of course." Ellen knelt before her. "With you assuming the difficult projects, I find myself with time on my hands. Would you like a shoe shine as well?"

"It does feel marvelous to be making a contribution." Kate batted away the polishing cloth Ellen produced.

"Well, there's no time now." Ellen pulled herself up from the floor. "I hear Walter coming to help you up the steps. How does he know when to come?"

"I possess special powers." Laughing, Walter bowed to both girls and then addressed Kate. "It is surprisingly warm for late October. Are you feeling strong enough for a walk outside?"

"I have not ventured out the door in weeks, Walter." Kate glanced at Ellen and chuckled. "Now that I have my shoes tied, I am ready to have a go at it."

"You are making a remarkable recovery." Walter adapted his pace to hers and offered his arm to lean on. "'Tis grand to have you walking outside with me, Kate."

"I feel my strength growing each day, but our first outing must be a short one. I'm sorry, but after working through the morning in the shop, I am exhausted."

"Of course, Kate. Let's head back to the bakery. You must take some time for a rest." He held her arm as they reversed their steps.

"It is a comfort to have your arm to guide me, Walter." She read the concern in his eyes. "I am fine, do not worry. Perhaps tomorrow we might adjust the time for our walk. I will rest through the afternoon, and then, we could set out after supper. Would that work out with your schedule?" She waited for his agreement.

"I look forward to it."

❋ ❋ ❋

From the time of their first evening walk, she began to confide in Walter, as she had with Patty Murphy. On a balmy evening on the last day of October, they walked to the park, the longest distance she had attempted thus far. As they strolled along, she tried to explain what she believed had happened to her. She wished him to understand, she wished to understand herself. What force or malady had worked so viciously to wear her body down as well as her spirit?

"You see, from the time each of the babies was born back home, Anne, Julia, and I were responsible for their care. They were more like our own children than brothers and sisters." She paused. She needed a moment. "When Jimmy and Maura died at such a young age, it was as if we had lost our own babies."

"Ah, aye, that is so sad, Kate." Walter tightened his grip on her arm.

"My years of grief for them gained nothing. My anguish failed to bring them back. After we lost our dear Lizzie last year, I pretended I was controlling my emotions. But I have never recovered fully from the sadness of her death. I searched for someone to blame. I tried to place the fault with my parents, but that notion was foolish. It brought me no satisfaction at all." Kate raised her eyes and gazed around at the quickly darkening skies. Her words came easier.

"I turned to questioning my own actions. I should have insisted on bringing them all out of Ireland with me. I should have worried about the young ones rather than concerning myself with proper clothing for the trip. I received no answers to my questions, and flogging myself brought no relief. Michael returning home seemed the final blow. I could not accept it."

"Have you prayed, Kate? You have only to ask, and our Father in heaven will provide you with peace and comfort." As they left Seventh Street and turned the corner onto Park, heading back toward the bakery, he took her hand.

"I know you are right, Walter. Before my collapse, I had begun to pray again. I suppose I did not pray long enough or hard enough." She stopped a moment to slow her breathing. "You, on the other hand, seem comfortable with prayer and comforted by prayer. Will you help me?"

He led the way, beginning with the *Our Father.* In his clear, strong voice, he offered praise to God and beseeched Him to heal Kate and fill her with serenity.

❋ ❋ ❋

"You must take the time to walk with Walter each evening." Ellen said the following week. "Your cheeks have taken on a fine glow."

Mary also joined in the attempt to rehabilitate her. "You must go about in the fresh air, Kate. We all want to see you strong and healthy."

The weather did not cooperate. "It is much too chilly to walk," Walter said that evening. "We will take the carriage." As the weeks passed, she continued to confide her deepest thoughts and the most fragile concerns of her heart to Walter.

Gradually, Walter began to relate details of his past life and his own concerns to her. "I've never shared these dreams before," he said on another cold evening.

Kate rejoiced in their friendship. *He trusts me...what joy this is!* In some of her most confident moments, she dared to dream it was something more. She had no notion of what love meant. Had she been the recipient of such a gift?

Chapter Fourteen

December, 1869

Kate stopped in Mary's room for a visit a week before the Christmas holiday. She removed a bulky bag from her shoulder and settled into a chair. Stretching, she allowed the bag to slide to the floor. She reached down and pulled one corner of an enormous afghan from the bag. Yards of deep green yarn rippled out, covering her from her knees down to her shoes.

"Ah, Kate, it is beautiful." Mary bent closer and examined the wool. "And, so soft." She rubbed an edge along her cheek.

"I have only a few more rows, and then I will be ready to add the fringe." Kate fingered one corner of the soft wool. "With so much in our lives seeming harsh and ugly, the beauty of this rich color and the elegant smoothness of the wool never cease to uplift me."

"'Tis the loveliest shade of green I have ever seen, and that's the truth. And your stitches are perfect." Mary inclined her head toward Kate. "I only wonder. Will it need fringe? Sure, I do not wish to interfere. The fringe is fine for a girl, or a young fellow like Tom, but—"

Kate burst into a hearty laugh. "Thank you, my dear teacher. I was carried away with my success with Tom's cover." She dabbed at her eyes with her handkerchief. "You've saved me from embarrassment and Walter too. I cannot picture him enveloped in soft fringe. He would have pretended to like it to spare my feelings." She broke into a giggle again. "I do want Walter to like it. I cannot wait for Christmas to arrive."

"I have been waiting for you to come and sit with me," Mary said. "The holidays are just what I wish to talk about tonight. I have an idea I would like to discuss with you. I wondered if, instead of our customary Christmas dinner, we might have a Christmas Eve supper."

"Christmas Eve? An interesting idea." Kate draped the wool across the end of Mary's bed and shifted the afghan toward her, seeking the easiest position to work on the bulky thing. "What made you think of it?"

"I want to consider Eddie, Grace, Ellen, and Cara. They could join us for supper on Christmas Eve. Later, I would attend services at St. Vincent's. You know, I look forward to Midnight Mass, but some of our folks may prefer to attend church in the morning. I thought I could prepare breakfast on Christmas morning and have it ready when they return. Then they will have the rest of the day to themselves." Mary held up one finger at a time as she presented her arguments. "Also, if Julia and Anne and their families come to us on Christmas Eve, they could spend the next day in their own homes. What do you think?"

"I believe it is a wonderful idea. As always, you think of others, Mary. Let us speak to the girls and learn their feelings. I am sure they will be pleased." They sat together, crocheting. Kate wondered at the mysterious green wool pieces Mary had not volunteered to share with her.

"I assure you Walter will love your gift." Mary examined one edge of the afghan and lifted it higher. "The color will be perfect in his room, and the abundant size of the thing will keep him warm all winter long."

"I pray you are right, Mary."

❄ ❄ ❄

By five o'clock on Christmas Eve, the Dempsey folks began to gather in the dining room. "Merry Christmas, Julia, Elizabeth, Maura." Kate was engrossed in arranging a centerpiece of shiny silver holders filled with wide, low candles, when her sister entered the room carrying her two little girls.

"Merry Christmas, Kate. Is this not a lovely idea to have a Christmas Eve supper?" Bright pink glowed from the cheeks of Julia and her girls, the effect of their short walk in the cold and wind.

"It is a wonderful idea." Anne came in right behind Julia, hugging her little Nell to her shoulder. "We all wish to be together at Christmas, but it will be marvelous to have an opportunity to rest at home tomorrow."

"Merry Christmas, girls." Walter entered the room with his new, green afghan thrown over his arm. "Have you seen the marvelous gift I received?" He looked at Kate. "It is a wonderful present. I cannot imagine the work that went into making this."

The girls moved closer to Walter to examine the afghan. "Ah, it is lovely." Anne gathered a section of the soft wool into her hand.

"A thing of beauty," Julia said. Exclamations continued as each new arrival passed through the doorway.

When the girls began placing steaming platters of food on the table, Walter turned toward the door. "I'll place my prize in the office, to keep it from harm."

"Wait. Allow me to help you." Eddie raised the afghan from Walter's arm and wrapped it around his head.

Laughter exploded around the room. Kate's eyes flew to Mary. "Thank you." Her words were only a whisper, but Mary dipped her head in understanding. Walter would have looked a sight with bits of fringe hanging from his forehead.

They had all gathered around the table, when he returned to the dining room, "Let us begin with a thanksgiving." He bowed his head. "We thank you Father for the wonderful meal and the good friends with us this evening. Please watch over our families back home in Ireland."

"Happy Christmas to all!" James raised his glass.

"Happy Christmas. Merry Christmas." Glasses were raised all around the table. "Best wishes to all."

Kate tapped a spoon on her glass. "It is a wonderful celebration, Mary. We thank you and Grace and Cara for preparing this grand supper for us."

"Here, here." Again, a cry went up from everyone in the room.

Kate studied the smiling faces around her, as Mary and her helpers passed around platters of steaming beef, potatoes, and vegetables. Was it the spirit of the holiday? Each morsel tasted more tender and rich than the one before. And the atmosphere was joyous, indeed.

"Well, we've cleared up everything." Julia hung her towel on the back of the door, a few minutes later. "I do not wish this evening to end, but we must go."

Kate helped Anne and James bundle their children into their sturdy coats and new woolen hats and mittens. "Well, Mary's secret project has been revealed, at last. Imagine hats and mittens for everyone, made by her fine hand." She handed Nellie off to Mary. "You are a marvel, my girl. Your gifts are wonderful."

"The Carty sisters have received a special Christmas gift." As Anne headed for the door with James and the children, she handed Kate an envelope. "A message came from Michael at last. When you have finished it, please pass it along to Julia.

Is it not a blessing to receive word in his own hand that he reached home safely?"

"'Tis grand." Kate shivered. At last she held a letter from her brother. "Merry Christmas, Anne, James." Kate waved them off and then turned to bid farewell to Julia and her family.

When the Duffs and Tobins were on their way home, she ran for the stairway. "Good night, everyone. Thank you, Walter and Mary, for the wonderful supper." She held the envelope tightly her hand.

Alone in her room, Kate changed into her night clothes and settled in her bed.

November 15, 1869

Blackwater, County Wexford

Dear Anne,

    We received your welcome letter. I was glad to hear you were all well. I never thought I would be here at this time. I cannot help myself at present. I cannot fix the exact time I can leave until I see what my father and mother may do.

    We are happy to hear of Kate's recovery. I hope she won't take trouble after the illness when God was so good to leave her alive.

    Remember us to Julia. Tell Kate to write and let me know particulars about her sickness. I hope with God's help she is over it. A great many of the neighbours are sick and dying.

    Give my regards to J. Duff and M. Tobin and the children and tell Mollie Whealen I am well. Please excuse my delay. I was waiting, thinking I could get away.

    Your affectionate brother, M. Carty

Chapter Fifteen

January, 1870

On a bitterly cold evening two weeks after Christmas, Kate sat at the table in the storeroom of the mission working over a pail of strawberries. She looked up, surprised, when Grace entered the room. "Good evening, my dear."

"How are you faring, Kate? And why are you working alone here in the back room?"

"I offered to prepare the berries. One of the parishioners donated several jars of strawberries she preserved last summer. My task is to open the tightly sealed jars and empty the contents into this enormous pail." She brushed her hand across the jars and lids spread about the table. "I am about to pour the contents of each one into the pan."

"But, is it not a cold night for you to be out?" Grace sat beside her. "Please take care, Kate. I could not bear it if you fell ill again."

"The idea of my volunteering at the mission was Ellen's, meant to take me away from the seamstress shop for a spell." Kate scooted her chair close to Grace. "It was a good suggestion, but I am not accustomed to all the bustle and commotion out there in the dining room. I yearned for a few moments of quiet. Since the strawberries were stored here, the task provided me with a few solitary moments."

"Do you wish me to leave you be?" Grace rose.

"Ah, no. Please, Grace, stay and talk with me a bit."

"How are you feeling, really, Kate?" Grace sat beside her again. "You know, we're not so different, you and I. I've had my moments of melancholy."

"But, you seem to have overcome your sadness. Is Eddie the full cause?" Kate closed her eyes a moment. Could she ever forget the years of sadness Grace had endured?

"Of course, Eddie is wonderful to me. Our being married and living in our own small apartment at the back of the bakery building has changed my entire life." A blush crossed Grace's face. "It was your fine nurse who offered me some advice that has helped keep my spirits raised of late. You might wish to try it for yourself."

"Mrs. Murphy is a wonderful nurse. I am ready to attempt anything she suggests."

"When Mrs. Murphy attended church services at St. Vincent's, she noticed me singing with the choir. She complimented me, and then she made a suggestion. She proposed that when I am alone, I try singing out loud, holding the notes as long as possible. She advised me to sing words of praise to God. Ah, I have found it is a grand thing to do."

"Do you mean: H-o-l-y G-o-d?" Kate sang in her natural voice.

"More like this: P---R---A---I----S----E!" Grace thrust her arms out, interjecting her full energy into her singing. The lovely notes soared to the ceiling. She held the last chord until it seemed the pure sweet sound would go on forever. "See now, one cannot dwell on sadness after such strong—"

"Well now, here is the source of the beautiful music." Father Burns, pastor of St. Vincent's Church, came through the door that opened directly behind Kate and her strawberries.

"Oh, Father, excuse me. I had no wish to disturb you." Grace's splendid smile crumbled.

"You are not troubling me. I've only come in to search for my shillelagh. I seem to spend more time tracking down the frightful stick than using it." The priest was bundled in a long, gray coat of heavy wool material with a matching cap pulled down over his ears. "Your voice is lovely as ever, my dear. You may sing for me whenever you like."

He turned his attention to Kate. "And, here's our girl. It is wonderful to see you looking so well." Concern spread across the priest's face. "I'm pleased you are recovered enough to come and work at the mission. Are you feeling your normal self? Has your full strength returned?"

"I am well, Father. With the help of my family and dear friends at Dempsey's, I'm near to recovered. Grace was demonstrating an exercise meant to lift my spirits." She glanced at Grace, and the two girls chuckled.

"It seems to work for me as well. My own doubts about going out on this cold night have floated right away." Father Burns looked to each corner of the room. "Now, if I could only find my cane, I will be filled with even greater joy. I must not be late for my meeting with the Archbishop."

Kate spotted the polished wooden stick with the curved end hanging over the doorknob. "Here it is, Father."

"Ah, thank you, my girl. Well, carry on with your singing and your cheerfulness. We all need some merriment now and then." With the handle of the walking stick hung over his arm, the priest disappeared out the back door.

"Nurse Murphy's suggestion seems to work," Kate said. "You have even cheered our priest with your lovely voice."

Still smiling, Grace worked with Kate, scraping the contents from each jar until they had removed the last tiny morsel. "I'll add the sugar."

"I'll try the singing myself." Kate stirred the mixture, careful not to allow any to spill. "I'll wait until I'm alone. My voice would wake the entire Dempsey's clan. I'm no Grace Donahoo...oh, excuse me...Mrs. Grace Kennedy."

Grace helped Kate tidy the work area, and they walked out to the dining room together. "I know Walter is coming by to bring everyone home, but I must hurry back to assist Mary with our supper. I will see you later, Kate." Grace waved a goodbye, smiling as she went through the door.

Watching her go, Kate marveled at the girl. She remembered Anne's account of how sad and despondent Grace had been when they arrived in America together some ten years ago. When Kate arrived six years later, Grace still clung to her wretchedness over the young fool who jilted her. The warm atmosphere at Dempsey's and her new position as their shop girl had been the beginning of the change in her. Her friendship with Eddie that eventually grew to love and resulted in marriage brought about the marvelous transformation Kate had just been privileged to witness. Perhaps she could do the same. Of course, her singing must improve.

"It's the strawberry lady, is it?" The former Bridget Rice, now the newly-married Mrs. George Blake, ladled soup from a deep stock pot into bowls stacked along the counter. A large group of immigrants had arrived on the afternoon ferry, and the good volunteers at the mission prepared to serve them a hearty supper.

"How are you, Bridget? The enticing aroma of your soup has been filling the mission since I arrived this afternoon. The tired, hungry immigrants are receiving a warm welcome to St. Louis." Kate placed her strawberries on the counter. "I thought marriage might curtail your work at the mission?"

"And, indeed, it has." Bridget's glow announced to one and all that her life with her new husband agreed with her. "I come to the mission only one day a week now. Ah my, I will surely miss everyone here when George and I leave in the spring."

"Your plans for your journey sound exciting. A new beginning in California will be a grand adventure, it seems to me." Kate settled the strawberries on a serving table and began to portion them into small bowls. Apparently Grace was not the only happy newlywed at the mission tonight.

"We are impatient to start out. As soon as the weather grows mild, we will be on our way. For now, I must rush back to work and serve these poor starving folks. Your strawberries look tasty," Bridget said, "and Mrs. Flynn has the cream ready for topping."

Bridget went from table to table serving soup, talking as she worked. "Tell me now, was it your fine voice accompanying our Grace back in the storeroom?" Bridget's eyes twinkled.

"I should never even attempt to sing with Grace around. She is a wonder." And, it seemed, marriage had not curtailed Bridget's penchant for teasing.

"How about dancing? Do you enjoy a reel, like your sister Anne?"

"No, I'm not much of a dancer, either." The folks at the tables were following Bridget's talk. "And do not even think it. You already know I'm not much of a storyteller like Julia. No talent at all. That is me." Kate laughed along with everyone.

"Oh, mercy me. Would you not consider your successful seamstress shop, your keeping three girls employed, and your own expert hand at creating garments a talent?" Mrs. Flynn crossed the room to stand with Kate, placing both hands on her hips and shaking her head. "You are a marvelous girl. Be proud of what you are doing."

"I heartily agree."

Kate turned to see Walter enter the mission. Had he come in time to hear the full of their talk? Her face grew warm.

"And now, you are finding time to help out here. That's grand, Kate." He smiled down at her. "Will I be of assistance?"

"Of course, you may help." Bridget handed him an apron. For the next half hour, they worked together, serving the soup Bridget and Mrs. Flynn made. Walter sliced the loaves delivered by Grace and placed small baskets of bread and pots of creamy butter on each table.

Kate served steaming cups of coffee to the adults and milk to the children. When everyone had their fill, she passed around the strawberries, and Mrs. Flynn followed behind her, with a topping of cream.

While their guests enjoyed the desert, Father Ryan, the young director of the mission, entered the room. He moved from table to table, checking with each group to be sure they had a place for the night. Two bedrooms were located at the far end of the mission hall. Kate had observed a young couple heading for the first room earlier. The other room was small and sparse, the only furniture being two beds. Sure, it would be filled before long.

"I will wash the dishes," Walter said. Mrs. Flynn dried while Bridget and Kate collected plates and utensils and cleaned table tops and counters.

"Good night, folks. Thank you." A group of immigrants headed out the door. "Your supper was delicious."

"Well, we have scrubbed everything." Walter reached for his coat. "Let us head for home."

Kate, Bridget, Mrs. Flynn, and Walter stepped out into the chilly night to begin their short journey.

"Rather than having you walk, I should have brought the carriage." Concern filled Walter's eyes. "The sun still warmed the air when I left the bakery. Sure, it has grown cold and windy now."

"No matter, now, Mr. Dempsey." Mrs. Flynn smiled down at Walter as she mounted the steps. "But please remember in the future we are grand girls accustomed to being pampered."

"Good-night, Mrs. Flynn." Kate called out as her friend reached her front door.

"Good night to you all and thank you for escorting me home." Curtsying to Walter, she sent one last taunt his way. "Even though I was required to walk."

They were all laughing as they headed for the Rice home where Bridget and her husband were staying until they departed on their journey. "Goodnight, Bridget." Kate waved, as Bridget moved away from them.

With Bridget deposited inside her door, they were alone. Kate took Walter's arm. A question had been tugging at her mind while they served the meal. "Are you troubled about something? You have been studying me all evening. Is there anything in particular you wish to say?"

Walter slowed his steps. He looked down at her, his eyes dark and serious. "I encountered Francis Reilly this afternoon. He asked after you."

Kate nodded her head. "He's heard about my illness, I suppose. Sure, everyone in the neighborhood has heard."

"Does it matter to you, Kate?" Walter stood in the road, unmoving. "Do you mind what Reilly thinks of you, or if he asks about you?"

"Oh, Walter, no. Not at all. It's more a matter of my self-esteem that responded to you. I pride myself on being strong and capable of handling my own care." She moved in closer. Could she make her feelings clear to him? "You know, when I was so ill, I suffered a world of grief because I was forced to depend on everyone at Dempsey's. Just to think of my helplessness brings embarrassment still."

"I remember." His face softened.

"About Francis, I never even think of him. You were present at the supper table that evening a few months ago when I explained my feelings to everyone. I must confess I left out part of the story." She held his arm with force now. She must make him understand. "When I allowed Francis to call on me, it was because of my concern over my family. Before I arrived in America, Anne and Julia had been working hard for so many years, saving to bring the children to America. I wished to help them, somehow. Francis appeared out of nowhere, seeming prosperous and charming. It was all wrong. I recognized that almost immediately.

"I am too outspoken. I never could have made him happy. I regret that my foolish mistake caused him pain, but I held no true feelings for him. I could not marry him, even to help my family." The admission of her folly brought a lump to her throat, but Walter deserved to know how imprudent she had been.

Walter said nothing.

Hopefully, his reaction was surprise. Well, it was a night for truth. She may as well ask her own question, one that had been in her thoughts for a long while.

"If I may, what of your own heart? Had you given any part of it to my sister Lizzie before we lost her?" Her question may be bold, but she must know the truth.

"No, Kate, not unless you are including friendship as part of the feelings. Your sister was a delightful girl. She loved working in the oven rooms and in the shop more than any helper we've ever had. It was a joy for all of us to have her at Dempsey's. I miss her, just as everyone does." A touch of a grin appeared. "I am surprised you thought there was anything more serious on my part."

"I wondered, is all. And of course, when something is on my mind, I must speak out. It is a particularly bad habit of mine." They were walking again, passing along an area where a cluster of factory buildings loomed high over them, darkening the streets in spite of the gas lamps. Walter reached down and took a firm hold of her arm.

She looked up at the same moment. Was it tenderness she observed in his eyes? Did his slight smile hold caring? Nothing for it, but a strong urge to experience the touch of his lips seized her. Without a thought to what she was about, she raised herself up, leaned in close, and kissed him.

For a sweet, brief second, Walter's arms came about her. He held her gently, as if she might crumble. Then he pulled away. "Kate, I apologize." Walter's expression grew serious again. "I had no call to do that."

"You didn't do it. I kissed you. I am shameless." She couldn't help it, she giggled.

"It is not proper. I am older than you. You are living under my protection." Walter stepped back.

"But, I must know if you enjoyed the embrace?" Certainly, she had been filled with joy. He could not be sorry. She would not believe he experienced no feeling when he held her close. "You see, other than a fatherly or brotherly peck on the cheek, that was my first kiss. I would like to know it will not be my last ever. Your indifference would not say much for the quality of my feminine wiles."

"Not even Reilly?"

"He barely touched my elbow when we crossed the street." Another giggle escaped.

Walter's laughter boomed out into the still, dark night. "You are an amazing, wonderful girl. I just cannot give in to my weakness of spirit. I have a responsibility to shield you."

"Is it because of my illness? Do you believe I am weak of mind or health?" Unsure, worried she may not want to hear his answer, Kate's words slowed. "Or, do you consider me ruined because I permitted Francis Reilly to court me? I wondered about that myself."

"Of course you are not damaged." Taking another step away from her, Walter began to walk again. "You are the most perfect, wonderful girl I've ever known. I just cannot compromise your good name. I will not."

What had started out as a magnificent walk grew silent and uncomfortable. If only she had not given in to her impulse. But then, if she had not dared to kiss him, she would not hold the warm, wonderful recollection of that touch and that embrace, as she did now. Was that all? Was she only to hold that one memory?

They continued on in silence, side-by-side, yet distanced from one another.

She did not stop at Mary's room that night, but instead climbed directly to the attic. She must sort out these new feelings and experiences. She set aside Walter's coolness to her. She wished to think only of the kiss and grasp the sensation of the touch of their lips and the feel of his arms around her. She would keep the wonderful memory hidden away, deep in her heart.

Chapter Sixteen

February, 1860

"Anne...hello." Was this a vision? The very person who had been in Kate's thoughts all morning stood just inside the seamstress shop. How strange, and how wonderful.

"Good morning to you, Kate." Anne struggled with the door, pushing against the fierce wind.

Crossing the room to help her sister with the door, Kate caught a glimpse of the heavy rain. "The children? Did you leave them home because of the weather?"

"I left them with Ceil. Tom has a cold and the weather is wretched."

"You will miss Ceil, when she marries, will you not?"

Anne nodded. "I am not sure I can manage without her, but she is so happy with her young man, Tim. I cannot help but be thrilled for her. We will find another helper, but Ceil has become a part of our family. I will miss her, indeed." Anne studied Kate. "Why are you sitting all alone? Where are your girls?"

"Ellen has taken Janey and Charlotte to the dry goods store to introduce them to our contact there. Ellen would make an outstanding shop manager. She is efficient and outgoing, much better at the job than me." Kate set aside her material and thread. She pushed things around, brushed the table with her hand, and waited. Just when she despaired of Anne ever hanging her coat on the tree beside the door and sitting with her, she received an enthusiastic hug from her sister.

"Nonsense. You created this business, Kate. Your excellent work made it grow." Anne moved toward the hearth.

Kate waved her hand in front of her. "And there lies my real talent. I'm much better at sitting here sewing away. Ellen is helping Janey and Charlotte learn all that is required to serve our customers. She is also training them to become fine seamstresses. And, with the growth of our business these last months, both Janey and Charlotte are kept busy full days.

"I am so happy you're here, Anne. The reason I was startled when you walked in is that I have been thinking about you all morning. While we have some time alone, there is something I must talk over with you. As you can see, I am nearly bouncing from the chair with impatience to begin my tale." She pulled the nearest chair over for Anne. When her sister was seated, she told her a little of what happened two evenings before, during her walk with Walter. She brushed over the part about how the kiss and the embrace made her feel.

"Walter? You and Walter? I am astonished." Surprise and then delight registered across Anne's face.

"Am I so unworthy?" Kate could not hold back a giggle.

"Kate, you are a fine girl." Anne placed a finger beneath Kate's chin and lifted her face until their eyes met. "Walter Dempsey or any deserving man would be fortunate to have your regard."

"I do not know if anything will come of it, so do not raise your hopes. We are taking far too much for granted. It was only a kiss. I have not spoken of this to another soul." She moved Anne's hand away. "Please, do not tell anyone."

"Julia?"

"No, please, let us keep this between us for now." Kate shook her head with purpose. "I will speak to Julia, as soon as I have anything definite to tell."

"Very well," Anne said. "But, you know I must tell James. I could never keep anything from him."

"I understand. That brings me to the favor I must ask of you. If you are agreeable, I would like to move in with you and James. I believe, at least for now, it would be best if Walter and I do not live in the same building." Kate's voice dropped. These words were difficult to express. "For the past two days, he has all but ignored me. He is concerned about shielding my good name."

"Walter is an honorable man, Kate." Anne threw her arms around Kate's shoulders. "I applaud him for thinking first of your reputation."

"I am a grown woman with a business of my own. I can well protect myself. But, if my residing at Dempsey's concerns Walter, I believe I should move." Kate leaned against her sister. "Would it be possible to come and live with you? Would James consent to it?"

"Of course. I speak for James as well as myself. We would love having you. You know how thrilled I was when Michael came to us. You could stay in the small room off the kitchen. Tom and Nell will share a room. They will enjoy being together." Anne moved away, pacing, clasping her hands together. "Our boarders are on the second floor, so you will be well away from them. I'll talk to James about moving your things. When do you wish to come? And have you talked this over with Mary?"

"No, I am not sure what to tell her. I am bound to guard Walter's privacy and at the same time refrain from hurting Mary's feelings. I must proceed with care and use the correct words. I will mull it all over a while longer. And of course, if I manage to convince Walter to speak with me, I will tell him about my decision." Voices were moving toward them. Kate whispered her next words. "We will talk again soon. And, Anne, thank you."

Ellen, Janey, and Charlotte entered the room amid a profusion of rain-soaked wraps and an explosion of chatter and laughter.

"Hello, girls." Anne laughed and talked with them, as if the two sisters had been in the midst of a trivial discussion. Kate applauded her sister's acting skill.

Preparing to take her leave, Anne bent down to hug Kate. "We will work this out. I will be back."

❊ ❊ ❊

For the second time in as many nights, Kate passed Mary's room. Her heart thudded with guilt. She was keeping a secret from her dear friend. After long hours of stitching and thinking, cutting, ripping, and pondering, weariness had overcome her. Nestled into her bed at last, she sought rest. She found none.

So many things had occurred in just these two days: the kiss, the change in her feelings toward Walter, his distance toward her, and her application to Anne to move to her home. And what would Ellen and the other girls think when she told them she would be moving?

She avoided thinking of Walter. She failed, utterly. Before she drifted off to sleep, she relived each moment of their walk together two nights before. Savoring the joy of it, she revisited each word spoken and every brief moment of their warm, magical kiss. If she held herself silent and still, could she recapture the feeling of his arms around her?

The last thing she remembered before she drifted off was that she must inform him of her plans to move. He must be told.

Keeper of the Flame

❁ ❁ ❁

She trembled as she descended the stairs the next morning, but she steadied herself. She must maintain a presentable appearance before the girls. Still, her thoughts spun about, and her stomach rumbled. In the past two days, her emotions had been unpredictable.

Had the girls wondered about her? Likely they were all worried her sickness had returned. More likely, they feared for her sanity. Her concern proved well founded. She had finished pressing a dress Janey Flynn made for her mother and she was taking extra time arranging the pretty frock on a hanger when Ellen walked through the shop door.

"Greetings, girls." Ellen's bright red hair fluttered behind her as she burst into the room. The incessant rain of the past few days had moved on, and bright sunlight poured through the doorway behind her. "I've brought an old friend for a visit." Holding a small package, Ellen appeared a bit nervous as she stepped away from the door. Patty Murphy, Kate's former nurse, stood in the entrance right behind Ellen.

"Nurse Murphy, Patty. Hello. It is grand to see you." Kate rose, surprise slowing her movements. "What brings you to our shop?"

"My cousin sent me some cloth from New York." Mrs. Murphy approached Kate. "I wish to have a gown made. Will you help me?" While the nurse made an effort to appear nonchalant, her eyes were examining Kate from every angle.

Kate's suspicions stirred. Her misgivings rose when Ellen, Janey, and Charlotte disappeared from the shop. "What is it, Patty?" Though she received no reply, she pretended to relax and submit to the nurse's assessment. Resentment grew within her.

"This soft, blue cloth will make a lovely gown." She held her voice even. Still, the furtive examination continued. "I believe a purpose other than sewing was behind this visit. Am I correct?" For once she must push away her anger and control her emotions. She owed this dear woman her life, after all.

    As she took Mrs. Murphy's measurements, Kate continued her questions. "Is everyone concerned for me? Is that why you have come?" She measured Mrs. Murphy's shoulders, arm length, and waist "Did Mary summon you?"

    Fixing her with a long, level gaze, Mrs. Murphy ignored her questions. "How are you, Kate?"

    "I am well, really I am. I have some matters I must sort through that have rendered me a bit distracted, is all." Kate pushed back her annoyance and held her breath. "Now do you really wish a new dress?"

    "I do, indeed, require a new garment, and I will hold very still and allow you to continue with my measurements. Please do not be upset with me, Kate. I am concerned for you."

    Concentrating on her work, Kate calmed herself, and soon they were chatting like the good friends they had become. They finished their negotiations quickly. "I will contact you if an additional fitting is needed. And it has been wonderful to see you again, even if you were brought here to inspect me." Kate hugged Mrs. Murphy, and the nurse took her leave.

    Ellen slipped quietly back into the room. "Kate, I am sorry."

    "Aha, the traitor returns." Kate's emotions swung between being annoyed by Ellen's meddling and touched by her friend's concern. Irritation won out. "You had no right."

    "Oh Kate, forgive me. It was not planned. I did just happen to meet her at the dry goods store." Ellen's face grew bright red. "It is only that I worry over you."

    "I am fine. Have I not worked my share since my recovery?" Kate could not hold on to the anger. Ellen was a dear girl.

"You work harder and accomplish more than anyone here. I am sorry for interfering. It is just that you have been distracted, and at times, explosive. Please say you are not falling into sickness again." Ellen stepped closer. "You are so dear to me."

Moved by Ellen's caring words, Kate allowed her vexation to slip away. She made an abrupt decision. "Are you able to keep a secret?"

"For you? I will lock your words away forever." Ellen raised her right arm. "If beaten, I will not tell."

Kate laughed. The tension dissolved. "There will be no beatings. My story is just the opposite. In fact, it is quite nice. Walter and I discovered we hold feelings for one another."

Shock and joy and concern settled across Ellen's face "Oh, Kate. You have lived here all this time. Did you and Walter never suspect an attachment until now? What will you do?"

"I am not sure how this story will end. Walter's concern is for my reputation. Right now, he pretends he does not even know me. He barely acknowledges my presence at Dempsey's."

"Oh, my word!" Ellen opened her mouth, then closed it.

"I have made one decision. I intend to move to Anne's as soon as possible." Kate swallowed hard. Apparently, this move was real, it would happen. "I will need your assistance, if I am to manage living away from the shop. Will you help me with this? I will not tell anyone but Mary why I am leaving. Of course, I will not lie and I would never ask you to tell an untruth, but I would like to leave the impression that I am still in need of care. Anne has always wished to watch over me and give me the attention she believes only she can provide. That part of the story is not at all an untruth."

Ellen appeared calm now, and her face returned to its natural pale beauty. "Oh, my Kate, I am so thrilled for you. I will do whatever I can to make this transition a smooth one."

"There is one thing more. I have not had the opportunity to speak to Julia about any of this. Please, Ellen, keep my secret safe until I have an opportunity to confide in my sister. I would not for the world wish Julia to hear of this from anyone but me." With Ellen's solemn nod, Kate hugged her, and it was done.

The last light of the winter afternoon was fading rapidly when Kate completed her work for the day. She decided on a short walk. She must find Walter and demand a moment alone with him. She wished to tell him of her decision to move. Starting off along the dim hallway that led to the back of the building, she stopped at Walter's office and peered through the doorway. No one was in the darkened room.

She moved on the few paces to the baking rooms. The space was made up of two large areas connected by open archways at either side of the room. As most everything at Dempsey's was, the entire area had been painted white. Ovens, tables, cabinets, and floors gleamed, likely all scrubbed before the place was shut down. Two small windows at the street side allowed a glimmer of light to pass through. Here, too, she found silence and an empty room. The men must have finished their work and gone off on their own pursuits. Where could Walter have gotten to?

Kate headed back toward her shop, her shoulders slumped in defeat. Then she twirled around and moved toward the back door. A bit of fresh air would revive her spirits.

She pushed the heavy door open and stepped forward. A gust of cold wind greeted her. Too cold for more than a few cleansing breaths. A loud thump, coming from the direction of the street, caught her attention. Walter stood at the curb, throwing hefty cardboard cartons into the back of his wagon. "Walter, I have been searching for you." She stepped outside, holding the door open with one hand. "Will you take a moment to speak with me?"

Keeper of the Flame

He turned. A hint of a smile crossed his lips. "It is very cold out here, Kate. You should be inside." He took a step forward. "Is there something you need?"

"Only to talk. I am aware you are avoiding me."

Walter returned to his work, throwing boxes into the wagon. "I have been busy."

Kate, a bit irritated at being disregarded, grew bold. "I must know your feelings. Am I so unpleasing to you that you cannot even speak with me?"

Walter picked up the last carton. Holding the box off to his side, he stepped toward her. "Not at all, Kate." He bowed his head before he spoke again. "You are so lovely I do not trust myself to be alone with you." He threw the last box into the wagon, walked out to the street, and jumped up into the driver's seat. With a wave, he and Josie started off down the street.

"Lovely." She stood in the silent street and stamped her feet. "He thinks I am lovely."

✸ ✸ ✸

Walter was polite to Kate at supper that evening, as he had been since the night of their kiss. Tonight, however, something new occurred. A worried look appeared across Mary's face, when Walter ignored a question Kate put to him. Certain now her move to Anne's was the right thing, Kate decided she could hold back no longer. She must share her decision with Mary before any more time passed.

When Mary went to her room, Kate begged the girls to excuse her from the cleanup and followed. She found Mary sitting in her chair beneath a gas lamp, holding her Bible. "Would you mind if we talked a bit?"

"I am pleased you have come, Kate. I am troubled. You and Walter have been such fast friends, what happened?"

"We are friends. We will always be friends. Now do not worry, Mary. Have you spoken with Walter?" When Mary shook her head, Kate pushed on. "Well then, I've come to explain. Faith, I've so much to tell you.

"You know, our strong friendship blossomed when we worked together during the expansion of my shop. Then, when the doctor ordered me to walk each day to restore my strength and Walter accompanied me on the excursions, our friendship changed forever." With some effort, she held her voice steady. She told Mary of the kiss, her part in it, and Walter's concern for her reputation. She explained her decision to move to her sister's home.

Mary cried through the recital of the entire tale. "Oh, Kate, you know I love you, do you not?"

Kate nodded. She could not speak.

"The prospect of you and Walter together would bring me great joy." Mary now turned to her usual caring response to any problem or difficulty. "What may I do to help?"

"Keep the secret. Pretend I am moving to Anne's to recuperate. Allow Walter and me the privilege of courting or just remaining friends or whatever lies ahead, in private." Oh, my word. What had she just done? She had bared her soul about her feelings for Walter, and she had done so to his sister. Though she had never fainted in her life before, this delicate conversation with Mary could bring about that one swoon. This entire matter had become an enormous web. Walter avoided her, he had not been told about her move to Anne's, and Julia knew nothing at all.

"I agree with keeping this a secret. It is the right thing to do." Mary's hug was fierce.

Relief poured through Kate. Of course, Mary would wish to protect her brother from any hint of gossip or scandal. Their talk ended with promises, Mary's of silence and Kate's to report any developments as soon as possible. They parted with hugs, tears, and a few chuckles.

But would she and Walter ever succeed in sorting through this intricate tangle?

Chapter Seventeen

Kate rested the iron on the hearth in time to see her sister enter the shop. "So you've come, Anne. And once more, no children. Will I ever see them again?"

"I am only stopping for a moment. The children remained at home because it is bitterly cold outside." Anne lowered her basket to the floor and unwrapped a heavy shawl from around her head and shoulders. "I spoke to Mary and extended an invitation to everyone at Dempsey's to come to us for supper tomorrow evening. Please ask your girls for me. Of course, we must have you with us. You will see the children then. I have spoken to everyone I could this morning, but please help me. I do not wish to leave anyone out."

"While it is only nine o'clock, I have already fitted three women for dresses." Kate held her order book before Anne. "We will work hard to complete our orders, and we will manage it. None of us could bear to miss one of your wonderful meals."

"I see one more customer waits to consult with you." Anne started for the door. "I will not keep you from your work. Come early if you can. We will take some time to talk over your move."

Kate had time for only a wave to her sister before she approached her customer. After the woman had been helped,

Keeper of the Flame

no other customers appeared, and the shop grew quiet. She and her seamstresses worked without interruption throughout the rest of the day. "Every woman in the city must be in need of new garments." Kate helped Ellen fold a lace dress and arrange it in a carton.

"Ah, likely they are anticipating lovely spring weather, as we all are." Ellen took the box from Kate and placed it on a shelf beside the door.

When the girls stopped for a cup of tea and a brief rest, Kate remembered Anne's request and extended her invitation to them.

"Supper at Anne's will surely be a wonderful thing for all of us," Ellen said. "I do hope we will finish our work in time to attend."

❀ ❀ ❀

As the sun settled behind the bakery building, the following day, Kate inspected the great volume of work they had completed. "We've finished the orders. We will be spending the evening at the Duffs'. I certainly look forward to it." Some of the others, however, reported difficulties with their schedules.

"I regret that I will not be able to go to supper at Anne's after all," Ellen said with a sad smile. She offered a lengthy, uneven excuse, involving a forgotten commitment. "I know Anne will understand."

Ellen's tale sounded vague, but Kate was preoccupied and the idea slipped from her mind. From that time on, she learned bits about one forgotten plan or engagement after another. Might she walk to Anne's on her own?

Grace came in the shop a few minutes later. "Do you suppose Anne would understand if Eddie and I do not attend? With everyone off somewhere, we wish to take this opportunity for a meal together in our own apartment."

"Anne will understand, Grace." Kate smiled to herself when the girl ran off to tell her new husband they could proceed with their plans for a rare evening on their own.

She closed the shop, turning down the gaslights and pulling the curtains across the windows. When she walked out to the bakery, she uncovered a new misfortune.

"Cara's rheumatism flared up." Mary turned down her own lamps and pulled her curtains shut. "I offered to stay back and prepare a healing soak for her feet. Beg Anne to forgive me. Tell her I will come by tomorrow for a visit. I must tend to our Cara. The poor girl works so hard for us."

Walter entered the shop and removed his hat. "Good evening, Kate." He stood before the fireplace, warming his hands.

She gazed at him, and he looked at her. "Hello, Walter." Could it be possible? "I suppose only the two of us will be heading off for supper at the Duffs' this evening."

Once outside, they walked along, attempting polite conversation. Kate shivered as the wind whipped right through her coat. "My customers might be intent on spring dresses, but the city stands entrenched in frigid weather." She wished to tell Walter of her decision to move to Anne's, but the walk was too short for a lengthy conversation. Still, she would tell him tonight. She mustered her courage and cleared her throat. "I have something I must discuss with you, Walter. It is important." She attempted a determined looked, and she must have succeeded.

"Of course, Kate." Walter ambled along, adjusting his strides to hers. "We will take some time after supper for a short walk and a few moments of talk."

"Thank you." She heard the grudging note in his voice, but he had agreed. She settled for that.

❃ ❃ ❃

Since no one answered their knock, Kate and Walter let themselves into the kitchen. Finding the room empty, they walked on through to the dining room. They found Anne and Tom awaiting their guests. The table had been set, and the room made ready for supper.

Ned Duff entered, and after a brief greeting, pulled a chair up to the table.

Patrick Tobin, Martin's brother, was not in attendance. An explanation must have been given. Involved in conversation with Tom who had been secured in his chair with a long towel, Kate missed it.

Baby Nellie had been fed earlier and was already asleep,

The gregarious James Duff arrived home from work and sat down at the head of the table. "Come, sit with me, Walter."

Kate watched as Walter and James immediately engaged in conversation. Well, he surely abandoned his uncomfortable manner in a hurry. She could not shake away her unease. She experienced an attack of nerves, thinking of the conversation they must have on their way home.

She spent a good bit of time explaining away the appearance of only Walter and her at supper this evening. "Everyone else seemed to be weighed down by complications and obligations." When the story required retelling each time someone new arrived, laughter rang out in the dining room. The situation helped to ease the tension between Walter and her, and soon they were both swept up in the pleasant talk around the table.

As soon as the prayer of thanksgiving ended, Anne faced Kate. "I realize the doctor prescribed walks for you, but I am concerned. Now that you are once again working long hours in your shop, I worry you are doing too much. And with the February nights so terribly cold—"

"Do not worry, Anne," Walter said. "I held the same concern. So, in the interest of improving my own constitution, I have been accompanying Kate on her walks. I encourage her to dress warmly, and we do not venture too far. If the night air is entirely too cold, I insist we go out in the carriage."

Kate stiffened. Anne and Walter discussing her well-being and not even including her in their talk was not appreciated. Had Walter forgotten that he had barely spoken to her in the last few days? There had certainly been no carriage rides. She lowered her head, and with her hands hidden beneath the tablecloth, she pressed an index finger into each knee. In the midst of inflicting pain on herself, the memory of their embrace, now three nights past, flitted through her mind. Aw, sure, Walter only looked out for her.

Another idea occurred to Kate. Perhaps Anne was acknowledging, before one and all, her need to watch over her until she recovered fully. Anne was providing the explanation for Kate's coming to live at the Duff home. She administered another prod to her knee. Surely one day she would learn to trust.

The talk around the table turned to Ireland, drawing everyone's attention. "I received a letter from an old school chum back home." Ned Duff placed his fork on the table and gazed around. "I am afraid it was a sorry message. Tim wrote of the hunger and disease that seem to be running amok throughout our beloved country."

"Conditions have not improved." James shook his head slowly. "The situation appears hopeless. I feel guilty I was able to come here and live this grand life we enjoy in America." He looked to Anne. "Many we left behind are suffering."

At their words, Kate turned to remembering. "I left my home without a backward thought. It proved such a shock when I began to yearn for the little cottage in Blackwater and our beloved family members remaining there." Though she addressed them all, her gaze rested on Walter. "I never imagined I would miss the cows and the chickens, but I do. And then, after I had been in St. Louis only a short time, I found my new life in America surprisingly agreeable. I discovered pleasant conditions I never dreamed I would experience."

"What of the many large buildings and the crowds of people?" Walter placed his glass on the table. "Does life in this large city not require some adjustment?"

"Those things have made little impression on me." Kate searched Walter's eyes. "In fact, I am so busy in my shop I've had few opportunities to look around at anything else. From what time I did spend in comparisons, I believe the sky is a deeper blue and the mossy hills a more vivid green in our beloved homeland than I have ever since beheld."

"Have you been working too hard? Are you indoors too many hours? We could, perhaps, manage additional walks."

Walter appeared concerned. Kate continued to hold his gaze. He behaved as if there had been no distance between them. Apparently, he had forgotten.

Anne turned to her husband. "We've been left out of this entire exchange."

"And at our own table," James said.

Kate did not miss the smile that passed between her sister and brother-in-law. She lowered her head to hide her own grin. Throughout the meal she struggled to hear any words but Walter's. By the time she helped Anne serve dessert, he was directing his entire conversation toward her.

She decided it was time to draw everyone into the talk. "I overheard an interesting conversation between two of my customers this morning. Mrs. Calley insisted that, even though she had been in America for many years, her dreams were always about Ireland. Another customer said her life in

St. Louis had been the setting for her dreams since the first day of her arrival."

"I remember, when I first came here," Anne said, "I dreamed I was walking along the road to the center of Blackwater. In another recurring dream, I felt the children tug at my clothing as I hung out the wash back home. I scarcely know what I dream about now. I will pay more attention from now on."

"At first, I dreamed of home too." Kate folded her napkin. The evening had slipped away. "Lately, I awake thinking I have just come from my shop."

"Sometimes, I believe you take pleasure in your time in your seamstress shop at least as much as I do in the oven rooms." Again, Walter directed his comments to her. "Can it be so?"

"It is true. You have already heard more than enough about my terrible experiences working in the dry goods store back home. I arrived at Dempsey's filled with apprehension. I assumed it was an establishment similar to Hogan's. Imagine my astonishment when I discovered how fine your home and bakery are. I have come to appreciate every moment of my time there. As James said, I feel guilty because I am comfortable here and often too busy to think of everyone at home."

"Kate is right, Walter." James broke into the conversation. "You and Mary have set an excellent example of how a business should be operated. You work hard and expect everyone to do the same. You treat your workers with fairness and consideration."

James turned to Kate. "You model your shop after Dempsey's. I admire you both."

"Thank you for the kind words, James." After Kate smiled her appreciation to her brother-in-law, she could not help herself. She turned again to Walter.

"I try to pattern my shop after your operation, Walter. I attempt to imitate the manner in which you deal with employees, trades people, and customers. You will do well to guard me. On occasion, I imagine I own the entire place myself."

"That's wonderful, Kate." A faint blush appeared across Walter's cheeks.

When they had finished the meal and enjoyed Anne's wonderful apple pie, the men carried plates to the kitchen, and Kate helped Anne with the dishes. A perfect opportunity to speak with her sister. "What did James say?"

"He thinks the idea of your coming to us is a fine one." Anne squeezed Kate's arm. "If you agree, he will pick up your things on Saturday afternoon."

And then, it was time to go. Kate thanked James and Anne for their hospitality and bade goodbye to everyone. She lowered her voice to whisper one last message to her sister. "I will be ready on Saturday."

❈ ❈ ❈

"Well, Walter, the evening turned into a grand occasion." Kate spoke up as soon as they headed for home. She could not risk losing her courage. "And now, I must speak with you."

"Kate, allow me to apologize—"

"Please, Walter, let me speak first. The apology must be mine. I am so sorry for my impulsive act the other night. I surely did not wish to bring you pain. While we have some minutes alone, though, I must discuss another matter with you. I must tell you about a decision I made."

"We'll walk for a bit, Kate, but not far. It is bitterly cold tonight." He unfolded a blanket Anne had handed him as they left and arranged it across her shoulders. "I will not have you catch cold."

"Thank you." She felt no cold. Heat darted from his hands as he wrapped the wool around her. Was there caring in his touch? Or did she read too much into his concern?

He took her arm again. "I know you've been trying to tell me something."

"The day before yesterday, I spoke with Anne and arranged to move in with her and James on Saturday." She darted a quick glance at him. Would he be angry?

"You are leaving Dempsey's?" Walter slowed his steps. "I am surprised, shocked. I never even considered you would move. I'm not sure how I feel."

"You and I may never experience more than a fine camaraderie, but some distance between us may help us sort our feelings. My living with the Duffs will also settle any questions of propriety in our friendship. Do you agree this move is wise?" Kate watched Walter closely. Unless the darkness was tricking her, his eyes softened.

"Will it not be an inconvenience to you?" Walter tightened the pressure of his hand on her arm. "Walking to and from your shop each day will take up a good bit of your time. You will continue to operate your shop in our building, will you not?"

"Yes, my shop will remain as it is. I suppose the exercise will be beneficial to me. Of course, on rainy days, I will likely change my mind about that." She glanced up at him, and they stopped walking.

"What will you tell Mary? And Ellen? Well, perhaps I should discuss the matter with Mary myself." Walter softened his hold, but did not remove his hand from her arm.

"Actually, I have already confided in Mary, a little. I told her I discovered I have feelings for you." Kate smiled up at him. Could he see her eyes on this dark night? "I hope you do not mind. I had to be certain Mary did not misunderstand my move. And of course, she will honor my secret. I thought I would just lead everyone to believe Anne wishes to take care of me and see that I do not work too long in the shop. That much is entirely true." She chuckled. "You heard her speaking of her concern for my health tonight. She believes only she can watch over me properly." As they passed beneath a street light, she watched a serious, sober expression cross Walter's face.

"Kate, if you are no longer living under my protection, do you think I should ask Anne and James for permission to court you?" A gleam appeared in Walter's eyes.

She had never witnessed such a look in a man before. Her heart pounded. Finally, she knew. She felt love in that look. She edged closer, until she could see his grin. "I believe we are already courting."

"Then, perhaps, I asked the wrong question and James Duff would be the wrong person to whom I should apply." They started on again, but proceeded slowly. Walter placed his arm around her waist. "I direct my question to you, Miss Kate Carty." They slowed their steps again. Walter bent closer. He captured her eyes with his own. "Do you love me, Kate?" Walter's powerful arms gripped her. "I am an old man compared to you and only a baker."

"I do love you. You are a fine, handsome gentleman and a respectable businessman. My affection for you has been growing these past months. I suspected the feeling was love. Just now, as we walked along together, I came to appreciate the depth of this new feeling. I love you very much. How old are you, anyway?"

"I am thirty-eight."

"A young man." Her teeth chattered. Love? The cold?

"Will you marry me?" His strong arms enveloped her now.

"Ah, Walter, yes. I would love to be your wife." Her heart thundered. "I would be proud to be married to you." She reached out and touched his face. Love for this wonderful man filled her being. Surely, nothing could keep them apart now. She shivered with the thrill of loving and being loved. There was as nothing for it, but she must have him kiss her. Was she not a brazen woman, standing on a street corner, wrapped in Walter's arms, absorbed in her own perfect happiness?

"We must head home, Kate. You are trembling." They started off again.

"I think it is only the excitement." While Walter still held her arm, she managed to capture his hand with her own. She relished the touch of his warm skin. "I enjoy loving you. I am thrilled by the notion that you love me. I am honored that I have now been awarded the privilege of holding your hand."

"You now have the obligation. I will require the touch of your hand on mine at every possible occasion." Walter smiled down at her as they moved beneath the light in front of the bakery. "Your move to Anne's is a grand idea. Conventions will be satisfied. And, it will not be long. We will be married soon and never be separated again. We will be together for the rest of our days."

"Ah, I look forward to our life together." She stopped. She wished to remain beneath the light and observe Walter's face while they talked of love and living together.

"We must never be at odds again. I could not bear it. I have been miserable these last few days." Walter held her hand tightly. "I wanted only to talk with you. Ah, I am shameless. It is worse than that. The truth is, I wished to kiss you again. I only worried about preserving your good name. I would never hurt you in any way."

"I felt dreadful, too. Since the night I kissed you, I was sure my boldness had sent you away. I was so unhappy. I wished to talk these worries over with you, but it is difficult to hold a private conversation at Dempsey's. And you were working mightily to avoid me." Kate stamped her foot. Would she ever gain control over that shameful habit? "Please, please, do not withhold yourself from me ever again. And, I promise you one thing. I will work at restraining my poor temper."

"I doubt it is possible." Walter shook his head, and they laughed together.

"And you, my dear Mr. Dempsey? I have bared my soul to you. I've told you about my first stirrings of feelings for you and of my longings for you. Just minutes ago, I described the moment when I was sure that the surge of strong emotions nearly overwhelming me was indeed love. And now, I would like to hear from you. When did the feelings begin? When did you know?"

"Do you mean in what year?" Walter squeezed her hand.

"Year? Have you been considering me that long?" Kate shook her head. Could it be true?

"The first day you arrived at Dempsey's, I thought you were the most beautiful girl I had ever seen." Walter touched the bakery door, but he still held her with his other hand.

"I am so shocked to hear this I can scarcely breathe. I do thank you for the lovely compliment."

"When you experienced trouble and sorrow, I suffered along with you." He held her face between his hands.

"I had no idea."

"When you began to walk out with Francis Reilly, I thought seeing you two together might crush me permanently." Walter held her chin with a firm grip.

"If only you had spoken. Those Sunday afternoons with Francis were some of the most painful hours of my life." She pushed her heels firmly into the ground and slipped her hand into his. "You might have saved me from that misery."

"I wish I had. But you scarcely spoke to me. You never even looked my way." Walter took her arm again and gave it a gentle squeeze. "Let us set that aside now. We have overcome our lack of action and our foolish mistakes. We are setting forth on a new beginning. I anticipate a wonderful life ahead for us."

"I agree." On this wonderful, perfect night, the fierce wind felt like a gentle breeze. The bitter cold brought Kate a sensation of exhilaration. "I have come to rely on our talks. Now, I may grow to need your fine hugs. Ah, I already depend on you so."

"Is this the strong, independent Miss Carty speaking? I would never believe it." Walter placed a hand at her elbow, and they climbed the steps.

"I would never believe it myself."

"I need you, too, Kate. I look into your lovely eyes, and the fire that smolders deep within you draws me in." Walter stepped into the darkened bakery shop and pulled her close. "I look forward to the time when I will be able to see you at every hour of every day. Do you awake each morning and coax the flame within you to a roar as you stomp down the steps from the attic? Does the fire burn low and flicker to embers, as you sleep? I have only seen you as a sturdy flame. The fervor you possess frightens me a bit, yet the passion and intensity you hold within you thrill me all the same."

"Thank you, Walter." She stood with him in the center of the shop, the warmth from the hearth causing a burning in her chilled face. "Will we speak to Mary this evening?" Moving apart from him, she rubbed her arms, missing his touch. But what an amazing spell of happiness had been cast all around her. Walter loved her. What had she done to deserve such perfect joy?

"Let's speak with Mary now." A question appeared in Walter's eyes. "What do you think her reaction will be?"

Chapter Eighteen

As Kate stood with Walter in the light of the dwindling fire, she discovered another surprise. Lights flickered in the vicinity of the parlor. Taking a few steps into the hallway, she saw Mary standing in the doorway, waving to them. A surge of relief passed through Kate, because she had not given in to her desire just then to move closer and kiss Walter's cheek.

"Why are you still downstairs?" She reached Mary first, with Walter moving right behind her.

"We intended to come upstairs to see you." Walter looked toward Kate. His laugh held a nervous edge.

Mary stood with a hand placed firmly on each hip. "It is a gift I possess, you know. The wee people have been whispering in my ear all evening. I've prepared for a celebration. Our tea is ready, and for the occasion, I baked brown bread. It was our mother's favorite, Kate.

"Now, I see by the magnificent smiles you both wear, my sources were right." After only a slight smile from Kate, Mary took her arm and drew her into a tight hug. "My dear sister."

Kate stepped back. Surely, she would hug Walter, too.

For her beloved brother, Mary showed only scorn. She administered a swift jab to his arm. "You did not tell me a thing."

Walter tickled Mary's chin until she grinned a little. "I could not be certain until tonight. And the story was Kate's to tell." He lowered his head until his great frame bent nearly in half. He faced his sister head on and blinked his eyes at her.

"Ah, Walter, I am happy for you." At last Mary relented and threw her arms around him.

"Ah, my, I am relieved." Kate said. Apparently all was well, and Mary approved.

"I am thrilled for you both. I could cry, but I will not." Mary poured their tea and handed around the cups. Then she settled in her favorite parlor chair. "Instead of tears, let us talk of arrangements. We must discuss Kate's moving to Anne's, your visit with Father Burns to set a wedding date, the wedding itself, and where you will live."

"I must speak with Julia before we proceed." Kate said. "After we have spoken with her and met with Father Burns, we will shout the news to the world."

Her state of love during her walk with Walter had masked the night's frigid air some, but the tea warmed her thoroughly. Lulled into a haze of comfort and caring, she could gladly remain here and enjoy the magnificent moment with these dear people. The hour had grown late, though. "We must say goodnight. The most wonderful day in my life has begun to slip away and I can do nothing to hold it back."

❁ ❁ ❁

"Good morning, Mary. Lovely to see you on this bright, sunshiny day." Kate rose from her chair to greet her future sister-in-law.

A determined look in her eyes, Mary swept into the dressmaking shop with Kate's cloak thrown across her arm. "We must walk to Anne's for a visit. I'm sure Ellen won't mind. We will not be gone long."

Kate folded her work, a gray suit coat. Thankfully those pesky flat felt seams were finished. With a broader smile than she intended, she applied to Ellen. "Do you mind? I will be gone only a short time."

"Of course I do not mind. Go." Shaking her material in Kate's direction, Ellen studied them, a question in her eyes. She said nothing.

"Ellen suspects something is amiss." Kate pulled the shop door closed and stepped down to the road. "She is a good friend, though. She will not indulge in gossip."

"I cannot contain my joy." Mary nearly skipped along the way to Anne's. "My suspicions were aroused in the past few nights, when Walter made such an effort to avoid you. Last evening, as I baked the brown bread, I was not so certain. My thoughts flew from 'it's sure' to 'impossible' and then back to ''tis a certainty.'" She shook her head at Kate. "I've dreamed that one day Walter would find someone to love. You are the answer to my prayers." She chuckled as they hurried along.

"Thank you, Mary. It means the world to hear those words from you." They moved swiftly, and Kate found herself standing on Anne's doorstep in no time.

"Ah, Kate, Mary, how grand it is to see you." Anne opened the door wide. "Come in. Come in."

"Mary convinced me to take some time to come and visit you, Anne. I've brought you a present, Charles Dickens' *Great Expectations*. Walter purchased the book at the new department store downtown, and Mary and I wish you to read it and give us your opinion." Kate handed her the heavy volume. "When you've had an opportunity to read the book, we will plan a get-together to talk about it. I am so pleased you included me in your group, and I look forward to our discussion."

"Thank you both. Thank Walter for me." Anne brushed her hand along the book cover. "I will begin reading tonight."

"Ah, I am just biding my time with talk of the book," Kate stood at Anne's kitchen table. "Something far more important has happened. Walter proposed marriage. We decided we must speak to our sisters before we set the date for our wedding." Kate stood with hands on her hips. "Well, Anne, Mary says she is happy for us. What have you to say?"

"Could I not have predicted this?" Anne faced her, matching her seriousness. "With you and Walter taking long walks together to help you regain your strength, spending time engrossed in discussion over every inch and facet of your shop renovations, and reserving the best of your smiles for one another, I could not help but notice. When you asked to move in here with James and me, my hopes grew. But, I promised you I would not speak of it to anyone, and I have not done so."

"And your feelings, Anne?" Kate couldn't help it, she giggled at Anne's grave look.

Anne ignored her and turned to Mary. "Did you not wonder? And do you not agree with me that marriage between Kate and Walter would be a marvelous thing?" A joyous laugh burst forth from Anne.

Mary nodded. "Well, of course, I've had my wee friends supplying me with information." They all chuckled at Mary's silliness. And then a serious expression crossed Mary's face. "I am thrilled for you both."

"We should not waste a moment." Anne moved toward the table where Tom and Nellie sat, drawing pictures. "We must walk over to Julia's and tell her right off. She will be ecstatic, and I cannot hold off telling her this wonderful story. Then, you will have leave to make your plans without further delay."

Kate and Mary gathered coats, while Anne searched for hats and gloves. With the children warmly dressed, they started off for the Tobin's house. "This will surely be one of our happiest tea times ever." Kate reached out to hug Mary, nearly toppling the cake she had carried from Dempsey's "I just realized Mary is now officially a part of our family group. There is no getting away from us now, my girl."

"I am delighted you consider me so." Mary sniffled.

❀ ❀ ❀

"Welcome, welcome." Julia ushered them through the hallway to the kitchen. "I am so happy to see you, and now Elizabeth and Maura will enjoy a splendid morning, playing with their cousins."

Kate took a moment to inspect Julia's kitchen. "The room is marvelous. The men have turned it into a spectacular, cozy place." The ancient wood stove that stood in the center of the room the last time Kate visited had been tossed out entirely. A new fireplace and oven, installed with the help of Mr. Flynn, had been placed along the outside wall, in the far corner of the kitchen. A new floor had been put down and a colorful rag rug, a gift from Mrs. Flynn, covered the center of the room.

She surveyed the bare windows. "I ordered material for the curtains, Julia. Let's measure before I leave, and we'll have new window coverings for you in no time."

"Thank you, Kate." Julia glanced over to Anne and Mary, who were making a pretense of admiring the kitchen, but at the same time casting smiles Kate's way. "You did not come here to examine my new stove." Julia folded her arms in front of her and turned Kate's way. "What brings these wonderful smiles to your faces?"

Kate could not hold the words back another minute. "Walter and I are planning to marry."

"This is marvelous news!" Julia commenced to march in circles around the children, who were settled in together on the floor beneath the back window.

"Are you well, Julia?" Kate watched her sister promenade. "I hope my news is not too much of a shock for you?"

"I am fine and fit." Julia raised her arm in a salute. After enduring two miscarriages, she was once again carrying a child. Because she was guarding her health, attempting to remain calm and quiet, she had not been to any suppers at Dempsey's for some time. "I am astonished and stunned, but at the same time pleased." She made a wide turn and whirled back to the kitchen table. "Walter will take good care of you, Kate. He is one of the finest men I know, and we already love him."

Julia turned to Anne with a mischievous smile spread across her face. "So, Mary triumphs, at last, with her long-awaited match."

"What is this, Miss Dempsey?" Kate nudged Mary's shoulder with her elbow. "Have I walked into a web?"

"It is a good thing, Kate," Anne placed an arm around Mary. "You know Mary loves us all and has long wished for a Carty sister to be a wife for her dear brother."

"Well then, I am happy to fulfill your deepest wish." She bowed to Mary.

"Your happiness brings us great joy," Anne said. "For years, Julia and I waited and longed for you to come here from Blackwater. Since you arrived, there have been so many sad times. Now we will move forward with rejoicing."

"I seem to be experiencing many happy moments these days." Even a simple thing like sipping tea together and chatting brought a grin to Kate. "I have had a wonderful time this morning, I am sorry to say, though, it is time for me to return to my shop. I am sure Mary agrees we must hurry back."

Her sisters nodded their heads, as well. They each had obligations of their own. "I promise I will bring you word of any new developments, Julia."

Kate held Tom's hand as they headed for Anne's. When they had helped her in the door with the children, Kate and Mary turned toward Dempsey's.

"Goodbye Kate, Mary." Anne stood in her doorway, holding a child's hand with each of her own. "Thank you for coming."

Kate focused her attention on Mary as they walked on. "You understand why I feel I must move to Anne's? You agree, do you not? You know how I love being at Dempsey's. I will miss the attic room. It has been a wonderful haven for me since I arrived in St. Louis."

"Of course, I understand." Mary held on to Kate with one arm and clutched the empty cake carton with the other. "Have no worry. You are doing the right thing. Before long, you and Walter will be married and you will be back home with us. Have you discussed a date for the wedding?"

"We have not had a moment to think of it, but now that I have shared the news with Anne and Julia, we are free to move forward. We will speak with Father Burns and arrange a date with him. There are so many plans to be made." She took the box from Mary as they crossed the street together. "I loved seeing the surprised look on Julia's face. She always fancies herself to be the first to learn any new happenings."

"It was indeed worth the walk to Julia's to witness her reaction," Mary's head bobbed. "There is no match for our Julia's enthusiasm. She was truly thrilled and happy for you."

"And I thank you, Mary, for accepting our decision to marry so graciously." Kate pulled her cloak closer. Even a state of love did not warm her entirely. "You could have held some objections, Walter being older than me, my foolish courtship with Francis Reilly, and my recent illness. Ah, I surely have a list, do I not?"

"You are a fine girl, Kate. There is no other in the world I love more. We will be true sisters." Mary attempted to wrap her shawl around herself, and when she failed, they stopped to pull the covering tighter. "Walter and I will be fortunate to become part of your wonderful family. And while we sat in the parlor last night, I rejoiced to behold my brother's beaming countenance. If I did not already love you, I would have begun to care as soon as I saw the amazing smile you brought to his face."

They turned the corner and headed down the last long block toward home. Kate grew quiet. Then, an idea she had been pondering burst forth. "Why do you suppose I have grown so fortunate, Mary?" Other questions seemed to rise up within her. "There have been so many changes in my life, and everything has happened so suddenly. Why am I feeling as if a different person resides within me? Where once I marched along, each footstep placed down with purpose, I now ease my pace. Where once I concentrated on the needs of my shop, I now have difficulty focusing on the many details I must consider in order to operate my business."

Mary's brows squeezed together. For a time, she said nothing. Then a wide smile crossed her face. "It is a gift from God, Kate. A true gift."

Kate nodded her agreement. She held her next thoughts within her heart. Something uncharacteristic, but certainly true, had been happening within her in these last few days. Walter had become her foremost concern. When their next conversation would take place or what she could do to make him happy was uppermost in her mind. Ah, these changes in her life had come swiftly.

She once prided herself in being independent, but she now wished to hear Walter's opinion on every question. She paused to consider his reaction to every matter. His smile of approval meant the world to her. The touch of his hand caused her heart to sing.

During each day at Dempsey's, there was always a chance she would encounter Walter, in the hallway, on the stairs, and of course, at Dempsey's suppers. After her move to Anne's, would they have opportunities for conversation? Would the days ahead promise such happy moments?

Chapter Nineteen

March, 1870

"It is a fine thing to be sitting down to tea with you, Mary." Kate added a spoonful of milk to her cup and stirred slowly. "Since I've been living at the Duffs' and we no longer enjoy evening crocheting sessions together, I've missed our conversations."

"I've not had a nighttime visitor since you moved." Mary set a cake on the table, pushing the plate away from Kate to the opposite side of the table and placing the cream and sugar beside it.

"I do appreciate the time I now spend with Anne." Kate settled back in her chair. "Before leaving each morning, I share breakfast with her and James. The warmth of their kitchen and the closeness and loving rapport I have observed between those two fills my heart with longing for a home and family." And for Walter… but she did not say that aloud. Mary was his sister, after all.

"Because of the long hours I spend in the shop, little Nell has been put to bed by the time I return in the evening for dinner. My encounters with my niece have been rare. She is walking everywhere, you know, and moving faster than any child I have ever seen. If you turn your head away, she is capable of pulling out the contents of a cupboard in a blink. She creates an entire disaster with the look of an angel."

"Her smile is sweet," Mary grinned, "but it seems there is mischief behind the innocent face."

"Well, she is a delightful child, trouble just happens when she is around," Kate said. "And I do thoroughly enjoy the company of Tom. I have been guilty of maneuvering a place beside him at the supper table whenever I have an opportunity."

"And has the walk between home and shop created a problem?" Mary drained her cup.

"The walk is no problem, but my move from the bakery building has precipitated some confusion. Adjustments must be made to my routine before things are running smoothly. The three blocks between the Duffs' home and Dempsey's loom large when I must retrace my steps to retrieve something from one place that I always seem to need at the other." Kate reached for the cake plate, but Mary pushed it to the edge of the table.

"What happened with Janey Flynn last night?" Mary rose from her chair to retrieve the teapot from the stove and pour them another cup. "Were you able to settle that mix-up?"

"Ah, it was my doing entirely." Kate rested her chin in her hands. "When it came time to close the shop and Mr. Flynn had not arrived to escort Janey home, I decided to walk her there on my way to Anne's. I'm afraid I frightened poor Mr. Flynn. A few minutes after I reached home, he and Walter appeared on the doorstep. I hastened to assure a frantic Mr. Flynn that Janey was safely at home. I apologized profusely and promised him that in the future Janey would wait for him in your parlor. I feel so sorry for worrying him."

"Aw, it was just a mistake." Mary proceeded to trim the edges from the sides of the cake. "Tim Flynn is overly anxious about his children. I am afraid he has never recovered from the loss of his dear young son in the war."

"There have been other incidents. Two evenings ago, a customer arrived at the shop after I had already left for Anne's. The woman insisted she had an urgent need for a dress that had been ready and waiting for her for weeks. With Ellen once again mysteriously absent, Eddie was dispatched to Anne's to fetch me. Nothing would do, but I must come back to the shop and deliver the dress to her." Kate turned a questioning look to Mary. "Where do you suppose Ellen disappears to?"

"I am not sure." Mary brushed cake crumbs into her hands. "I have noticed that once the kitchen cleanup is finished in the evenings, she vanishes. Do you suppose she has a beau?"

"It is a mystery." Kate said. "We must observe her more carefully in the future. You know, I miss our evenings working together and discussing these important matters. And I have not crocheted anything since I moved from Dempsey's. I need a project. Perhaps I will create something special for Anne, to thank her for allowing me to move to her home. She may appreciate an afghan for her parlor.

"What are you up to, Mary?" Kate pulled the plate across the table and examined the cake carefully.

"I purchased a beautiful silvery blue yarn last week. Eddie seemed to appreciate the afghan I made for him, so I thought I would make one for George." Mary dropped the darkened cake edges into her apron pocket. "Since I no longer have my partner with me in the evenings, I, too, have found it difficult to begin. With George and Bridget anticipating a late spring departure for California, I suppose I must put my hands to the work."

"I will miss them both." Reaching into Mary's pocket, Kate removed a crumb and held it up to the light. "Do you know what George intends to do?"

"He plans to buy land with the money he saved while working here at Dempsey's." Mary captured the burnt edges from Kate's hand and pushed them back in her pocket. "He told Walter he has enough to purchase a small ranch. A ranch surprises me a little, but he did tell me once his father owned a farm outside of London…

"Now Kate, I must have your promise. If Walter learns I allowed the cake to burn, there will be no end to it. It was the fault of the oven, you know."

"Bridget will adapt to whatever life they choose for themselves," Kate said. "I wish them well. While he has been here, poor George endured abuse and scorn because of being a Brit. And now, that same small-mindedness has been turned toward Bridget because she married him."

"And is she not the one girl in the city who has devoted her entire life to helping others?" Mary folded her napkin. "The worst of it is, they would receive the same abuse if they lived in a community of British folks. Ah, it is a sad thing."

"Well they will have a new start in California. And Mary, dear, your burnt cake secret is safe…although you will be forced to suffer a few snickers from me." Kate chuckled.

"I believe I will manage a few of your worst giggles. And as for Bridget and George, I pray it will be a happy time for them." Mary grinned. "It is Walter's taunts I could not abide."

"Thank you for the tea, Mary. I will tidy up here at the sink and then hurry on back to the shop." Kate rose from the table and began to collect teacups, spoons, and napkins. "We must sit and talk more often. I was about to add that I will bring the cake, but you are so dear to me, I'll not say a word."

"I am available tomorrow." Mary stopped in the doorway.

"If we do not receive rush orders for draperies from three hotels, I will be here." Kate poured hot water in the sink, and chuckling to herself, she added slivers of soap.

❈ ❈ ❈

"We've hardly had a private moment together since I moved here to Anne's." Kate pulled on her coat. At last, on the coldest night of the winter thus far, Kate and Walter prepared to set out for a walk to the park, their first since declaring their love. "This move has certainly fulfilled its purpose of placing distance between us. Were you able to slip away from the bakery unnoticed?" Kate raised her eyes to Walter. Chills moved through her being, the result of the smile he offered.

"I walked right out the door of the bakery, and no questions were asked. I suppose everyone at Dempsey's is more concerned with their own pursuits right now than with me." Walter's hearty laugh bounced along the walls of the entryway, but no one was around to hear. "My destination did not appear of interest at all."

"I am pleased to hear it. We have so many things to talk over, so many matters to resolve." A long list of details needing to be discussed and questions wanting answers floated through Kate's mind.

"More important to me," Walter said, "I wish to walk beside you, hear your voice, and touch your hand. Well, I would like to have the privilege of doing those things every day. So, let's hurry and plan our wedding. I suppose we must settle on a date. I will arrange a meeting with Father Burns, and once we record our wedding date on the parish calendar, we will make an announcement of our betrothal. I wish to tell the entire world that I love you." Walter bent down until their foreheads touched. "I wish to shout to one and all that the beautiful Kate Carty loves me in return."

Kate had been longing for this opportunity to share an evening with Walter. Excitement surged through her. His smile erased any doubt. He was as impatient as she to spend time alone. She wrapped a heavy shawl about her shoulders, to shield herself from the fierce wind.

Walter pulled on a hat and gloves, and they stepped out the door together and moved across the wide front porch of the Duffs' home.

Descending the steps, Kate glanced up the road in the direction of Julia's house. Off in the distance, a slight, blurred figure approached, moving swiftly. The form drew closer, almost running toward them. In the next moment, Peggy, the young girl who lived with Julia and Martin and helped with the children, came into view. "What is it, Peggy?"

"It is Julia. She has fallen ill." The girl gasped for breath as she reached the porch. "Mr. Tobin asks that you come, please."

They climbed back up the steps. "I'll fetch Anne and James." Kate ran inside, leaving Walter to continue the questioning.

"Peggy? What's happened to Julia?" Anne pushed through the door first, with Kate and James following. "What should we do for her?"

"Mr. Tobin asked that Anne and Kate come to help." Her breathing still shaky, Peggy lowered her head. "I am frightened for her."

"Of course, I'll come at once." Anne turned back to James. "I promise I will send word to you as soon as I am able."

"I will come with you, Anne." Kate shivered.

Walter extended his arm to Peggy. "Lean on me. I will attend you and the other girls to the Tobins'"

"The children?" Anne walked back to the door.

"Not a worry. I will watch over them." James hugged Anne and headed inside.

❊ ❊ ❊

"Cholera." Kate repeated the word in a whisper. Just the sound of it brought a shudder. She and Anne stood beside the bed of the sleeping Julia, while Martin and Walter walked Doctor Gallagher to the door.

"Her fever is high." Kate touched Julia's cheek. Their spirited, jovial sister had grown silent and still. She paced about the room, twisting her hands together. "She will respond to the medicine the doctor prescribed, will she not?"

Anne nodded her assurance, but worry showed in her eyes.

Kate knew the water was suspect. A murky brown stream poured from the pump at Dempsey's, and she had discovered much of the same in her short time at Anne's. Well water was also tainted. They had all been forced to boil their drinking water. An outcry had arisen all over St. Louis, demanding city officials act quickly on the completion of the new water system. The project had become entangled in money shortages and political battles. With little progress made, the terrible illness raged throughout the area.

"The deaths this dreadful disease has caused cannot be ignored," Kate said to Anne. "Julia's illness terrifies me. I worry for her, especially as she is carrying a child. I am also concerned for anyone who comes in to care for her. Of course, I will not abandon Julia, no matter how frightened I am. I only mean to say that we must all be very careful."

Kate and Anne removed Julia's clothing and pulled a nightgown over her head. She did not awaken. "If you sit here beside Julia," Kate said to her sister, "I will help Peggy with the children."

With the little girls settled in for the night, Kate and Anne prepared to leave. "I will be back early tomorrow morning." Her voice trembled as she attempted to reassure Martin. Poor man. His concern tugged at her heart. "Try not to worry."

"She will recover. I feel certain of it." Kate could not see Anne's face or Walter's as they walked home. Surely they were as worried as she was.

"We must pray." Anne's whispered words nearly drifted away with the wind.

"We will all pray." Walter took Kate's arm and then Anne's as they hurried along.

❋ ❋ ❋

Kate arrived at Tobins' at six o'clock the next morning. She met Dr. Gallagher in the parlor, pulling on his coat. "How is Julia?"

"She is the same as last night, but no worse. She has been sleeping since I arrived."

"Please, before you go,' she said, "I have a few questions. I hold no nursing skills. Will you provide me with advice on how to care for my sister?"

"Of course." The doctor headed back toward the bedroom. "Come along with me. There are just a few basic things you must know."

Anne came in later that morning, and Kate shared the information with her. "Dr. Gallagher is certainly a kind man." Kate watched for Anne's reaction to her next words. "He said you should remain at home." When her sister only lowered her head, her suspicions were confirmed. Anne, too, was expecting her third child.

"He also suggested we hire a nurse for Julia, but I have found that with all the illness in the city, nurses are in short supply. I contacted our old friend, Mrs. Murphy, but she is caring for another patient and will not be available for at least a full week. I have Mary inquiring at the bakery and Ellen in the dressmaking shop, but anyone with nursing skills seems to be occupied." Kate placed a hand on each of Anne's shoulders. "Promise me you will remain at home, Anne. I will care for Julia until Nurse Murphy comes."

She raised the matter of caregivers the next time the doctor came to see Julia. "We've had many offers of help, but I must be sure no one else falls ill. Please provide me with specific instructions for the best manner of protecting the people who care for Julia."

Dr. Gallagher shook his head when he heard the number of people who had offered their help. "I strongly discourage such an arrangement. This malady is passing through the city like wildfire. We cannot take the chance of adding any new cases."

When Anne came later that morning, Kate again repeated what she had learned. "The doctor said anyone who tends Julia must wear a mask. Also, they must boil their clothing and scrub their exposed skin after they leave her room. He strongly advises against allowing several people to share Julia's care. He is extremely concerned with the spread of the disease."

"I could take the twins home with me."

Kate shrugged. She could not make that decision.

Anne arrived again that evening and made the offer to Martin. "We would love having them with us. What do you think?"

"I appreciate it," Martin said, "but I would like to keep the girls with me, if I can manage it."

"Well, I am ready to welcome them, if you change your mind." Anne buttoned her coat. "I have alerted Father Burns and Father Ryan. They will inquire after someone who could help us."

❁ ❁ ❁

The following evening, when Kate walked to Julia's room to prepare her for the night, she found her sister awake. "How are you feeling, dear?"

"I am sleepy. I have been trying to remain awake, because I wished to talk to you." Julia lifted her head, but it fell back almost immediately, and Kate fetched another pillow and eased it beneath her head. "I thank you with all my heart for caring for me. I feel comforted to have you here. I worry, though. I am taking you away from your time with Walter. I am so happy for you both, you know."

"Do not worry over me, Julia." Kate smoothed the covers around her sister. She wished to help her. If only she possessed the knowledge and the skill. "Our Mrs. Murphy will be here in just a few days to nurse you back to health. I will then return to mooning over Walter."

A tiny smile appeared, the first Kate had seen from Julia since her illness began. "Thank you. I would laugh out loud, if I were not so weak. You have come a long way, Kate. It is grand to see that you are so happy you are attempting to make me smile."

"Now, do not struggle to remain awake any longer." Kate bathed Julia's face and hands with a cool cloth. "The doctor said rest is the most important medicine for you."

"May I ask one more question?"

"The girls? You wish to know about Elizabeth and Maura?" Kate sat beside the bed.

"Please?" At the mention of the girls' names, a grin appeared on Julia's face.

"They are both wonderful. Perfect, in fact. Peggy is doing a magnificent job with them in the nursery. Do not fret, Julia. The doctor thinks you will conquer this terrible ailment with no problem. So, sleep all you can, and it will not be long before you are well and strong again."

"I will do my best, Kate. I believe I may even fall asleep right now."

"Good night, dear." She watched her sister closely. Had she observed a wink, before Julia's eyes drifted closed?

Each morning, Kate rose early and walked to the Tobins'. She cared for Julia while Peggy saw to the children. While her sister slept, she prepared meals and tended to the house.

At midday, she visited her shop. After a short stay there, she returned to Julia's, bringing along hand sewing she could manage while Julia rested. She remained with her sister until Martin returned from work and Julia and the children were settled in for the night.

Walter appeared one evening later in the week to walk her home. "Hello, Walter. I am so happy you are able to walk with me to Anne's. The prospect of spending a few minutes talking with you offers the only bright spot in my day." A week ago, her thoughts had been filled with her love for Walter or her next opportunity to hold his arm. Now, she could not even touch him. She would not take a chance of passing the illness along to him. Once again, her life had taken a peculiar turn.

❦ ❦ ❦

At the end of the first week, Nurse Murphy had still not been freed of her prior duties. "If you are to be here for a longer period," Dr. Gallagher said, "I suggest you revise your arrangements. I apologize for giving orders, but the spread of this illness has not eased in the city. It would be best if you remained here, Kate, rather than returning to Anne's each night. I understand how difficult this is for you, but in the end it will be for the best. You must consider that if you carry the disease to anyone at Anne's, you will only acquire another patient to nurse. For the same reason, I suggest you avoid going to Dempsey's.

"And there is one more thing." Dr. Gallagher's face grew solemn. "I am aware Anne has been coming for occasional visits. Please insist she remain at home until Julia is out of danger. If she contracts the disease, she could lose the child. If she resists, speak to James.

"I also thought the children were being removed from the house." The doctor shook his head. "I should not burden you with the question of the children. I will take that up with their father."

❊ ❊ ❊

When Martin returned from work, she met him in the hallway. "As soon as you have seen Julia, I must speak with you. The doctor advised some changes in her care."

"She seems a bit better," Martin said when he returned a few minutes later. "She even spoke a few words to me. Or am I just being optimistic? Is the doctor apprehensive about her condition?"

"No, not at all." Kate placed a hand on his arm. Martin worried so. If only her words would reassure him. "In his usual cautions tone, the doctor said she is somewhat better. His concern is the contagion. He worries I may carry the illness to everyone at Anne's. He strongly advised that I move in here and stay until Julia recovers. Of course, it is your decision, Martin. Do you think I should do that?"

"It is a good idea." Martin rubbed his chin, brushing at his short beard. "I should have thought of that myself. Of course, we will be happy you are here. I will do whatever the doctor recommends. Anything that will hasten Julia's recovery. I know this is difficult for you, Kate. We are keeping you away from your work—"

"That brings me to another thing the doctor advised." Kate said. "I am not to go to Dempsey's for the duration of Julia's illness."

"Ah, Kate, I am sorry." Martin walked a few paces away then returned, still rubbing his beard. "I will never be able to thank you properly for what you have done for Julia. Just tell me what I can do to help you, and it will be done."

"If only Julia recovers. Then none of us will even remember this difficult time." Kate bowed her head.

"I agree." Martin hugged her.

The simple gesture brought tears to Kate's eyes. The reserved Martin Tobin had never hugged her before. "She will rally." She patted his shoulder.

"If only she pulls through this. I need her so, Kate." Martin pulled his hand through his thick, black hair. "What will I do to help?"

"Mrs. Flynn will be here to prepare supper for you this evening, but because of the doctor's orders she will not be able to care for Julia. If you will watch over her, I will go to Dempsey's and ask Walter for his help. I will need a few things from my shop and a few things from Anne's." She paused and folded her arms. "I will go in through the back door at both places, so I do not encounter too many people."

"There are two shopping bags and a basket in the kitchen. Will those help with carrying your things?" Martin started toward the back of the house. "I will ready the back bedroom. Will that do for you?"

"It will be fine, Martin." Kate started to press his hand then pulled back. "It will not be for long. We'll have our Julia well and strong in no time."

❋ ❋ ❋

"Good evening, Kate. How are you?" Walter appeared on the Tobins' back porch a few evenings later. "I am here to collect the laundry."

"I've just placed it in the corner there." She pointed to the post where two bulky laundry bags rested. "Thank you for arranging this." Walter's friend at the laundry, Hap, had developed a method for cleaning linens used by patients with cholera and other such diseases, and Kate would be forever grateful to both of these dear men. Of course, she held some bias, but she believed this act of kindness by the laundry man and by Walter helped her to survive this entire ordeal. "The laundry service has been a world of help to me."

"Anything I can do to help you, Kate—"

"Oh, Walter." She placed her hand on his face then drew it back. "I must not touch anyone. Dr. Gallagher brings a new directive each time he visits Julia."

"He attempts to stop the spread of this vicious disease. The city's doctors are all working without rest to help people, but the epidemic rages on. Hundreds of new cases are reported each week." Walter held her arm lightly.

"Then I shall not touch you." Kate stamped her foot and backed away. "Here, I've only learned what a thrill and a comfort the touch of your skin can bring. Will we ever know that joy again?"

"I understand what you are saying, Kate. I am still a bit shocked and surprised that we are intending to be married. I am a little in awe of this wonderful love between us." Walter followed her into the kitchen and removed his cap. "Do not become discouraged. Julia will pull through this. Our time will come. I love you so and I long for the day when we will be together."

"It is only the third week since I have been tending to Julia," Kate said, "but it appears we have been apart much longer. While I worked at my shop, I could look forward to meeting you in the hallway or stopping at your office for a talk or enjoying an occasional supper with you. I miss you terribly." She folded her arms, resisting the urge to reach out and kiss his cheek.

"Is Martin home?" Walter stepped to the doorway and gazed along the long, empty hallway.

"He has not returned from work." Kate wrapped her arms around her own shoulders. "He wishes to be here, and yet he feels an obligation to his employer who has treated him with such kindness."

"Well, I will see you tomorrow night." Walter went through the back door and lifted a laundry pack to his shoulder. "Perhaps we will have some encouraging news to share then."

"I am so grateful we have found this wonderful love we share. I am impatient to be with you. I wish to be your wife, share your home and your life." She gave in to the urge and brushed her cheek against Walter's. "And then, my next thought is guilt for these selfish desires. I do not begrudge Julia the time I am spending with her. I insisted I must be the one to provide her care. In truth, we have engaged in some marvelous talks when she was feeling strong enough to have a conversation."

"Ah, my Kate, it is only these two laundry bags keeping me from seizing you up and carrying you off, but—"

"I never imagined I would ever be so dependent on another person." She chuckled. "Here I am, though, yearning for you like a foolish school girl."

"Well, I love to hear it. We must have faith that Julia will rally. It will not be long. The moment we become convinced she is recovered, we will proceed with our wedding."

Chapter Twenty

April, 1870

"We all felt so encouraged. The cautious Dr. Gallagher reported a slight upward turn in Julia's condition." Kate discussed the events of the last few hours with Mary, on a morning in the fourth week of her sister's valiant battle. She pulled a handkerchief from her sleeve. "Our time for rejoicing was brief. Less than thirty minutes after the doctor left, our dear little Maura suffered a nosebleed."

"Maura and Elizabeth have been healthy since birth." Tears filled Mary's eyes. "Poor little girl, I pray her tiny body will be strong enough to hold off the terrible fever now surging through her. Has Elizabeth been moved to Anne's?"

"Yes, Martin took her there last evening. He has been worried Elizabeth would carry the illness to someone at Anne's. The doctor advised it though, and he agreed." Kate moved to the sink and began to dry the dishes stacked there. "Poor Martin, he blames himself for Maura's illness. He feels he should have taken both girls to Anne as soon as Julia took sick. Little Elizabeth is suffering, too. She misses her twin, and of course, she does not understand any of it. She has no idea what has befallen her mother and sister. My heart aches for Julia, Martin, and the children."

"So much sadness. On my walk here, a team of horses pulling a long hearse passed me by. I've heard they move through the streets day and night, retrieving bodies of the poor souls." Mary abandoned her handkerchief and dabbed at her eyes with a towel. "If only we could have improved the water quality."

"There is one good outcome of the need to move Elizabeth." Kate placed her arms around Mary. "You know the doctor advised Anne to stay home. It is dangerous for her and her unborn child to be exposed to the disease. Still, she clings to the notion that it is her duty to tend to Julia. With Elizabeth at her house, Anne will be required to remain at home. She will be safer there."

"I insist you allow me to help you." Determination filled Mary's voice.

"Thank you, Mary. It will ease Anne's mind to know you are here, and with Julia and Maura to nurse, I will be grateful for your help." Kate administered a firm pat to Mary's arm. "If the doctor discovers you are here, though, he may not allow you to return to Dempsey's."

"He's a good man, our Dr. Gallagher, but we have a need here. And if I've a mind to outsmart him, he won't even know I've been in the house, and that's the truth." Mary winked at Kate as she walked toward Maura's room. "Aw, I will take care. I will not go into the oven room or the bakery shop. I would not for the world want to pass the illness to anyone else."

❀ ❀ ❀

While Kate tended to her sister the next morning, Julia begged to know about her little girl. "I know she is ill. Please tell me the seriousness of her condition."

Kate evaded her questions for a few hours. She wanted to do what was right. The little girl was weakening. Should she tell her sister the truth?

"Please go and check on Maura, Kate?" Julia sat up in the bed and gazed at her with a pleading look.

When she returned from the nursery, she could hold back no longer. "Her condition is grave." Kate sat on the bed. She did not cry. Her tears would only upset Julia. "I fear for her."

"Help me walk to the nursery. I must see her." The once energetic and full of life Julia rested in a chair beside the bed, leaning heavily against the arm of the chair and holding to Kate with a desperate grip.

"Perhaps we should wait until this afternoon. Mary will be here to assist us." Kate helped Julia back into bed and watched as her body sank down into the soft mattress.

"I will rest until Mary arrives." Julia immediately drifted into a deep sleep.

When Kate entered the bedroom that afternoon, with Mary right behind her, Julia was awake. "How are you feeling now, dear? You've had a nice, long rest."

"I have not forgotten your promise, Kate." Julia waved to Mary. "I am glad you are here. I've been waiting."

"Let's each hold one of Julia's arms, and perhaps we could manage to walk her along the hallway to Maura's room." Kate wrapped a blanket around her sister's shoulders.

Julia took a few steps, but the effort brought tears to her eyes.

"Ah, Julia, I worry we are hurting you. Your limbs are so weak." Kate shook her head.

"You are not hurting me. Please, try just once more." Tears continued to course along Julia's cheeks. She took two steps and then slipped to the floor.

"It is no good, Julia." Kate and Mary helped her back to bed.

"Perhaps we could wheel Maura's bed to your room. If we combine our strength, we can surely accomplish that feat." Kate applied to Mary for agreement, and soon the small bed rested against the substantial one, and Julia held her baby's hand.

"I am not sure this is wise." Kate sat in a chair and Mary rested beside her. "Julia longed for Maura, and I could not find it in my heart to deny her this small consolation."

"I agree," Mary said. "They will comfort one another. In truth, I cannot imagine Maura's condition could become worse than it is now."

❀ ❀ ❀

For the next week, Kate rarely left the Tobins' house. As the doctor had advised, she did not go to her shop. She placed the responsibility for her dressmaking business in Ellen's capable hands. She had no choice. She rose early each morning and tended to Julia, helping her wash and put on a fresh gown. She changed the bed linens and cleaned the bedroom as time permitted.

"Our Mary will be slipping in at any moment to help us." Kate dressed Maura in a clean gown while Peggy placed the soiled clothing in a laundry bag. "She is a dear to come to our aid."

"Is Mr. Tobin not proving to be an excellent cook? Of course, we have a world of food brought in by our good neighbors, but he warms something for our supper as soon as he arrives each evening and prepares breakfast before leaving for work." Peggy lifted the bulky laundry bag and started for the door.

"I am gaining a whole new appreciation for my brother-in-law." Kate held the little girl close. Surely they would not lose this precious child. "The man accomplishes more with one arm than most people I know, handicapped or not."

Days of fear and dread crawled by. Maura's breathing weakened. Kate worried the little girl's life could be nearing its end. Again and again she offered a silent prayer for the child.

Please dear God, spare her. We have already lost so many.

❀ ❀ ❀

At the end of the week, it happened that they were all visiting Tobins' at the same time. Anne had managed to stay away for two weeks, but she had come today, insisting she must see Julia. Martin came in from work earlier than usual. He sat on the bed, cradling Maura in his arms. Kate, Anne, and Mary stood a little apart. All were wrapped in sheets, their faces covered below their eyes.

"I am shocked at the change in the baby." Anne lowered her voice to a whisper. "While Julia shows signs of improvement, Maura's condition seems to have grown so much worse since the last time I was here."

Kate's thoughts followed her sister's. Had the finality of the situation occurred to everyone? And how strange that they were all gathered here at one time. Grief registered across each bowed countenance. A glance around the room confirmed that tears soaked into the protective cloths they each wore. The little girl, the image of Julia with her blonde ringlets and soft blue eyes, rested quietly in her father's arms.

When the doctor arrived a few moments later, his sad sigh and the slow turn of his head confirmed Kate's fears. Could nothing more be done to help the sweet baby? Was it too late?

"Oh, dear God, she is our precious daughter. Please do not take her from us." Martin prayed aloud. "Please, God," he said again and again.

Kate stood beside Martin now, and each word of his prayer battered her heart. His pleadings pounded across her shoulders, as if she received rapid jolts. Kate recalled the pride he displayed when he held Maura and Elizabeth on the day of their births. His grief now seemed unbearable. "I am so sorry, Martin."

Finally, his voice stilled.

Father Burns arrived, and he stepped in and assumed Martin's place with the prayers.

Maura whimpered.

Kate watched, overcome with helplessness, as the tiny body trembled and an eerie rattling sound escaped through her small lips. The shudders continued on and on.

Julia's eyes had been cloudy and vague in the past weeks, but in the last few days she had remained awake for longer periods and she now blinked with alertness and clarity. Kate worried her sister would not be capable of withstanding this overwhelming grief. If only she would be drawn into a deep sleep.

The baby's breathing stopped.

Kate stood with her family, watching, waiting. Maura did not breathe again.

"No!" Martin choked out a harsh sob. He held the baby close for a moment, and then he placed her in Julia's arms and rested his hand on her shoulder.

"Ah my, it cannot be." While she stood by and watched Julia say goodbye to her baby girl, Kate remembered the dreadful day they lost their dear Lizzie. Now, as then, she worried this sorrow would be more than she could bear.

After what seemed an eternity, Martin took Maura from Julia and handed her to Kate. Cradling the silent bundle, she led Anne, Mary, Father Burns, and the doctor from the room, leaving the heartbroken parents alone. She placed the lifeless child in the spare crib at the back of the room. They were all milling about in the parlor when Martin rushed in after them.

"Doctor, come! Julia...! The baby...!"

"You go and assist the doctor," Mary said to Kate and Anne. "I will remain here with Maura."

Kate brought the news to Mary a short time later. "Julia has given birth to a stillborn son."

Father Burns, who had come for only a short visit with Julia and Maura, baptized the new baby and offered final prayers for both children. "May they rest in peace—"

Quiet, sorrowful "Amens" echoed around the room.

"Please fetch a glass of water, Kate." Once she poured water from the pitcher, Doctor Gallagher mixed powder into the glass. "I apologize for being abrupt, but I have another sorrowful family waiting for me. This will help Julia rest."

Kate held the drink to Julia's lips, but she did not finish it all. After the first sips, she fell back in a deep slumber. If only the sedative would help her sister sleep, at least through the night. Sure, she would need her strength to accept the loss of her two babies.

As Dr. Gallagher prepared to leave, he placed a hand on Martin's shoulder. "Haven't I watched this terrible fate strike too many? This same tragedy has befallen many families throughout the city. Our water situation is a disgrace. Dozens have died in just the past few weeks, deaths that are entirely unnecessary. Something must be done to stop this terrible sickness."

The poor, sorrowful Martin opened his mouth to respond, but no words came. He shook his head.

The doctor patted his arm and approached Kate. "Use your anger and outrage for a good purpose. Rally your family and your neighbors and friends. Demand the completion of the new waterworks. It has taken far too long for the city to obtain safe drinking water. Please, do what you can."

He turned toward Martin with renewed vigor in his plea. "The improved water system could be a memorial to your children."

The impassioned words seemed to penetrate Martin's grief. He managed a brief reply. "I will try."

❃ ❃ ❃

Early on Saturday morning, the family gathered at the Tobins' home. Maura Anne Tobin, not yet two years old, and her tiny, unnamed baby brother were placed together in a small coffin.

As Martin prepared to leave, he appealed to Kate. "Julia is not strong enough for the ride to the cemetery. Will you stay with her?"

"Of course." Kate helped Martin into his coat. "Julia has always been the one to provide strength and encouragement for all of us, but remaining behind while her children are buried will render her sorrow near to unbearable. If I can offer any comfort to her at all, I wish to do it."

She and Julia stood in the doorway together as the mourners, accompanied by Father Burns and Father Ryan, climbed into the vehicles assembled by Walter. Following behind the wagon bearing the tiny coffin, they proceeded slowly away from the house.

Julia leaned on Kate for support. "She is gone. I will never rest my eyes on her again." They stood, straining to see, until the last second when the wagon and carriages turned the corner and disappeared from sight.

Then Kate helped the sobbing Julia to a chair. "I will make some tea."

"Thank you, Kate. I must gain control of myself and my tears." Julia placed her elbows on the table and rested her head in her hands. "Elizabeth is sure to awaken at any moment and I would frighten her in my present state."

"I, too, will dry my tears." Kate pulled a handkerchief from her sleeve and blew her nose. "You know, our beautiful Elizabeth might prove to be our answer."

"I understand your meaning. Perhaps Elizabeth will lead Martin and me out of this valley of grief. She does not understand what happened to Maura. She walks through the house, opening doors, searching for her sister. Maybe, in her neediness, she will help us bring peace and joy into our home once again." Julia leaned her head back, and Kate hurried to fetch a damp cloth and place it across her eyes.

"You know, Julia," Kate pulled up a chair and sat down beside her sister, "I must apologize to you."

"Whatever for, Kate?" Julia sat up. Some of the redness had already faded from her face. "You have seldom left my side in these past weeks. I owe you my life. There is no need for an apology."

"I am speaking of the past. In the days when we lived together in Dempsey's attic room, I could not understand how you could maintain a constant state of cheerfulness. We faced so many disappointments over the children not being sent to America and endured so much sadness with the deaths of our brother and sisters." Kate placed her hand on Julia's shoulder. "I must confess, I was impatient, at times, when you persevered in being merry while my own spirits were low."

"I knew you did not always approve of my exuberance." Julia smiled sadly. "I sometimes agreed with your assessment of me. Many times I berated myself for my foolish ways."

"No, Julia. I am the one who has been mistaken. Since you fell ill," Kate moved her chair around to face her sister, "I realized how wrong I have been. Your strength comes from your optimistic attitude. When I fell ill this past winter, I had time to examine my own life. I found I had allowed my anger and bitterness to pull me so low I had become weak. I learned that the strength of your spirit carried you through every hard and difficult thing in your life. I finally came to understand. I am truly sorry, Julia."

"Thank you for the kind words, Kate. I only pray I will be capable of regaining that vitality. Right at this moment, I do not feel so mighty or spirited." Julia bowed her head.

"You will recover." Kate rose. She took Julia's hand and helped her to her feet. "It may seem impossible right now, but we have already decided you must recover for Elizabeth. She needs you."

❦ ❦ ❦

"I will miss you, Julia." Kate had packed her things, preparing to return to Anne's. "I must return to the Duffs' house and to work in my shop, but Mrs. Murphy will take good care of you." She walked to the back door, her arm around her sister. "I will visit you tomorrow evening on my way home."

A few days later, Kate and Anne decided on an early visit with Julia. "Mrs. Murphy will soon be leaving for another assignment." Kate hurried along. Spring had arrived, but the morning breeze was brisk.

"I know the doctor declared Julia out of danger, but will she be strong enough to stay on her own?" Anne held her arm as they hurried along the quiet streets. "Of course, Peggy will be there, and we will continue our regular visits."

"Good morning." Martin answered Kate's knock and ushered them into the parlor. He held his hat, twirling it around his finger, placing it on his head, spinning it again.

"What is it, Martin? Is Julia all right?" Kate's heart began to roll and thump.

"She is feeling sad this morning. She seems worried about the family in Ireland. Please do not mention anything about home. The doctor warned she must be kept free from cares, and I know how news from Blackwater upsets all of you girls. Any further distress could reverse the small gains she has made."

"I agree with you." Kate removed the shawl she had wrapped around her head and shoulders. "We will take care to introduce only happy subjects this morning." She and Anne waved as he went off to work, and then they moved to the kitchen.

"My concern right now, Kate, is you and Walter." Julia sat at the table with Elizabeth. "You have set aside your own life in these past weeks to take care of me and my family. My wish is that you move forward. Speak with Father Burns and make your plans. Set a date for the wedding. You and Walter postponing your marriage will not bring my babies back. We will hold the memory of our precious Maura and our dear little baby boy in our hearts as we celebrate the marriage of two of my favorite people." Though she smiled, Julia's eyes filled with tears. "They will be our own dear little angels at the wedding."

"Ah, Julia, thank you. We do have a kind and thoughtful sister, do we not, Anne?" Pulling a chair close to little Elizabeth, Kate sat down beside her and brushed her fingers through her curls. "Walter and I have talked about the wedding these last few evenings. We would not wish our celebration to bring you and Martin any additional sorrow. Now that you are recovering, though, we thought we would speak to Father Burns and set a date for a few months off.

"We also need some advice from you, Anne. Would a September wedding allow you time enough to regain your strength after adding another wee one to your nursery?" Kate smiled at her sister. "Will that be agreeable?"

"Late September or early October should be just fine." Anne laughed. "And this news is grand." She jumped to her feet and pulled Kate along in a spin around the room. They both turned to Julia.

"Are you up for a whirl?" Kate asked.

"Of course, I am. It may only be a short spin, but I would like to try." Elizabeth watched, with wide eyes, as her mother and aunts danced around the room. Anne moved a little behind the others, but her dancing talent made up for any slowness of foot. After a short reel, they collapsed on chairs, laughing and gasping for breath.

"It is good to see you smile." Kate touched Julia's cheek. Had they diverted her attention with their foolishness?

Julia took in deep breaths and blew the air out slowly. "Something has been preying on my mind." She stood again and walked the length of the room. "We have had no word from home in so long. I suppose Michael will not be coming back to St. Louis anytime soon."

Oh my. Just as Martin predicted, she was worried about home. "But, Julia, you must stay quiet—"

"We seem to be losing touch with them all." Julia ignored Kate's plea. "Why can they not write one line?"

"Now, you must not upset yourself." Kate had to smile. "Things have certainly been tossed about. It is usually me who becomes impatient and paces, Julia. It has always been you entreating me to be calm."

"I only wish they would write. We do not even know if Father has recovered." Julia folded her arms.

"I understand your dissatisfaction." Anne sat beside Julia and held her arm. "That same frustration has taken hold of my thoughts on many occasions. From friends who came to us with messages from home, we have learned Michael has begun to farm our small place. Imagine the depth his spirits must have reached. He was unhappy the entire time of his indenture to the farmer outside of Blackwater. And he loved working here in the city. He would be content to make his home here."

Kate took Elizabeth's hand and demonstrated a few of their dance steps for her. No more gloomy talk. She must divert their attention. "We do know James's brother Dan will arrive soon. He will bring us news of our family."

"At one time we thought they would come together," Julia said. "I suppose we cannot hold out any hope that it will happen now?"

"Pray, Julia." Kate held Julia's hands between her own. "You always encourage us to pray. On our walks together, Walter and I have been praying for you and for the folks back in Ireland."

"You and Walter are praying together? That's wonderful, Kate. A true blessing." Anne held Elizabeth in her arms, and together they danced around Kate and Julia.

"You are doing a fine job, my girl." Kate clapped for Elizabeth as she attempted to imitate their dance steps, and she received a tiny smile from the solemn little girl.

"You must bring Nell to dance with us, Anne."

Anne held out a hand to Julia, but she waved her away. "I've no more dancing in me today." Her smile had returned though, bright and shinning.

Kate's hope for her sister's recovery rose. In spite of Julia's deep sorrow, she still possessed the strength and the spirit to rejoice for her and Walter and wish them well. Would they all possess enough fortitude to bear the disappointment of James's brother, Dan, arriving on his own, with no one from the Carty family with him?

Chapter Twenty-One

Blackwater

April 4th 70

Dear Sisters,
I received your welcome letters which I should have answered before. I do thank you for thinking of me. I often think of you although I have not the heart to write. I promise to never be so long from writing again.
Kate, I hope you will not get married until I see you in America. I hope the day is not far distant. Your affectionate brother, M. Carty

May, 1870
"How are you feeling?" Kate asked Julia as they sat in her parlor one morning shortly after her recovery. She brushed her sister's hair back from her face. "Will I pin your hair up for you?"

"Yes, please. That would be grand. I do feel well. If only my full strength would return. I am impatient to take command of my home and care for Elizabeth as I always have. I complete one small chore, a simple thing I have done all my life, and then I must make my way to a chair for a rest." Julia drummed her feet on the floor, her head bobbing with each measured step. "Ah, pay no mind to my complaints. I am fortunate to be here with you."

"I know it is difficult for you, but have patience." Kate held Julia's knee to halt the shuffling. "You will regain your former stamina in no time."

"Martin's efforts to gain completion of the new waterworks have given me a spark of hope and an incentive to go forward." Julia sat erect in her chair, glancing over at Elizabeth from time to time. "I've worked with him some, on petitions and proposals. When I fall to despairing, it comforts me to know Walter and James attended meetings with him and they are using their talent for persuasion with the city's leaders to demand the project be completed."

Kate reached out to Julia and held her hand. How comforting it was to see even a tiny spark returned to her sister's eyes. The moment passed quickly.

Julia pulled away, holding herself erect again, a serious, determined look in her eyes. "At a recent meeting Martin attended, he learned the city could have decent drinking water by the end of this year."

"That is wonderful." Kate stood and clapped her hands to acknowledge this important achievement. "It is amazing, and Martin has been largely responsible."

"And now, we must move forward." Julia tapped her fingers on the side of her chair. The spark in her eyes rekindled. "Have you and Walter made any new plans?"

"Actually, we have." Kate paused. Holding back a grin, she took a long drink of her tea. "We visited Father Burns and arranged our wedding date for the fourth Saturday in September. It is now official. Since the folks at Dempsey's had never been told about our plans to marry, I joined them for supper last evening and we made the announcement."

"Were the Dempsey girls and Walter's helpers astonished?" Julia asked. "It must have been a joyous evening."

"Apparently, we had not been as clever at hiding our feelings as I thought. No one looked too surprised, I'm afraid." Kate felt a blush spread across her face. "The spilled secret did not lessen the celebration, though. We were showered with congratulations and good wishes. It was a lovely time. What a relief it is that we no longer must avoid one another and hide our plans."

"And what of your wedding arrangements?" Julia asked. "Have you decided anything?"

"We did settle on living quarters." Just the thought of living with Walter filled her entire being with joy. Would Julia read the delight in her eyes? "Walter had the idea that I would wish to reside in my own home, apart from the bakery building. Since I have lived away from my dressmaking shop these past few weeks, I could put his mind at rest on that point."

Kate studied Julia's serious eyes. "Though it was a difficult time, I loved living with you. I also enjoy being with Anne and her wonderful family. You have seen, though, how inconvenient it has been walking back and forth between two places. At times I have been forced to make the trek more than once a day and I almost always have my arms filled with material, patterns, or anything else needed for my sewing."

"Walter only wishes you to be happy." Julia's smile broke through for the first time that morning.

"I know he does." Kate poured another cup of tea for them. "During this time of making decisions and discussing plans for our future, he has been kind and thoughtful. He considers only my comfort and my wishes, never a thought for himself. Still, I could feel his sigh of relief when I assured him living in the attic room with him would thrill me." She giggled and her sister laughed with her.

244

"What a joy it is to have you join with me in this silliness." Kate patted Julia's cheek. "To hear you laugh is delightful, even if it is only a little chuckle."

Julia reached out and pulled at Kate's apron strings. "Continue. What will Walter do with the attic room?"

"Since we made the decision to live there, Walter has been busy every moment, drawing up plans to renovate the place." Kate placed the teapot on the side table and walked back to Julia. "The room served all of us well, but Walter intends to expand the space to include the storage room. We will use that area as a parlor. And then he will raise the ceiling, so he will be able to stand up straight."

"Oh my word!" Julia burst out in a full, hearty laugh. She rose from her chair and ran to fetch a glass of water. "Walter moving around in the attic room is the best story I've heard in a long time. Imagine his long frame in a permanent hunched state."

"Your mother and I are only being silly." Elizabeth's eyes had grown wide and Kate stopped to pat her curls. She did not wish to frighten the little girl.

"Our dear Walter insists I must have the finest living quarters." She felt a blush coming on again, but Julia seemed to enjoy talk of the attic room and she continued on. "He has many grand ideas toward accomplishing that goal. He told me last evening that the remodeling is proving to be more than even he and his trusty helpers could manage. He will be forced to hire on some additional help to finish the work in time for the wedding."

"Ah, Kate, it will be magnificent." Julia sat back again. "I cannot wait to inspect your elegant new living quarters. I am happy for you both. You deserve a fine life."

❁ ❁ ❁

"I love these long evening excursions," Kate said to Walter as they walked together one warm May evening.

"With the hired workers taking on the better part of the renovations, we have more time to talk than we've ever had before." Walter took advantage of the ample shawl Kate had draped around her shoulders and slipped his arm around her waist. "Where shall we walk?"

"To the sports field." Kate stepped into a brisk pace. "This new love we share is so fresh and unexpected to both of us, but we must come to know one another in a different light. We're no longer landlord and tenant. I look forward to the prospect of marriage, but this is an all new world we will be experiencing."

"A marvelous new life as partners." Walter took her hand, as they approached the field.

"It looks wonderful." Kate pointed toward the grassy area. "The surface has been leveled and the grass is coming up nicely. Have you had an opportunity for a game of hurling or soccer?"

"The other evening George and a few of the men from church conducted a soccer demonstration, and I came along to assist." Walter stopped to pull up a few weeds. "Actually, I learned more than I helped. It was great exercise."

"When will the games begin?"

"James advised me to hold off until next year," Walter said. "Allowing the grass a full year to take root will result in a sturdier field. We will hold demonstrations this summer and plan for a full schedule of soccer and hurling beginning next spring."

"I can see it now. It will be a marvelous thing for children to have such a fine place to play. Perhaps one day our own children will come here." Kate felt a blush rising within her, and unable to push the embarrassment back, she lowered her head.

Keeper of the Flame

Walter stopped and looked down at her. "The color growing across your face is lovely."

"Thank you." Still a bit disconcerted, she changed the subject. "Do you suppose I could learn to play soccer?"

"I will instruct you personally." Walter's laugh rang out across the empty field. "As soon as I become proficient myself, of course."

When they headed back toward Anne's, she wished to raise a new topic but she was unsure how to begin. She hesitated. She chose her words carefully. "I often have difficulty believing we've received this wonderful gift." Shameful girl. She only wanted to hear him say that he loved her.

"I agree, Kate. I must constantly remind myself that this wonderful thing that happened between us is real and true." Walter shook his head. "I had begun to feel I would never find someone who loved me."

"I understand what you are saying." Kate held Walter's arm. "I became so discouraged after I made that embarrassing mistake with Francis Reilly. I thought I might never marry."

"You should never have considered such a thing." Walter grinned down at her as they walked along. "Any man would be fortunate to have you for a wife. It is too late for all those other sorry blokes now. Your hand is already won.

"I love you, Kate. I will never tire of saying those words. I am the luckiest man in the world to know you love me in return. Every day I thank God for your love."

"I love you, Walter. I'm just so surprised to be saying that. To think we lived and worked together in the same building for more than three years before we...well, before I discovered our love. I, too, have begun to thank God for this happiness we have been granted." She held his arm as they climbed the steps to the front porch. How had she grown so bold? She had coaxed an "I love you" from Walter and she took every

247

opportunity to take his arm or hold his hand. A thrill passed through her each time she felt his touch.

❃ ❃ ❃

James waited in the entryway, his expression serious. Kate and Walter followed him into the parlor.

"What is it, Anne?" Her sister sat before the hearth with a coffee tray at the ready.

"James has..."

"I learned some news," he said. "I encountered Francis Reilly this afternoon. He told me the partnership he entered into with Dermot Fortune and a few others has been dissolved. Fortune embezzled money from the partners, and he is now in prison, somewhere in Illinois. Francis admitted Martin and I were right when we objected to his doing business with the man."

"That scoundrel." Walter paced the room. "Jail is where he belongs."

"Do not upset yourself over it, Walter." Anne rose from her chair and walked over to hand him a cup of coffee. "You warned me to remove our savings from Fortune's grasp. If I had listened to you and acted to set up an account in Julia's name, this entire incident could have been avoided.

"Besides," Anne returned her tray to the table and placed her hands on her hips. She gazed at Walter, directly. "It is time we allow the matter to rest. I believe Kate will agree with me. So many years have passed and so many things have happened, it is best to leave Mr. Fortune to God's judgment."

"And apparently now, to the State of Illinois." Walter patted Anne's shoulder and went to sit with Kate.

"I agree with you, Anne." The feeling of calmness Kate experienced surprised even her. "I am ready to forget the Fortune matter and concentrate on bringing the rest of our family here."

She turned to James. "I wish they were all coming with your brother. If only we could have drawn some hope from the short letter we received from Michael. Alas, the few words he wrote gave no information on Father's health or if they had made any plans to leave Blackwater." Gazing around the room, she searched for some small sign of expectation. She found only hopelessness.

"While I believe your brother is a fine fellow," Walter said, "he is not much of a correspondent."

Chapter Twenty-Two

Mary entered Kate's shop a few mornings later with a cake box in one arm and a shawl across the other. "Since Anne held Julia's betrothal party in her home, it is my turn to hold the celebration for you and Walter here at Dempsey's."

Kate opened her mouth to defend her sister, but no words came.

"Please come with me to Anne's." Mary's eyes held pleading, but a tiny upturn at each side of her mouth suggested she was experiencing only mild distress. "The time is short, and we must talk over the details for your celebration." When Kate rose readily from her chair and folded her work, Mary's grin spread across her face. "Shall we fetch Julia?"

"Julia grows stronger each day, but she is still recovering her strength. I think we should leave her to rest as much as possible." Kate placed her work on the ironing board and followed Mary out the door. "We could make a few plans, and then perhaps next week we could visit her and bring a full report of every detail."

"Mary is right." Anne conceded with grace when they settled in at her kitchen table. "She supported me when I prepared for the party for Julia and Martin. I will gladly do the same for her." With that important detail settled, Kate relaxed her hold on the teapot, and Mary began to plan for the supper.

"I predict this will be your finest feast ever, Mary," Kate said when they had worked over a menu.

"Try this chocolate nut cake. If you like the taste, we could include it with the—"

A sharp rap sounded at the front door.

"I am not expecting a visitor." A curious expression spread across Anne's face.

Kate and Mary followed her into the hallway, and the children trailed behind them. Through the glass in the door, Kate could see a bulky figure standing on the front porch. As soon as Anne opened the door, Kate recognized him. Sure, she and James's youngest brother had been schoolmates. She moved past the others and took his arm.

"Is it our Dan, then?" Before them stood a younger, shorter copy of James Duff, with a full head of the same sandy hair. Dan had not waited for anyone to fetch him, but just as Michael had done, he appeared at the door on his own. Kate pulled him inside. "Welcome to St, Louis, Daniel. I am so happy to see you after all these many years."

Anne moved in closer. "I am your sister, Anne." She offered Daniel a smile and a hug. "Your brothers will be overjoyed." She introduced him to Mary and then to Tom and Nell who pulled back wearing shy smiles. "Come out to the kitchen, please. We were just sitting down to tea. We will have a grand opportunity to become reacquainted. Then, we will settle you in the room we have waiting for you upstairs."

"I did not expect this splendid house," Dan gazed at each of the rooms as they passed through the hallway. Sitting down at the table, a look of relief shone across his face. "And a room of my own is grand, but more than I need."

"Well, Anne and James have prepared a marvelous bedroom for you upstairs. It was intended for someone from your family or ours to occupy. It appears the Cartys will not be coming anytime soon." Kate placed a cup of tea and one of the chocolate squares meant as a sample for her betrothal supper before him. "Forgive me, Dan, I did not intend to sound abrupt. I am truly happy you are here. It's just that you bear a touch of Ireland in your voice, your clothing, and your smile. When you walked through the door, you brought a bit of our beloved homeland with you."

"We are thrilled to see you, Dan." Anne placed a hand on his shoulder. "Even though we knew the truth of it, we all held out hope they would come. It is difficult to still the disappointment that at least one of our dear ones did not walk through the door with you."

"Aye, I wish I could have brought them all out. I am truly sorry." Then, avoiding meeting their eyes, he rushed ahead. "Michael wished to bring them, all of us come together, as James asked. Your mother refused. Your father, Maggie, and Michael begged her again and again, but they could not sway her. I handed over the money you sent for their fares to Michael. He asked me to tell you he holds out hope she will consent to come in the fall."

Remembering Daniel's recent loss, Kate spoke softly to him. "And you've lost your own dear father. I am so sorry. He was a fine man. He was always kind to me."

"James and Ned were broken hearted to learn of it." Anne jumped up from the table to pour tea for everyone.

"Sure, it has been a great sorrow," Dan said. "I had convinced him to come to America with me, when he fell ill."

Kate held back, until a brave smile appeared across Dan's face. Then she questioned him about everything back home, family, friends, church, and the condition of the country.

"I have been remiss, Dan," Kate said, after they had talked of Ireland for a while. "I must explain our relationship to our Mary here. Anne, Julia, and I all lived with Mary and her brother Walter. They have been our benefactors since we arrived in St. Louis. And now, Walter and I are to be married."

"Don't I know all about the Dempseys?" Dan rummaged in his bag. They waited a moment as he pressed deeper into the valise, shifting things around, rearranging them. Finally, he pulled out a small, wrinkled envelope. "'Tis from your aunt and uncle. Nothing would do but I bring you the letter myself." When he grinned at Mary, Kate recognized in him the same engaging manner his brother James possessed. Apparently his charm worked well with Mary, too.

"Thank you for the letter, Daniel." Mary placed it on the table. "We must also account for our gathering here. Our Kate is to marry my brother, Walter, and we are planning a betrothal supper for them on Saturday night." She paused and looked to Kate and Anne for agreement. "Now we will all be expecting you to attend the party. Your two brothers will be there. And newly arrived from Ireland as you are, you will find everyone eager to speak with you and hear every bit of news from home. You will be surprised at the number of Blackwater friends you will encounter seated around the table."

"I see how weary you are, Dan." Anne stood beside her brother-in-law as she scrubbed Nellie's hands and placed her on the floor. "We will cease our questioning and explaining and allow you some time to rest. Why don't I take you up to your room? I promise to wake you when your brothers return from work."

"And we must take our leave and hurry back to Dempsey's." Kate rose from the table and began to clear away the dishes. "I am sure Anne and Mary will agree your arrival and the news from home are more than enough excitement to take in for one day.

"Our next outing will be a visit to our sister Julia. You will want to come along with us, Dan." Kate extended her hand to him. "Rest up now. Though she has been tossed about recently by illness and by some trying times, our sister's high spirits are beginning to blossom again. You will need your full strength for a visit with Julia, that's sure."

Dan laughed, a hearty guffaw that again reminded Kate of James. "Yes, of course, I do remember Julia. She was a few years ahead of Kate and me in class, but we all heard stories of her escapades. My favorite was the tale of the summer afternoon when she gathered up all the children in Blackwater and led them on a fishing expedition."

"I do recall that day." Kate dried the dishes, thinking back, remembering the story. The sound of the lapping water, only a short walk from their home, filled her mind then drifted away. "The fishing resulted in a greater catch than the Blackwater folks had experienced in a long while. Julia organized the children. The older boys made fishing rods out of the reeds they found along the water's edge. I was in the group of girls assigned to attach twine to the end of the rods."

"I remember like it happened yesterday." Anne turned her attention to Tom and began to scrub his fingers. "The older girls, including me, were meant to clean the fish. I can attest to the fact that there were many fish caught that day. Ugh, it was an unpleasant chore. I do have a favorite memory of that evening, though. The families of the village all came together to cook and eat the fish. It was an unplanned gathering that grew to include nearly all of the folks around. I believe it was one of the grandest parties ever held in Blackwater."

"And, indeed, the story is being told in the village even now." Dan smiled at the girls. "I do look forward to seeing your Julia again."

❁ ❁ ❁

By the time Kate had walked back to her shop, the disappointment over her family not coming with Dan had settled deep in her heart. She could not concentrate on her work. Thoughts of Michael and Maggie, waiting to come with little hope left, danced before her eyes. A powerful feeling of sadness slipped over her. Even with her eyes pressed shut, her tears escaped and ran down her cheeks.

Not wanting to explain it all to the girls, she walked out the door to the street that ran along the side of the shop. She forced herself to gulp deep, cleansing breaths until her tears stopped flowing and her body ceased to shake. She moved back inside, but she did not take up her sewing. With no urgent work before her, she settled on cleaning the shop.

"I will help you, Kate." Ellen approached her as she gathered cleaning supplies.

"No, dear, thank you. I would rather work on my own." Proceeding at a feverish pace, she moved from ceiling, to walls, to windows, shelves, and floor, scrubbing and shinning in quick, determined motions.

Why? Why? One question followed another at a furious pace. Three remained in Ireland. Michael went back. Four! They had sent the money for them all to come with James's brother. Still, Mother refused to leave.

Janey and Charlotte each offered her their help, but when Kate shook her head, they slipped out of the room.

"Will I do anything for you before I go?" Ellen held Kate's eyes with her own until she gave in and stopped working. "If you tell me you are all right, I will leave you in peace."

"I am fine, Ellen. Thank you." Kate turned to wave to her friend then returned to her reflections.

Had she, indeed, become her mother? No, not exactly. When Mother became upset, she set the children to cleaning. She, on the other hand, took on the entire task on her own.

A tiny grin had begun to cross her face when she discovered Walter standing in the doorway.

"I became curious when the chairs and tables appeared in the hallway." He moved into the room. "Is it Dan's arrival that upset you so?"

"Please forgive me, dear, for making such a ruckus. I just had to make peace with the disappointment." The energy she expended cleaning the entire shop and the ruminations about her mother had helped Kate gain control over her emotions. Calm now, she felt ready to talk it all over with Walter. "In my heart, I knew my family would not come with Dan. Still, when he walked through the door at Anne's, I could not push down the regret. I cannot bear the thought of the distress and heartbreak Michael and Maggie must be experiencing."

"Perhaps Dan's notion that Michael will bring them all here in a few months is right." Walter took her hand. He rubbed his thumb along each of her fingers. "He holds the fare money, and your mother may consent to the trip by then. Let us just wait and hope. I will do anything to bring them here, Kate, but I have begun to be of the same opinion as Michael. Your parents have found it easier to send their children out of Ireland than to break the tie and leave their homeland themselves." He moved closer and wrapped his arms around her. "And too, with your young brother and sister buried in Blackwater, your mother may believe she is bound to the land."

"Our Lizzie is buried here, and now, two grandchildren." Kate gazed around the room. The place was, indeed, spotless.

"Your mother is not thinking clearly, Kate. We must pray that her wish for Michael and Maggie to come will be stronger than her fear of separation from home. I am not imposing harsh judgment." Walter released her. He stepped back but still held her hand. "I just believe we must be realistic about our expectations."

"I agree with you." Kate moved closer to Walter and placed her hand on his sleeve. What a comfort the touch of his arm had become. "We can only wait now. They have the money, and Michael has been to America and seen for himself how comfortably they could be settled here. I pray Mother will listen to him and allow them all to come. As I worked through my sorrow and distress today, I cleared my thoughts and reached a conclusion. I will leave their care in God's hands. I will hold you and the new life we are beginning together first in my heart."

Walter hugged her again. "I know this responsibility for your family weighs heavily on you. I only ask that, now that we have been blessed with this wonderful love for one another, you allow me to worry with you. I fear the anxiety will make you ill all over again."

He stopped a moment, squeezed his eyes shut, and pursed his lips. He coughed a little. "I can see myself in the floors." His laugh rang out now, loud enough to be heard throughout the building.

She smiled at him, and when he draped his arm across her shoulder and smiled at her in return, her sorrow began to dissolve.

"Would you like me to help you put the room back to order?"

"That would be wonderful. If I didn't already love you, I would begin right now with your strong arms." They enjoyed a laugh together as they moved tables and chairs back to their rightful places.

❋ ❋ ❋

The bustling and preparations for the betrothal celebration proceeded at a great pace. "I would like to help, but I am not allowed." Kate handed Ellen a long, blue skirt she had just finished pressing, "I feel a little left out."

"Enjoy it." Ellen placed the skirt on a wooden hanger and held it high. "You will not be pampered so after you are married."

Kate closed her eyes and permitted her favorite dream to drift before her. Walter Dempsey loved her. She looked past tonight's betrothal supper. Their glorious wedding could not come soon enough.

"Kate? Kate?" Anne stepped into the dressmaking shop. "Have I found you daydreaming again? Ah, my dear sister, it is wonderful to see you so happy. But I must not tarry. Before I head off to the kitchen to help Mary, I have a message to deliver. Julia told me to tell you she is gathering her strength so she will be able to attend your celebration. Other than short walks, tonight's supper will be her first excursion out of the house since her illness. I assure you, she looks forward to the evening with great eagerness."

❈ ❈ ❈

When the time came at last, Dempsey's dining room looked more beautiful than Kate ever remembered. A profusion of spring flowers and flickering candles were scattered along the center of the table. China, crystal, and silverware that belonged to Mary's mother sparkled at each place.

Kate and Walter stood just inside the doorway, greeting everyone. She rejoiced when her sisters and their families arrived. "The brothers" of their group, now expanded to include Martin's brother Patrick and James's two brothers, Ned and Dan, came in with them. Kate's seamstresses were all in attendance. Ellen helped Mary, Grace, and Cara place platters of food on the table. Janey Flynn entered the room with Mr. and Mrs. Flynn, and Charlotte arrived with her parents, Gus and Tilda Mueller. Walter's helper, Eddie, was in the kitchen, lending a hand to the cooks.

"God bless all here." Father Burns' voice rang out as he entered the dining room.

"God keep us all." Father Ryan followed behind him, leading them in the familiar response to the prayer that had journeyed with all of them from Ireland. When they had gathered around the table, each of the priests offered a blessing.

Kate's emotions nearly overwhelmed her. This moment and these prayers were for Walter and her. If she had the need to speak right then, it would have been impossible. The kind and wonderful Walter Dempsey had declared his love for her. At last, she believed it was true.

Thank you, God, for this precious gift.

Though he did not partake himself, Walter served a fine wine to his guests.

"Wine or no wine, it matters not at all to me," she told him in a whisper. "In my childhood, we were fortunate to have fresh milk while Father owned a cow. After the cow had been sold to settle the taxes, we had nothing to drink but weak tea. Sure, I have tasted only a few sips of wine in my entire life.

"Dessert, I do appreciate. Gus and Tilda Mueller's apple strudel, sweet apples layered into a flaky crust that melts on your tongue, is delightful."

With a broad smile, Walter tipped his fork to the couple. "The strudel is magnificent."

Praises for the strudel filled the room. "Wonderful dessert, delicious," and "a tasty dish" were heard all around the table. The Muellers' daughter, Charlotte, beamed with pride.

"I do miss Bridget and George tonight," Anne said. "I wish they were here to join their voices with ours, as we offer good wishes to Kate and Walter."

"I miss them, too." Kate felt a catch in her throat. Another beloved person who would not be attending her wedding. She looked around at her guests and brightened. "I am sure they are well on their way to California now."

"Let's wish them well." Walter raised his coffee cup. "I see a wonderful life ahead for those two fine people."

Cries of "hear, hear!" circled the room.

Kate could not remember a happier celebration in her life. She wished the evening could last forever. The hour grew late, though, and everyone prepared to take their leave, donning wraps, offering thanks to Walter and Mary, and adding more good wishes to Kate and Walter. "Good night, good night," she called out to each one.

"Come to the parlor with me." Mary motioned for Kate, Anne, and Julia to follow her.

"What is it? I know something is on your mind." Kate sat beside Mary. It had been a perfect evening. What could have happened to upset Mary?

"I wish you girls to know how happy I am Kate consented to marry my brother." Mary placed her arm around Kate. "I believe this is the proper moment to speak. I pray you agree. I must say my peace, so you know how I love your Kate. I am pleased she has come along to make Walter so happy. I have already told Kate how it thrills me to see the joy shining in his eyes. I am also delighted to observe the measure of happiness that has settled over our girl right now." She took Kate's hand.

"Thank you." Kate rose from her chair and favored Mary with a curtsy, low enough and formal enough to suit a queen.

"Oh, I know some wondered if I was envious because Kate would assume my place in the shop and with Walter. Some even said it right out. The poor fools must have been suffering from blistered ears as they walked away from me, I'll tell you." Mary giggled.

The three Carty sisters broke into peals of laughter.

Keeper of the Flame

"Walter has begun to expand the attic into a spacious new apartment for them. Kate has already chosen a marvelous blue material for draperies for their parlor. It will be a grand, cozy place, and I couldn't be more pleased."

Kate hugged Mary. With smiles and tears and many more hugs, the wonderful evening came to an end. Would she not be happy to enjoy a lifetime of grand family evenings such as this?

Chapter Twenty-Three

September, 1870

A glance out Kate's shop window on the morning of her wedding revealed an entire, unending stretch of gloomy grey sky looming over the city. The color of the sky and the threat of rain would not quell the excitement that had built inside her. She attempted a serene pose, but she failed entirely. Had a giggle become trapped deep within her being? Her smile would not be suppressed. She avoided conversation with the girls. The laughter she held back might erupt if she attempted to speak.

"Walter closed down the oven rooms as soon as he returned from his delivery rounds." Mary hurried into the dressmaking shop. "He and Eddie cleaned the entire place." With her face flushed and her arms in constant motion, Mary's sweet, calm ways had disappeared this morning. For the last few hours, she had been rushing from room to room in a state of frenzy.

"Though I have been hearing the sounds of work coming from the oven rooms, I have not seen a glimpse of Walter all morning." Kate placed an arm across Mary's shoulder and felt her trembling. "He must be busy."

"The notice he placed in the paper and the signs he posted in both shop windows that the entire operation would be closing at noon today brought in a constant stream of customers."

Mary threw up her hands. "Oh my, I must rush to help Grace. She will be overwhelmed out in the shop, I've no doubt of it." Mary ran from the room without a backward look.

"Have you and Walter put everything in place?" Ellen walked up behind Kate and whispered in her ear.

"Walter tells me he has every detail in order." Kate pulled Ellen to her. "I do thank you, dear. Our trip would not be possible without your managing everything here in my absence."

"With the time we spent together, compiling lists of orders and the dates they must be delivered and developing estimates of the work expected in the coming weeks," Ellen said, "you have organized everything. Do not worry. Your shop will be just fine."

"Well, missy, the news of your own engagement to Martin's brother Patrick was surely a surprise." Kate pinched Ellen's chin. "I admit I did become suspicious. A few times I wondered where you had disappeared to. I am happy for you. Patrick is a wonderful man. I will never forget the care and devotion he extended to Martin after his accident."

"The hospital is where we came to know one another, you know." Ellen lifted the iron from the hearth. "By chance, I sat with him in Martin's hospital room one afternoon, when no one else was around. Another evening he walked home from the hospital with me. From that time forward, our friendship grew. Ah Kate, I have been alone so long. This new love is the sweetest, most exciting thing that has happened in my entire life."

"That is magnificent, Ellen." Kate searched Ellen's countenance and recognized a gleam of happiness she suspected was shining from her own eyes today. "I wish you and Patrick a lifetime of joy."

"Thank you, Kate. Now that we have kept each other's secrets, I feel wonderfully close to you. It's as if you are the sister I never had." Ellen moved right back to work, finishing up one last dress before they closed the shop. Certainly there would be no problem with leaving the shop in her hands.

With her own sewing completed, Kate worked with her young helpers. She held the cloth steady while Charlotte hemmed an expansive, layered skirt. She peered over Janey's shoulder, as the girl worked to ease a bulky sleeve into the armhole of a woolen dress.

While Kate watched Janey work, the girl's mother entered the shop from the hallway that led out to the bakery. "Ah, here's our fair bride. Are you ready now to adorn yourself in your beautiful gown?" Mrs. Flynn walked over to hug Kate, pulling her away from Janey and her sleeve project. She wore a full, flowing coat and a wide brimmed hat. Protection from any coming rain, perhaps. With the front panels of the coat falling open, Kate caught a glimpse of the blue dress she helped Janey finish the day before. As Mrs. Flynn turned slightly, she also recognized a spray of magnificent, ecru lace spilling out from between the folds of her dress and the coat. She remembered the lovely veil Mrs. Flynn had worn to both Anne's and Julia's weddings.

"I am honored to see I rate your wearing of your mother's veil to my wedding."

Mrs. Flynn turned back to give Kate her full attention. "Thank you, my dear. I am happy it pleases you."

"Now then, I am off to collect Mary and start out for Anne's." Kate assembled pins, thread and scissors, articles that might be needed for any wedding emergency. "My gown and Mary's are already there, and Anne wishes to oversee my dressing."

"Well, hold on a moment before you head out to the bakery." Mrs. Flynn placed her three bags on the table. "A few of our foolish neighbors are out in the shop. They have been discussing what happens to a bride who allows a drop of rain to fall on her head. When I left, your Mary was chasing them out the door, a loaf of bread held high in each hand."

Kate's laughter would be suppressed no longer, and everyone in the shop now stopped their work to join in with her. With the tension released, a cool wisp of peace and calm settled over her. "Thank you, Mrs. Flynn. Your story swept all my anxieties and heart flutterings clear away. Your Janey has finished her work now. Take her home, and I will see you both at the church."

She turned to Ellen. "We've accomplished enough for today. You and Charlotte close up the shop and hurry on to dress yourselves."

Her excitement billowed up within her again as she turned and headed for the bakery. She found Mary alone and the shop closed, at last. They hastened to collect their things and prepared to depart for Anne's.

"Wait for a minute, Kate." Before she could pass through the door, she was surrounded by Ellen, Janey, and Charlotte from the seamstress shop and Grace, Cara, and Mary from the bakery. Mrs. Flynn had remained as well, waiting for Janey and joining in with the others. Ellen, flushed and smiling, handed Kate a white square package with a silvery bow tied at the top. "'Tis a token of our love and best wishes for you on your magnificent day."

Kate opened the package. Buried in layers of tissue, she found a small, delicate, cream-colored silk handbag trimmed with pearl accents. The gift was so lovely, the gesture so dear, her breath caught. "It is elegant. I've never had a handbag I've not made myself." It required a great effort for her to speak. No tears, she commanded herself. She never cried. But tears had begun to run down her cheeks. Whatever was happening to her? "Thank you all. This is the finest, most thoughtful gift I've ever received."

The girls nearly pushed Kate and Mary out the door. "We'll see you again in only a few hours." Ellen waved one more time and then shut the door behind them.

"We are finally on our way, Mary." Kate clutched the precious purse under her arm, as they hurried along. She marveled at the girls' thoughtfulness. "I am happy to have this opportunity to extend a few private words of appreciation to you. You kept the secret of this wonderful present all along. It is a lovely thing."

"I had no part in the selection." Mary huffed a little as they walked. "It was all the girls' doing. I do agree with you. It is a beautiful handbag, unlike any I have ever seen."

"Even more important, you've held a world of confidences for Walter and me." Kate held Mary's arm. "I thank you for your kindness."

"I love you and Walter." Mary spoke through her sniffles. "Your happiness means the sun and the moon to me."

Kate gave Mary's arm a squeeze. Before they reached Anne's door, she had one thing more she wished to say. "You have been grand to help me plan the wedding. I must be sure I have not injured your feelings with my decision to hold the supper at Palmer House. I only wish our celebration to be free of work for you. You have done so much for all of us. On this one occasion, you will be our honored guest with everyone attending you."

"I do understand, Kate. It will be a magnificent day altogether. I will sit at the table like a fine lady and allow some grand server to bring my tea. Ah, my, such a business." Mary slipped her arm through Kate's, and they hurried along. "I love you for thinking of me."

"And I already love having you for a sister." They had arrived at Anne's, and Kate stepped quickly up the steps and approached the front door.

Had someone been stationed at the window? The door flew open, and Anne greeted them and ushered them into the parlor. "This room looks amazing." Her sister had transformed the space into a dressing room for the day. White sheets had been draped over each chair, and the floor was covered with white paper. Where had all the paper come from?

"And my little mother, are you feeling well?" On September 1, Patrick James Duff had arrived. He was a cheerful boy who had been filling their lives with joy for the past four weeks. "And our brand new baby, Patrick, how is he faring?"

"We are both fine." Anne spun in a circle. "I feel grand. And our wee Patrick is enjoying the attention of Julia's Peggy, who volunteered to watch over him today."

"That is wonderful, Anne." Kate bowed to her.

"Well, if a new baby and this marvelous wedding are not enough," Mary removed her coat, "I have learned some surprising news I am now at liberty to share with you. I will try to hold it until Julia arrives." She turned to offer a hug to Anne's little Nell. The tiny girl sat in a chair in the middle of the room, dressed only in a shift.

"I am waiting for my cousin, Elizabeth," she said to Kate and Mary.

As if summoned by Nell, Julia entered through the kitchen door holding Elizabeth's hand. "I know you came to tell everyone the same story, Mary, but I am bursting to pieces with it. Our Ellen and Martin's brother Patrick are to be married." An apologetic expression crossed Julia's face. "Oh, I am sorry, Mary. I could not contain myself a moment longer."

"Have no care, Julia. I worried over telling the tale at all." Mary looked so uncertain Kate rushed over to place an arm across her shoulder. When Julia reached out and squeezed Mary's cheeks with her fingers, they all laughed.

A glow that now seemed to be a permanent part of Mary spread across her face. "Ellen intended to withhold the announcement until after the wedding. She had no wish to take anything away from the celebration for Kate and Walter. Now that you have taken over the task and announced the news, my mind is eased."

"Do not fret," Kate said. "Walter and I are so thrilled our wedding day has arrived, at last, we are happy to share our joy with Ellen and Patrick."

"Well, if you will permit me," Mary appeared a little apprehensive still, "I am here to invite you to an engagement party, to be held next Saturday."

Kate bowed her head to hide her grin. Mary knew full well she and Walter would not be in attendance at the celebration.

"We suspected something was amiss with our Ellen." Julia removed Elizabeth's sweater and placed her on a chair beside Nell. "Here I am Patrick's sister-in-law, and I admit I had no idea he was making the girl blush. We rejoice for these two fine people."

"Sure, Ellen is the sweetest girl in the world." Anne glided across the room toward the little girls. "And of course, Patrick is a wonderful young man."

"It is a grand thing, indeed." Julia expressed joy, such as Kate had not seen from her in a long while. "I am thrilled for Ellen and Patrick, and now I have gained yet another sister. With our Mary, that makes two new sisters in one year. I could not be happier."

"Julia, dear, I cannot refrain from worrying about you." Kate studied her sister's face. Her eyes seemed a little too bright, her talk too cheerful, unnatural, even for Julia. "Are you certain our celebrations are not wearing you down, or causing you undue sadness? I would not for the world wish to bring you one minute more of hurt or pain than you have already experienced. I would not want my wedding day or this news of Ellen and Patrick to upset you...or, should I not have raised the subject at all?"

"Do not give it a thought, Kate. Martin and I talked the entire matter over this morning, and we decided on a gift for you and Walter." Julia placed her hand over her heart. "We pledged we will set aside our sorrow for the day and think only of your happiness. Seeing the peace and joy that have settled over you both has filled me with gladness. I promise you I will remain in this happy state for the entire day."

Kate still worried. Was Julia pretending for her sake? Was she pronouncing herself happy to ease her mind? She wished it was more than playacting. She prayed her sister had recovered enough to share in her joy today. Remembering the surprise that was to come, she breathed deeply. She had come this far, and she had not revealed a word of it. Perhaps the news would help cheer Julia.

"Mrs. Flynn is one happy person we can speak of." Mary grinned. "Sure, she is almost as pleased as Ellen. She is the reason the news leaked out. It seems Patrick and Ellen contacted her Andrew and his wife Marie out in Denver. They plan to meet them there and find a home near their place. Mrs. Flynn could not keep the secret from me. She is assembling gifts to send along for Andrew and her new daughter-in-law. Ellen says by the time they depart they will need an extra trunk."

"They are moving to Colorado? I cannot believe it. I did not even know that." Julia removed two tiny pink dresses from their hangers and approached the little girls.

"There are grand tidings for our Cara, too." The worry lines on Mary's face had eased as her joyful words burst forth. "With Ellen set to leave us soon, Walter plans to divide the girls' large second floor sleeping room and provide Cara with her own quarters. She assures me she is happy, though she has done naught but cry since I gave her the news."

"I am pleased for Cara." Kate rushed over to Julia to help her with the little girls' dresses, but Anne had already taken Nell's and she was slipping it over her head. "What a wonderful thing for our dear girl to have a room to call her own. I cannot wait to congratulate her myself."

"Did you know about the engagement?" Julia aimed an arched eyebrow at Kate.

Kate could not turn away and escape her sister's scrutiny. She inclined her head toward Julia and nodded.

"Well of course, you must have known. With you being Ellen's employer and the two of you working side-by-side in your shop each day, you must have heard something." Though busy with dressing Elizabeth, Julia followed Kate with her eyes.

"I did know, though I only learned the full story last week." Kate retrieved her own dress from the closet and swished it in front of Julia. "Ellen's mysterious disappearances each evening were my first inkling that something was amiss."

"What will happen to your shop with both of you getting married?" Practical Anne worried over her, as always.

"There's more to this tale than I am able to tell right now. I have been authorized by my soon-to-be-husband to reveal only that we have a surprise for you. I will say no more." Kate folded her arms. "The secret will be revealed at supper this evening.

"Now, help me into this dress. I wish to be a bride, Walter's bride." The girls went to work, slipping the dress carefully over Kate's head and shoulders and fastening the buttons. The gown, made of a cream silk which she had ordered from her connection in New York, was very near the color of her new handbag.

"It is lovely." Julia arranged the skirt, fluffing and smoothing.

"You are lovely." Anne brushed her hair.

"Ah, it is magnificent!" Mary moved closer to admire her.

"I hope you don't mind that I made it on my own." Kate gazed at each of her dear sisters. "You all did wonderful work on the dress that Anne, Julia, and Grace wore. It is just that it has ever been a dream of mine that someday I would create my own gown. Sure, it was only childish folly, but now, it seems all my dreams and fantasies are coming true."

"You've done a splendid job," Anne said. "The dress is wonderful. Perhaps one day Nell or Elizabeth will ask to wear it?"

"Thank you, all. I seem to gain your agreement today, no matter what I say." Kate allowed them to work over her, arranging the dress and fixing her hair to their satisfaction. Anne brought her a small mirror. Holding it at all different angles, she could see most of the dress. She had attempted to create a simple design, with long slim lines, free of any extra adornment. Had she achieved that look? Her wish was to appear stately and elegant enough to make Walter proud.

Julia began to sing. "Our Kate is perfect. Nothing more needs to be done." The girls left her on her own a few moments while they went off to finish dressing themselves.

Then, as Julia and Mary turned to see to the little girls, Anne slipped over to whisper in Kate's ear. She waited for her nod, and then she ran out of the room. "I will just check on the progress of James and Tom, and yes, of baby Patrick, then I will rush right back.

Anne returned to the room, her arms all but hidden by the large box she carried. "We have one more surprise." She handed the box to Kate with an exaggerated curtsy.

Kate marched toward Mary and placed it in her arms. "For our dear new sister."

"Oh my," Mary fingered the smooth white box, a look of true surprise shinning from her eyes. "Whatever is this?"

"It is just a small token, meant to show you how much we love you." Kate kissed her on the cheek.

"We do all love you," Julia bowed low to Mary, "but Anne and I cannot take credit for this gift. It is the product of the skilled hands of our Kate."

Mary's hands shook as she untied the large pink bow and lifted the lid from the box. The trembling increased as she removed a small, fluffy mound of white wool from its protective tissue. "Oh, Kate, it is beautiful." Mary stretched out the exquisite, white shawl, looking the stitches over carefully. Kate stepped forward to help her arrange it across the shoulders of the rose colored gown she and Ellen had made for her.

"It is so soft and wonderful." Mary's tears began to fall as she held a panel of the shawl out for them to examine. "Where did you find this marvelous soft yarn? And look." Mary held the other front panel of the shawl toward Julia for closer inspection. "Just see the delicate silver flecks."

She turned back to Kate. "What is this unusual stitching? I have never seen anything like it."

"It is called a shell pattern. My contact at the dry goods store obtained the yarn, and his wife demonstrated the stitch for me." Kate produced a handkerchief. "Now, no more tears. It will soon be time to leave and you must look your best today."

"Ah, do not worry, Mary." Julia slid her arm beneath a corner of the shawl. "You will be the most beautiful girl at the wedding."

Keeper of the Flame

"Thank you, Julia." Mary whirled around for a moment, holding her arms out, allowing the shawl to float around her. Then, she turned to Kate. "You are a wonderful girl, and you have given me a perfect gift—"

The sound of a carriage pulling up in front of the house interrupted their talk. "Walter offered his buggy to take us all to church." Mary rushed to the window. "James held firm, though. He insisted he would care for Kate until she arrived in church and he formally handed her to him in marriage.

With everyone surrounding her and helping guard her dress, Kate climbed into the carriage. "James is so kind." She squeezed Anne's arm.

"You both have grand husbands." She reached out to Julia and took the part of the veil her sister had draped across her arm.

"And very soon now, you will be blessed with an equally fine man for your own husband." Julia stepped into the carriage, and Martin handed Elizabeth in to her.

"It is still dark and dreary, but there has not been a drop of rain. In only a few minutes we'll have you inside of the church and your dress will be safe from the threat of the dampness and grime the rain would bring." Anne held her hands palms upward, as if to push back the rain.

Soon Kate stood in the vestibule behind closed doors, safe and dry. "You must wait until everyone has been seated." Julia issued her command in a firm, no nonsense tone. Then she and Anne left Kate and proceeded along the side aisle to take their places in the front pew with Mary and the Dempsey girls.

Chapter Twenty-Four

Standing alone at the back of the church, Kate clutched the door handle to steady herself. It had grown extremely dark. She stamped her feet a few times.

She had not seen Walter the entire day. Now she anticipated her first sight of him at the altar. Peeking into the church through a crack in the wall, she kept her eyes on the narrow door at the side of the altar. She watched Walter and Eddie emerge through the archway and walk over to stand beside Father Burns and Father Ryan.

The organ music began. Her cue to move forward. Kate pulled the heavy door open and stepped out into the aisle. James appeared on her right side and Martin took her arm on her left. Had they been waiting just on the other side? They proceeded slowly down the aisle toward Walter, while the voices of Ellen and Grace blended in a hymn. Beautiful, but the title escaped her and she could not make out the words. Was she more excited than she realized? Kate had so loved the singing at Julia's wedding that she and Walter asked Grace and Ellen to sing for them. Ellen, who loved to perform, agreed immediately. The shy Grace took a little coaxing. Finally, Grace could not say "no" to Walter and she agreed.

As Kate drew nearer to Walter, she rested her gaze on him. Luck? Providence? Surely, a gift from God? She was about to marry the kindest, most generous man she had ever known. Now, with the skies growing murkier each minute, the entire church had been thrown into darkness. The candles on either side of the aisle cast the only light. Her family and friends had all come. She could see shadows moving throughout the church, but it would have been difficult to make out a particular face in this dim light.

Candles filled the altar, and her bridegroom appeared as if he had become encased within an archway of flickering lights. A blurred halo surrounded him. They both seemed framed within the glow of the candles. Staring straight ahead, Kate's eyes found Walter's. She imagined they were the only two people in the church. *I pray he is experiencing this same incredible image. What an extraordinary beginning to our lives together.*

The ceremony proceeded swiftly. When they had pledged their lives to one another, Father Burns offered a final prayer for a blessed marriage. Each time she looked at him, Walter smiled down at her. The love shining from his eyes warmed her. She could not resist dreaming again. She imagined residing with him in the attic room, now a splendid apartment, and spending her life at his side.

And then, the organ blared forth with a joyful flourish. They turned together, her hand on Walter's arm, and walked back down the center aisle. "You are my wife," he whispered.

"I love you," she said.

The back doors had been thrown open to reveal a steady driving rain now pouring from the skies. "Aw, Kate, I am sorry." Walter placed his arm around her shoulders.

"It matters not at all. Nothing could spoil my joy." She whirled around in surprise as men from the church appeared and held a heavy tarpaulin high over them, and she and Walter rushed down the steep church steps together. Her new husband held the train of her dress over his arm, guarding it carefully from the muddy water coursing along the streets. Kate's heart pounded with happiness. She could feel her cheeks flame with delight as he helped her into the buggy. Walter had arranged a hired carriage for them and turned his own over to Eddie to transport the Dempsey group for the day.

A cheer went up from their family and friends, and Kate and Walter turned to wave to them. She watched the small parade of carriages and wagons follow them the short distance from the church to the hotel. Walter had both hands occupied with handling the unfamiliar horse and carriage, but Kate moved closer to him and held fast to his arm.

"Ah, Mrs. Dempsey, you are a lovely girl." Walter's smile was warm.

"Thank you, Walter. I cannot believe I am now Mrs. Dempsey. Kate Dempsey. The sound of it is marvelous." Perhaps the delightful rays he sent her way would dry her a little.

"Are you ready for our grand adventure?" Walter took his eyes from the road for a moment and gazed down at her.

"I am ready for anything with you by my side." Kate could not contain her joy, but they had pulled up in front of the hotel and their private moment ended for a time.

Walter jumped down to the street. "I will care for you now." He placed his arms at her waist and lifted her from the carriage. Drawing the train of her dress away from the puddles, he carried her the short distance to the hotel's doorway.

❀ ❀ ❀

Kate and Walter stood beneath the hotel's canopy observing the procession of vehicles approaching the hotel entrance. She waved to Anne and Julia and their families, the first to pull into place. Even with the rain coming down in torrents, she could see nothing but beauty all around her. What a perfect, glorious day this was.

Walter escorted her through the magnificent lobby. The entire area appeared edged in gold. "Everyone is here." They moved to the dining room, with family and friends filing through the entryway behind them.

A gasp escaped from Kate as they entered the room. The hotel had everything in readiness, and the place looked enchanting. "I have been in this room many times," she said to Walter. "When Palmer House reversed their decision and requested that we make the draperies that now hang at the windows, Ellen and I came here to measure and then to supervise the hanging of the draperies. It was full daylight, with the room empty of furnishings. Seeing the place now, on our wedding day, the room fitted out with white cloths on the tables, china, and glistening crystal and silver, and the flickering gas lamps at the side walls illuminating it all, nearly draws the breath from me."

"Our drapes look magnificent, do they not?" Ellen leaned close to whisper to Kate as she and Patrick Tobin moved past to find their places at the table.

"They do, indeed." She answered Ellen, but she rested her eyes on her husband.

"We are in a dream." Kate placed her hand in Walter's as they settled in their places at the head of the table.

He squeezed her hand. "No, I believe we are real, just incredibly fortunate and happy." He bent his head to keep his words only for her. "You look beautiful, Kate. I love you."

"I love you too." She kept her voice down, but she cared little if anyone heard her. Walter's happiness was spread across his face, and she had observed jauntiness in his walk as they entered the hotel a few minutes earlier. He always moved about with confidence, but she did not remember ever seeing such delight in him before today. Surely her own face reflected that same love and happiness. Were their feelings obvious to everyone in the room?

As soon as they were all seated, Father Burns offered a brief but heartfelt prayer. "We thank you, Father, for the meal we are about to receive, and for the gift of love Walter and Kate are celebrating on this special day..." At the end of his prayer, their family and dear friends joined together in the "amen."

The grand cook, Mary Dempsey, took tiny tastes of each dish. "I must be the first to acknowledge that this fine meal is a masterpiece."

"After the many marvelous suppers I have been privileged to enjoy at Dempsey's, and at Anne's, and Julia's," Kate waved to Mary and her sisters, "I felt some nervousness about ordering a meal at an unfamiliar restaurant. I must say, I need not have worried."

"I believe the cook must have apprenticed in Mary Dempsey's kitchen." Julia shook her finger at Walter seated across the table from her. "I am sure I recognize the aroma of the bread being served. Has it come from Dempsey's own oven rooms? Have I found you out?"

Walter nodded his head. "It is true. You have uncovered my secret."

Kate giggled. Had the joy she could not hold back signaled her wish to celebrate? The room erupted in laughter.

When it was time for dessert, another surprise awaited. Walter's dear friend and Charlotte's father, Gus Mueller, had insisted he would provide a wedding cake. "Oh my, how beautiful!" Kate rose from her chair to get a full view of the enormous white cake the waiters carried toward them. They arranged the cake carefully at the center of a table behind Walter and Kate. Three deep layers were covered in sparkling white icing and decorated with intricate scrolls and flower designs. It was magnificent. Many of their guests rose from their places at the table for a closer look, but they had only moments to admire the splendid creation The waiters sliced and served generous portions to everyone.

The servers appeared again with coffee and tea, and then the toasts began. After listening to a few testimonials, Kate could remain quiet no longer. She stood. "I do thank you all, but believe not a word of it. You are caught up in the spell of this wondrous day. I am not that good or kind."

A chorus of "nays" answered her statement, but she only shook her head and went on.

"I do agree with your kind words for Walter. Praise for him has come from his priests, his workers, and his friends, and every word of it is well deserved." While the cheers went on, Kate sat back a moment. She had not exaggerated about Walter. He was her husband; she could not believe it. Somehow, he had come to love her. Why? She did not understand it, but she thanked God for the gift she had received.

The celebration drew to an end, and everyone prepared to take their leave. Kate held fast to Walter's arm, excitement making it hard to be still.

"Are you prepared to reveal our secret?" Walter leaned close.

Her breath caught in her throat. "If I am forced to wait much longer, I will burst. I am ready to shout out the news to everyone."

Soon, all their guests had gone but their family. "Please stay for another few minutes," Walter said. Their number also included Eddie and Grace, and Ellen and Patrick, whom Walter had asked to remain with them.

"Let us gather around one end of the table." Kate heard a hum permeating the air. Did everyone suspect a huge secret was about to be divulged?

As she and Walter had discussed their plans on their walks each evening, Kate remembered saying that she might explode into tiny pieces with happiness. He laughed at her then. Even now, he was joyful, but calm. As the waiters served another round of coffee and tea, he began with their announcement.

"Kate and I have something to tell you…"

Chapter Twenty-Five

Four Days later...

"I have been saving something to share with you." Kate shifted closer to Walter. They sat out on the deck. Strong rays of sun shone directly on her face, but the wind also whipped around them.

Walter unfolded a blanket and tucked it around them both, obscuring the fact that her hand rested in her new husband's sturdy one.

"Imagine, Kate Carty, stretched out comfortably in a deck chair." She scooted down in the chair and glanced around furtively. "Well, at least there are no steerage passengers on this run from America back to Ireland. I am not sure I will be capable of sitting out here on our return voyage. Looking down at our poor countrymen, jammed in steerage, would be more than I could bear."

"It is Kate Dempsey, you know." Walter's smile held a hint of mischief. "You are Mrs. Dempsey now."

"Fancy that. Mrs. Dempsey, herself, just recently come from spending her nights as a guest in luxurious hotels, first in St. Louis, and most recently in New York." Kate wrapped her shawl around her head. Sun or no sun, it was chilly. "I had never stayed in an establishment so fine. They were both lovely rooms."

"Nor had I." Walter sat up straight and faced her. "You are teasing, making me wait for your pronouncement. What is it you have to tell me?"

"I've forgotten. Our talk of the hotels turned my thoughts back to our wedding and the marvelous supper at Palmer House. It was a wonderful celebration, was it not?" She narrowed her eyes at him, but she could not hold back her smile.

"It was grand. My favorite part of the entire affair came when we told everyone we would be journeying back to Ireland." Walter rubbed his chilled hand along the outline of her jaw. "I will never forget the surprised expressions of our family and friends when we told them of the task we would attempt."

"Anne was shocked at first." Kate closed her eyes, remembering. "She never imagined I would return home. Once I convinced her we intended to come back to St. Louis, she was pleased."

Walter's expression turned serious. "Poor Julia. I do believe the surprise of our journey pushed her sadness away for a time. If that is true...if anything at all could lift her from her sorrow...our entire trip will be well worth the effort."

"Learning we were going back home brought her hope." Kate pulled her hand from beneath the cover and reached out to touch Walter's cheek. "The thought that we may be successful in bringing our family back with us to St. Louis has given her something to look forward to, a cause for hope. She was surely right in saying we three sisters will have no peace in our hearts until we bring our family to America."

"She is the one I am concerned for right now," Walter said. "It is my prayer that she will rise up from her sorrow over her lost babies. I sure do miss our bright, joyous Julia."

"In truth, it is Mary who is most in my thoughts." Kate's hand had grown cold, and she slipped it beneath the cover again. "We left the burden of two businesses on her shoulders."

"I have long believed Mary could run the entire operation. And she will have an abundance of help. So many offered their assistance. James pledged he will come every night to work in the oven room. Anne promised her help out in the bakery shop. Eddie and Grace have become a part of the operation and of the family, and they will manage the bakery as if it were their own. And, with our former helper Will returning to St. Louis to assist Eddie, they will be fine." Walter edged his chair closer. "Are you concerned about Ellen and your shop?"

"Ellen will be a grand manager." Kate's shoulders relaxed. "It is just that I have concentrated my entire time and energy into the seamstress shop these past years. It is an impossible thing to push the business from my thoughts. In truth, I know everything will be fine."

"We will spend some time, while we are away, thinking of a proper way to thank Mary and Ellen." Walter rubbed his hand along his chin. "What do you think?"

Kate smiled. "We do have a few weeks. We will come up with something splendid."

"I will never forget Mary's words." Walter laughed and pounded his hand on the arm of his chair. "She told everyone she would likely not realize we are gone. She said she would not miss me, even a little."

"I think she will miss me." Kate couldn't resist grinning up at Walter.

Walter removed his hand from hers and started to rise. "Are you ready, now? Have I waited long enough to hear what you have been saving to tell me?"

"I wrote to my family." She said the words quietly, but his expression told her he heard.

He sat down again. "Now, I am the astonished one. You have not written to your family in a long time, have you?"

"No. I have been so angry with my father and mother, I've only written two letters since I arrived in America."

"What changed?"

"Many things. The passage of time, I suppose. And, Lizzie's death and the deaths of Julia's babies. I began to feel my parents sorrow at losing so many. I believe I can now understand the sadness and hopelessness they must feel, after enduring one tragedy after another." Kate took Walter's hands and held them between her own. "The greatest change was you. You brought love into my life. Oh, I suppose it was there all around me and I just could not feel it or accept it. Somehow, your love broke through the wall of bitterness I surrounded myself with. I thank you for it."

"Are you up to a walk?" Walter kissed her fingertips and then held his arm out to her. "We should begin to plan for our meeting with your family. It is grand that you have already written. Your communicating with them should make our first visit easier."

Kate looked out across the endless ocean. As far as she could see, the waves lapped and rushed. "We have weeks ahead of us, gazing at the ocean and planning what we will say to my parents and how we will convince them to accompany us back to America.

"Do you think your aunt and uncle will consider coming back with us?' Kate paused. She had been considering this question. "And will the Dempseys be content to have us stay with them for a few weeks?"

"I wrote them we were coming." They walked along the railing, Walter holding her close. "Though I did not receive a response, I know they will love having us. I have no doubt that they are looking forward to our visit. And, we can surely ask them to come to America with us. I hold out little hope, though. I believe that, like your parents, they are too firmly entrenched in the green hills and valleys of Ireland.

"Our mission is Michael and Maggie." As Walter spoke, Kate rested her head against his arm. "We must concentrate our energies on your young brother and sister. We will take these next few weeks to make a plan."

❦ ❦ ❦

They spent the warm afternoons walking on the deck, talking of their coming visit to the small village of Blackwater, planning what convincing arguments they could put forth to encourage them all to come to America.

"If your father and mother refuse absolutely," Walter said one afternoon, "we could offer them enough to pay their taxes and live simply. We could hire someone to help. Would that remove any guilt from Michael over his leaving?"

"I believe it will." Kate slowed her steps, and Walter held out his hand, waiting for her. "I hope and pray Father will recognize the wisdom of our offer."

Another afternoon, Walter turned their conversation in a different direction. "What if they all refuse, Kate? Will you accept it?"

Kate reached out to hold his hand. "Yes, Walter, I will. In the weeks we will have with our families in Blackwater, I will do all I can to encourage them to come to America. My hope is that having you at my side and allowing my parents an opportunity to see for themselves what a solid, successful person you have become will sway them. If they absolutely refuse, I will do all I can to persuade them to allow Michael and Maggie to return with us.

"We can make the journey possible for them. We can make them feel welcome and wanted and needed in America. And then, they must make the decision." She gazed into Walter's eyes. "I will at last be at peace with the fact that the resolution lies in their hands.

"When we are back on the ship, headed once again for home, our job will be done. The years we spent, my sisters and I, saving our earnings, collecting the funds in Anne's immigration canister, will be over and done with. The promise Anne made to Father, now over ten years ago, will be fulfilled.

"In a few weeks, we will be ready to leave Ireland and return home again. As much as I anticipate our visit to Blackwater and the reunion with my family and yours, I am equally ready to return to St. Louis. I am already looking forward to spending my days and nights with you at Dempsey's."

"That is wonderful, Kate." He kissed her lightly on the cheek.

"Working together, operating the bakery and the dressmaking shop, seems more wonderful and fulfilling than any adventure I ever dreamed I would experience. In truth, that time cannot come soon enough. I long to settle in our lovely attic apartment in St. Louis and begin our lives together."

The Carty Sister Series, Books One and Two are also available from Mantle Rock Publishing.

Keeper of Coin
Book One

In 1859, John Carty sent his sixteen year old daughter, Anne, from their impoverished home in Ireland to meet with his brother who had established himself in Oregon. Anne, who was good at holding on to her money, promised her father she would make a home for her brothers and sisters and bring them all out to join her.

When she made that promise, Anne could not have known she would come as far as St. Louis and lose touch with her uncle in Oregon, or that James Duff would arrive from their home in Blackwater to pledge his love and support, or that the Civil War would interrupt their plans.

Anne could not have foreseen that, while she saved every possible penny, her father would time and again be forced to spend the passage money she sent him for food for their starving family and taxes on their land. She was determined to bring her family out of Ireland, but how much time would pass before she succeeded and how long would James Duff be willing to wait?

The Carty Sister Series, Books One and Two are also available from Mantle Rock Publishing.

Keeper of Trust
Book Two

Julia Carty resolved that she must change her ways. Her father had called her "flighty" and sent her younger sister to America ahead of her. Her beloved Martin referred to her as his "beautiful butterfly, flitting from one adventure to another."

She had come to St. Louis in 1861 at the start of the Civil War. In the intervening years, she worked hard at the church mission and at Dempsey's Bakery to prove she had put aside her childish habits. With the arrival of her young sister Lizzie though, she realized she had not contributed her share to the immigration fund. She left it to her sisters Anne and Kate to save the majority of passage money to bring the children out of Ireland's poverty.

When Martin suffered a life-threatening accident and faced disabilities that would alter his life forever, he needed her love and support. When additional tragedy struck the Cartys, her dear family turned to her for strength and encouragement. Had she matured, at last? Would she be capable of sustaining them all?

If you loved *Keeper of the Flame*, check out the other historical romance novels from Mantle Rock Publishing.

A Most Precious Gift - Dinah Devereaux, New Orleans-born slave and seamstress, suddenly finds herself relegated to a sweltering kitchen, though never cooked a day in her life. When she accidentally burns the freedom papers of Jonathan Mayfield, her fear of the fields becomes secondary.

Jaqueline Freeman Wheelock draws on her southern roots to create to create this intriguing love story.

A Light in Bailey's Harbor takes the reader to Wisconsin in the 1880s where Kate Kippling struggles with taming her abundant personality. New lighthouse keeper, Blake Strawberry causes Kate to question her faith.

Bethany Baker writes a heart-warming romance in the lakeside Wisconsin town of Bailey's Harbor.

Callie's Mountain brings the struggles of 1790s living in the East Tennessee Mountains to life. Callie finds herself in a marriage arranged by her father which makes her life in a new area more difficult.

Katt Anderson sheds light on prejudjces in rural areas. The second novel in the series, *Susannah's Hope* is also available.

Mantle Rock Publishing
www.MantleRockPublishing.com